TH
PRINCE
OF
SNOW

L.B. DIVINE

First paperback edition April 2023
Cover by Kelly Carter
Map by Natalia Junqueria
Editing by Poisoned Ink Press LLC
Interior Design by Lorna Reid

FIVE YEARS AGO

he weight of the crown crushed every bone in his body and shoved the air out of his lungs in a crippling fire. He was choking, gagging, and fighting back sobs. He was drowning in the fear that wrecked his body.

At last, his father had broken him.

Blood crusted over his fingers as he repeatedly dug them into the marble floors. To no avail, the knights continued to drag him backward, savagely yanking on his legs. An unbearable sharp pain pulsed through them, his screams more frantic by the second.

You can't lock me up, you can't lock me up. What are you going to do to me?

A mere hour ago, he was the Prince of the First Kingdom, inheritor to the Ten Kingdoms and merely a boy. Now, he had become an endangerment to his father's rule, a destiny bigger than anyone could have foreseen.

He was the Prince of Snow, inheritor of his grandfather King Cian's throne.

The Prince fell in and out of consciousness; that boyish strength turned to icy brutality as the knights picked him up and slammed him against the wall. He made out the shouts of his father through the madness. He saw nothing but his father's familiar scold, reminding his knights who they were manhandling.

As if he cared.

"He is the once and future King," his father hissed above the chaos. "You have no permission to eliminate him, only remove him."

His father's anger was a scorching flame that decimated all in its path, and the Prince was the target.

Hatred bloomed in the Prince's blood. Tears dripped down his lashes to his face; blood smeared, mixing with his sadness. His nose throbbed with pain from the knight's hard hit. The brutes his father deemed worthy to be his men did not give a shit about the well-being of the Prince. They only cared for power and how they could usurp it.

My father does not love me, not anymore. Maybe he never did. Why have a son if you are not to love him? Why even have a son if you do not want someone to continue your legacy?

A sob escaped him, bloodcurdling.

The smirks, the beatings, the intense training reserved for me due to my exceptional rank and birthright. My father did not respect me nor did he respect my birthright.

The Prince was not celebrated by his father. He was an obstacle. He was bred to be slaughtered. It was a miracle that he had made it as far as he had. He was not to have power. He was a threat. *So, why was I born?*

An iron fury overtook the Prince. He thrashed his appendages wildly. Gasping, he wrangled free of one of the guards. His arm's pain lessened as he dashed toward the door.

The temperature dropped in the throne room. The breath of life sucked out of him by the King who destroyed everything he touched. The Prince shook with fear he could no longer control. He moved with all of his might as the guards fought to regain a hold on him.

"*Princeling.*"

"*Bastard.*"

"*Dalton.*"

Their insults rang in his head—violent and hurtful. Each word was interchangeable. Every insult, every name, even his own—it was a curse on their lips. The Prince saw nothing, heard nothing, but his own racked sobs, as his fingers slipped, wet with tears and blood. His own mother was not even there to see him treated as such, for she did not care. Her lack of love was not a shock to him.

He was to be *the* King one day; the Thinkers had just told him. His father overheard. The destiny that had held since King Cian was overturned. The Gods no longer sang it in their songs to the Thinkers.

A fifteen-year-old-boy had shifted the tide of the world.

Cyril, the castle Thinker, reiterated the song that had always been sung to him. He spoke of it to the Prince, his eyes on edge, but his voice calm. "*The King of Snow is coming. He will Rise from the death of his Father. The Ten Kingdoms will fall. Fire will scorch the lands. A Violet Queen will Reign, and the light that holds the Kings of Old will go out.*"

His father's anger was explosive; his face unab' to mask the distraught he felt over his son's success *What does this mean, Cyril? He will Rise from the d/ of his Father…*"

Cyril spoke of the prophecy as if it w' curse. He looked at the King, his eyes filled with a r'lue disdain.

"*My King, King Ronan, there is r*'pping destiny,"

3

Cyril replied, his voice thinly laced with hostility.

His father lost it then. The King's grievances against the Prince were a rivaling hatred of the famous King Finn, his great-great-grandfather, who had been so dangerous his own daughter destroyed him.

His father bested that abhorrence now; his anguish over something as trivial as prophecy demonstrated the true madness within. The Prince tried to speak out, moving closer to his father. The King's rage had been quelled before with reason. The Prince saw no reason as to why it would not work this time.

That is when he struck. The Prince thrusted his hands forward, letting the Kings of Old's strength take hold.

He knew without a doubt that this was the beginning of war.

The knights huffed and puffed as they wrapped their arms around the Prince's torso. Stupid bastards who assumed he was nothing more than a boy. Damn his father for using his own birthright against him.

The King of Snow is coming.

He willed himself to be destroyed by the magic that had awoken. His heart beat in spasms, irregularly due to the pressure of the Knights' limbs.

The Prince hoped he would die there.

His father's diamond shoes clicked on the floor as his black cape slithered behind him. His father crouched down. A long, jeweled finger moved against the Prince's jawline methodically, taunting him with his inability to fight back. Above all else, this monster was his father. He was the King. The Prince had to bend the knee.

"Take him to his quarters, where he shall remain."

The Prince's shoulders relaxed and his head hung. He was defeated. His father had broken him.

4

Again.

He turned around, the scene humiliating. His father lifted his fingers to let the guards know to grab his hair— the most demeaning way to lift a royal's head. The King clicked his tongue against his teeth rhythmically, studying. He moved closer, his lips an inch from the Prince's ear as he took a breath to speak.

The Prince seized from within. His rage turned to sheer vindication as he tried to unleash himself upon his father. Again.

The King's eyes fell to the Prince's fingers first. They were covered in ice, a thin layer encapsulating them. The Prince's eyelashes suddenly were heavy; a white lining barely visible on his horizon.

Is that snow?

He was kissed awake by the breath of a first winter. He had been brutalized, but he was *alive*. The Prince's inner fire was frosty; his anguish and turmoil a full-fledged winter.

The room around him froze in time. The throne room's marble became a glistening spectacle of frozen beauty. His teeth chattered; his skin burned with the need for warmth.

"Ten Kingdoms," he whispered as he turned to see the knights behind him.

They had turned to ice sculptures. Their faces were frozen in permanent disbelief. He turned back to face his father, praying he had met the same fate. To his disappointment, his father still stood before him. However, there was a light dusting on his shoes, as there was on his hair. He had been kissed by the power of snow too.

"Father... I..." He was speechless. *How did this happen? Who had I become?* Magic was *illegal*.

His father's face faltered and changed to complete

disbelief. He stared at him with a softness that alarmed the Prince. However, the moment was brief. His eyes shifted to pure darkness, and the Prince's heart thundered within his chest. Louder now than ever before.

"That's my Dalton," he said, as snow fell from the ceiling, dusting the wicked throne.

I

THE INVISIBLE GIRL

ONE

Dalton Saphirrus crept out of the castle with ease. He trotted down the mountainside's pebbled road that wound to his dreadful abode on the hillside. The way was slick. Rocks slid as his boots carelessly crunched on the pavement. It must have just rained, which did not surprise him because that was something he would not care to notice anymore. He was always inside. *Why bother with the formalities of weather?*

Sneaking out in the evening had not been a struggle. He never floundered under pressure. His wits and abilities remained intact, despite the stressors of daily court life.

Looking right and left, he smirked. No servants crowded the halls, no knights on guard outside his chambers. Not even Cyril had come by to take a crack at breaking his solitude this night.

As the town of Thallgan came into view, his heartbeat quickened. The break of evening left the village center quiet, despite the hustle he had heard about from the servants. The servants always headed off to Thallgan for pleasure, despite it being simplistic. Thallgan supplied the royals with the necessities. Desserts, vegetables, meats; all the delicacies which were cultivated and sold.

Or so he had been told. Pride beamed through him at the recognition of this tiny village, despite just laying eyes on it now.

Dalton readjusted his tunic, praying to the Gods that he would remain incognito. He cursed his magic—not for the first time—for turning his hair white. There was no record that the first King of Snow's coloring had changed. Cyril found it peculiar that the change had not reached his eyebrows or eyelashes. It stopped at the ends of his wild hair, wavy, turning to curls at the end. His hair was the physical change he let happen because he had no control.

Most of the time.

Dalton was just *lucky*.

He crossed his arms over his chest and continued toward the entrance. Taking note of the stars and their precise location, he embedded it into his memory. He was no astronomer, but he would not be caught coming back late due to a lack of timing. Tutoring had to be good for something.

He saw the faint outline of his Gods-damned tower from this viewpoint. He scoffed, his irritation overthrowing momentary happiness.

You are here. You are out.

He breathed deeply as he basked in all that Thallgan had to offer.

Cinnamon, wine, horses, freshly baked bread: it was love, life and happiness. His vision clouded, blinking away tears. Pleasures had not been privy to him over the last five years.

As Dalton passed through groups of people inside the town, he knew he was different. It was not his hair or his simplistic garb that singled him out: it was the joy he was sure was plastered over his face that could not be wiped off. Being out in the open like this was a blessing. He had not felt the wind on his face nor the wind at his back for five years. He did not forget the life that he had once lived, that of freedom and choice. But he had forgotten what it was like to be free of restraints.

The people of Thallgan probably thought he was a fool. He embraced it, smiling at them in greeting.

If they thought him a fool, they were not wrong.

Dalton stopped as a little boy cut into his path. He guessed he was five years old: his cheeks chubby and his blue eyes the epitome of innocence. His hair, black as night, offset his sun-kissed skin beautifully against the moonlight.

Dalton had never been so close to a child before. He steadied his breath as his power gripped against the fragility of his nerves. His chest constricted. The fear of being out of control near someone so fearless left him in pieces.

The child spoke softly, "You be to Thallgan?" He craned his head to the side as if his question made any sense in the world.

Dalton scrambled to remember what it was to be five years old, and found it rather difficult, since he blocked most moments of his life from memory. "I am from the First."

The boy nodded and smiled, reaching out his hand with a rock no bigger than his palm in it.

Dalton touched the rock in his palm and the boy pushed it forth as if to tell him that it was a gift. It was his.

Dalton's own personal rock. He could not wait to tell Cyril of it.

"Thank you, my boy," he said softly, weirdly overtaken by emotion with the gesture.

"You look like King in songs," the child said before

wrapping his hands around his neck in an embrace.

Dalton stiffened, but did not dare get up. He saw the outline of the boy's parents now behind him, beneath the porch of their cottage. They smiled at the child as if the four of them were involved in the world's best kept secret.

Dalton smiled at them softly, acknowledging it.

They broke apart. The boy turned back to look at him as he ran to his parents. Dalton touched the rock that had been given to him, put it in his pocket, and smiled. He could not remember the last time he had been given a gift.

Onward, he frolicked and hunted for a tavern to pop into. The familiarity of wine was a phantom taste against his tongue as he dreamt of his daily indulgences. He looked back at the castle's shadow now, fearful of missing his window of opportunity, but also terrified of who he would become if he surrendered his time to the embers of his father's punishments.

And so, he continued.

Rounding the corner of the opening street, he was met with thunderous excitement before he noticed the door to the tavern swing open. Without thought, he plunged into the madness of dancing and intoxicating bards with sultry voices.

And he reveled in it.

His face was flushed within moments from the sheer crowd which existed among the tavern walls. The floor was sticky with ale, the walls a furnace for all the bodies which plagued the room.

The Beloved King, he muttered to himself, laughing at the irony of the tavern's name.

He danced over to the bar nimbly, acquiring the ale which he sought. He wished it was wine, but he often thought of many things that did not come true. He lifted it to his lips immediately upon throwing a few shillings at the bar owner, relishing with a groan the familiar taste of freedom. He had snuck out of his chambers many times before, but this was the first time he successfully made it off the castle grounds. He laughed as he threw his head back and watched those who had already been there.

Paranoia set in without warning. Dalton's dark blue eyes scanned the tavern.

He was being watched. He continued to stand, drinking his ale faster and faster as he fought the urge to run. To return to the safety of his confinement. To return to Cyril.

Just as he was about to tip back his pint and finish the ale, a soft voice crooned in his ear, "Well, well, what do we have here?"

He snapped his head to the side, facing the voice which had acknowledged him. His eyes narrowed as he tried to place the man who stood before him, the familiarity of his green eyes shocking as they were strikingly similar to that of his servant boy.

Athelred.

Ten Kingdoms save me. "Athelred, my darling, do you frequent this fine establishment?" He backed up toward the door, but the masses of people who crowded the room made it near impossible for him to blindly maneuver an escape.

Athelred's green eyes blazed with fear.

Athelred must have been sent here by my father.

"Now, if you'd just let me *go*," Dalton said. The coolness that he often tried to radiate left him as Athelred followed him step for step as they exited the tavern.

"He already knows," Athelred said softly, shame plaguing his eyes.

Crack. The thundering of the rope against his back splintered his skin into fragments. No noise escaped him, for he was turning to dust. Dalton's spine gave way underneath the pain, which erupted on every nerve ending in his body. He heaved, vomiting his innards in a most un-Princely manner.

> *Pain is mental.*
> *You have nothing to fear.*
> *You are a survivor.*
> *You are not broken.*
> *Cyril loves you.*
> *You will be free one day.*
> *Think of the little boy.*
> *Think of Carinthya.*

Dalton awoke the next day to a hand wrapped in his.

Cyril leaned on the edge of his bed. His head was bowed in prayer; the light chanting the only noise that revealed to Dalton that he was awake. He forced himself to stay still as the memories of the night before thrashed through his vision. He was suddenly queasy. Raw understanding took over. His own father had ordered his beating for sneaking out to Thallgan.

Cyril sat up, for he either finished his prayer or heard Dalton's back uncomfortably wrestle with the sheets that donned his bed.

Dalton looked down at himself, red clouding alarmingly around where he lay. His bandages had soaked through. Dalton could only assume that his bed looked like the outcome of an assassination attempt. *It would not be a wrong assumption.*

14

"My *boy*," Cyril choked out, hesitant to touch him.

"That's me," Dalton replied, running a thumb over Cyril's cheek.

TWO

"o, lift it with your arm, rather than your wrist, Char. That's it. Pivot your foot in the back and *lunge*. There you go, sister, looking like a member of the King's guard already."

Charmaine Grimes huffed a laugh, lifting her brother James's long-sword with precision. She had been at it all day, her back sticky as the sweat clung to her corset. Pins of pain jotted within her wrists, but she could not relent.

James would never let her live it down if she quit.

The First Kingdom was unseasonably hot the past few days; the finality of summer bringing the worst out of the weather. Her hands were swollen, her fingers fat with heat. She was slow today. She missed her marks as her mind wandered aimlessly. She was not sticking to the methodologies they had been practicing.

"So bossy today," Charmaine chided, her feet steady on the grass. They had been at it for weeks at this point, correcting with a maddening drive for perfection.

James was determined to teach her the way of the sword, be it that the mercenary attacks had been arriving closer and closer to the citadel of the First Kingdom in recent months. James and Charmaine were the only two members of their family left and were rather determined to stick together.

And sticking together meant survival.

"You know I have my reasons," he said with his hands behind his back, inspecting her movements with the sword.

Charmaine was not particularly blessed with the blade, nor were her fighting skills something to pride herself on, but they were acceptable. It was James who was lethal with any sort of weapon and who had a love for swords unmatched for anything else.

Other than that of Charmaine, of course.

"I know," she said, gasping as she finished up the routine. *Shoulders up. Chin up. Slash with your shoulder muscles. Flick the wrist to move it to the side.* She finished, breath heavy as she threw the sword to the ground with a clang.

"Well done, sister."

Charmaine smiled softly, her back aching despite weeks of hard work. She had gone from reading all day to training like a man in the King's Guard.

She supposed they had to be ready; the mercenary attacks were becoming no coincidence. "They attacked Gordfrick the other day, James," Charmaine whispered.

"I heard," his voice was laced with venom. She winced, aware that he was probably thinking of the knights who had infiltrated the Dragon's Egg last night.

Her cheeks flushed with more than the heat of the spar. The knights who served the King's Guard were characteristically handsome.

"Do you think they'll come here?" she asked, despite knowing the answer.

Gordfrick was a mere fifteen miles away. Their passage through the lands was mapped many times by the council leaders of Brinn. It was clear they were headed for the capital of the First, the castle of King Ronan.

She prayed her brother would lie to her—tell her that no such thing could possibly happen, that the mercenaries would be directed elsewhere.

Instead, he looked at her head-on and replied with no love in his voice, "More than likely, Char."

"I wish you'd lie to me."

"And where's the fun in that?"

Suddenly, the doors to the shop opened, and a red-headed boy with blue eyes strode in with impertinence. He smiled; his white teeth beamed against the contrast of his sun-kissed skin. He was wearing a red tunic and black leathers, as if he had just come from training and work.

"Tommy boy," James said, instantly brightened by the arrival of his best friend. "Where have you been, lad? Dampening in the latest pub dispatch of lily root?"

Charmaine snorted. Lily root was a powerful potion that anyone could brew. The effects of which, however, were those which not everyone would enjoy. It lowered inhibitions and infected the mind with poor decision-making. She was fortunate enough to never have crossed paths with the nasty brew, but James and Tommy were not so lucky in life.

"Around about the borders, doing checks with my father." Tommy's father was a member of the privy council of Brinn, a group of men who reported to the King. They had received instruction from King Ronan's knights a few weeks ago to keep a weathered eye on the horizon. Tommy had volunteered to serve with a small group of men from Brinn who would become a part of the servitude to the King.

They had asked James, but Tommy forced him to turn it down. James had come home that night rather ruffled with his face red, upset. Charmaine inquired what Tommy had said to him, and all he replied was, *"It's you and me."*

Tommy told Charmaine a few days later that he had convinced James to stay behind and look out for her. Charmaine wept. She was all he had left and he was all that she had left. James was her emotional tether to this life, and without him, she did not know who she would be or who she would turn into.

She owed Tommy for helping him stay alive and stay out of the mercenary's mess.

"And how did said checks go?" James asked Tommy, his eyes heavy with worry.

"Not as we hoped. No sign of them, but that doesn't mean they aren't nearby."

Her eyes went wide, fear in her voice thickening as she asked, "Did they find anyone in Gordfrick?"

Tommy kept his voice steady, but he did not take his eyes off James as he said, "No survivors and burnt to the ground like the others."

"But *why?*" James asked as he sat down. His violet eyes matched her own blaze of fury and grief.

"Some darkness is at work here. Even the bloody King doesn't know how to fix it."

"It certainly seems like he could try harder," Charmaine whispered.

James stood up and walked toward her. "You can't speak like that, Char. It's treason."

"Treason or truth, I don't see a difference. If they come, we're dead. All of us."

"We won't be dead if we keep training," James spat, irritation lighting up his voice.

"I will be dead if I change, Jamie," Charmaine admitted, too low for Tommy to hear. She had a secret, one that her mother had died to protect. A secret that her father had taken with him to the grave. A secret that plagued every breath she drew because it put her brother at risk.

Charmaine Grimes could turn invisible, and it could happen to her at any moment without any warning. She was a target anywhere she went in the First Kingdom, and only feared for the worst if she were to come in contact with the mercenaries. She was at risk among her own people and had been for years. Despite knowing them her whole life, cruel fascination overtook the masses. She had seen far too many people enslaved to those who did not believe that anyone should have magic. They followed the whim of the King, instead of following what they believed to be true in their hearts.

Charmaine never knew why she had this power. Her mother, who had magical abilities as a Cipher, had tried to teach her to live with it, but it still happened of its own accord. It was sporadic but consistent enough that it was a living fear within her. The fear of being overtaken by invisibility, vanishing from sight of the world, was crippling.

She could not imagine anyone ever dreaming of vanishing from the world.

"Then let us hope they don't come," Tommy chided, his blue eyes stuck on them.

"Hope hasn't helped anyone else," she spat.

THREE

t had been three years since Randolph killed.

Three years since he unleashed himself in his primal ways, the ways of his people, and once again inked himself with their despair.

Randolph never forgot their faces, their screams. It was his madness. In the night, he still heard them, felt their warm blood coat his hands. He awakened like clockwork in the middle of the night. The same fear pulsated through his veins. He never wanted to be violent, never wanted to take a life.

But there were choices to be made in this world, and he made this choice every single time.

He blinked, brought back to reality. He hated the forsaken explorations that King Ronan set them on. He was grateful for time away from court, time with his fellow knights, but lost parts of himself when he was away from the castle. Randolph needed the structure of rules to keep himself grounded. If he was not a knight, he was a murderer. He was trying to be a better man. For himself. For his Kingdom.

It had been a long three years since he formally

declared his path—this intent of servitude—so he often forgot why he did it to begin with. *Was it to escape the Seventh? Was it to be praised? Was it for the glory? Was it for redemption?*

Randolph was not sure anymore.

It was the end of summer. The full bloom of the First Kingdom's evergreen plants and trees was utterly cruel to his nose. The views were absolutely spectacular, views which he truly found to be enjoyable on these trips. He was able to appreciate the land that had cured him of his sins, gave him purpose again that was worth fighting for. The pollen in the air was thick with rebirth and planning for the treacherous fall that laid ahead.

And frankly, he welcomed the chaos.

Sweat pooled on the palms of his hands as he rode his horse, Gregoria, through the field that lay between Hammen and Brinn. Gregoria's brown hide was slick with sweat; her hooves pounded on the grass. Gregoria was another steadying constant that he needed, his traveling companion that kept him sane the further he got from the First Kingdom's castle.

And a reliable friend when the men of his legion tested him.

Focusing on the surroundings quelled his never-ending mind, which was determined to never sleep.

This would be their fifteenth village in seven days, a backbreaking tour designed by King Ronan to get a grasp on the devastation that had beset his lands. Randolph was in denial until he set out on this murderously fast-paced journey to examine what they already knew.

The mercenaries had not slowed. *But why were they here at all?*

For what seemed like the millionth time on the tour,

Lawton yelled behind him, "Rand, when can we stop for something?" Originally, he had asked for ale, then he asked for women, then he asked for men, then he asked for a wee. There was absolutely no end in sight for the absurdities of his questioning.

If he were to survive this journey, Randolph would need to take care of Lawton. Randolph would rather have the bloodthirsty mercenaries who they had been scouting these last days be the newest members of their journeying squad. He would rather sit back to think about his time in the Seventh.

"For the last time, Lawton, when we get to Brinn, you may have your women, your men, your ale, your wee, and your *something*."

Lawton sighed the most egregious of all sighs, one which Randolph was sure if a mercenary were within sixty villages, they would have heard. "My *lord*," he said, trotting his horse up toward Gregoria. "We don't even know what we are looking for."

"We are looking for mercenaries," he said point-blankly.

"Yes, *Eniar*, but I don't know what in the Ten Kingdom's that even is. Who are they? What do they look like? Who hired them?"

Randolph turned, willing to fire back unprofessional commentary for being in the rank he was, but he did not have any ammo. He seethed at the mention of his long forgotten last name.

Randolph did not know the answers himself. The truth was he did not know what in the Ten Kingdoms he was looking for either. It was exhausting, and something which he had asked King Ronan about privately before he left on the expedition with no specifics.

Ronan had only replied, *"That's the business of the King."*

Randolph left and proceeded to drink an entire bottle of wine. If he had to give his men no answers, then he would try to find them. It was his sworn duty. Randolph could not go back to the Seventh, not after all he had done. Not after all that he had destroyed.

So, following Ronan it was.

"You really don't know?" Lawton whispered.

He looked away from him, squinting to see Brinn's outline in the distance. They had arrived.

"I know enough," he whispered as they trotted forward.

He hated to stop at these towns, feeling the weight of their presence against the simple people who lived there. All of them had suffered enough, and this one-sided war seemed ceaseless against the stroke of time.

Brinn was a town of a simplistic nature. He never heard much about it until he moved to the castle of the First Kingdom. It was the town of healers and creators. They were crafters typically: hardworking and rather poor compared to the rest of the villages. The world was rather disgusting that way. Those who had the most to give the world did not make it the way they deserved to.

Riding their horses through the town square, Randolph noticed the amount of looks the legion received. Men, women, and children stopped what they were doing to watch them pass. He tried to look forward, but their kind faces seemed to draw his attention. They smiled and some even saluted.

The heat rose in his cheeks, a reminder of the role he often forgot he played in the world. He should have been used to this attention, given his background, but it had never felt right for him.

He swung off of Gregoria as they approached the pub in the town square. A round sign hung off the door and was labeled, *The Dragon's Egg*. Randolph scoffed at the name, noting that there had not been Dragons in these lands for over a hundred years.

They entered a rather empty pub, for it was the middle of the day. Two men sat in the corner, laughing with pints and swords strapped to their backs. One man had bright red hair, his eyes full of light and humor. He held the pint in his hands without grace, clearly spilling everywhere as he told whatever story he was in the midst of. The other man was definitely that of a skilled swordsman for the ale was balanced seamlessly in one hand, as he intently watched his friend boast about whatever it was he found so hysterical.

A girl sat with them, only she had a bowl of stew in front of her. She, too, had a sword strapped to her back. Her set posture indicated she was uncomfortable. Randolph sensed that she was nervous being in such a public place. Her midnight black curls dangled down her back and caressed the sword with a darling entanglement. Randolph could not see her face. He noted there was an aura about her that could not be placed. It smelled like lavender and mint, and he felt the familiar urge to walk over to understand it better.

Randolph was trained in the ways of the Thinkers, magical beings gifted in foresight and chosen by the Gods themselves. He forgot so many of their formative teachings and idealisms. They had taught him in the reformation that there were different energies and pulsations that radiated from different people, and that these were expressions of their soul which had manifested.

These energies were that person's story and their secrets.

Except the problem was that he had not practiced his skills since his mother died seven years prior. Therefore, he had lost his own gifts. A few, luckily, remained. The ability to sense and read people lingered, but it was like seeing through smoke.

As they sat down and ordered ales from the bar, Randolph tried to keep his eyes on his men. He was particularly watchful of Lawton, trying not to draw attention to the girl he could not see from this vantage point. He did not need his men calling attention to anyone in the town, especially people whose pulsation he did not understand.

Lawton tapped his fingers on the table with a fever that had Randolph's blood boiling.

"What is it?" Randolph nearly hissed in his direction. The four other men with the legion were quiet, but would not dare play around. Not on a mission.

Not with Randolph.

"I'm just bored, your Majesty," he said, too low for the other men to hear.

Randolph erupted. He gripped the table with his nails, digging into the wood, threatening to draw blood.

"Watch yourself," he growled at him. He would not lose it, not here. Not with Lawton baiting.

"Suit yourself, pretty boy." He flashed a smile. His eyes crinkled as though he found himself charming. Randolph would show him what it felt like to be—

"Are you members of the King's Guard?" a velvety voice said to his right.

Randolph swiveled his head; his nails released from the table and freely bled at his sides.

The girl with the black hair stood before him. She was more beautiful than he could have imagined. Her midnight black curls draped down her back. A plump but symmetrical mouth was appeased in a smile. Her nose was round and soft featured. But it was her eyes that left him speechless: the violet irises that rendered him unable to do anything but gape.

Thankfully, Lawton had *some* semblance of sense. "Why yes, we are stopping through on our brigade on official business."

The girl smiled; her white teeth shone as she nodded graciously. She bent her head slowly, a sign of respect among the common folk to those who were above them in station. For some reason, it upset Randolph when she did as such; the regality of her without a crown was prevalent. This girl must have been the daughter of a member of Brinn's council: her manners too proper and her voice too genuine.

This was no commoner.

"May I offer to ask the owner of the Egg for a round for you on the house? He's a dear friend of my family, and you look as though you've had quite the journey."

Randolph's fellow knights almost fell over.

Ten Kingdoms save them all.

"Absolutely," Perceval muttered.

The night raged, thick with music and laughter. Randolph shed one of his many skins, something which he had not done in years. He did not quite feel himself—for he did not know if he would ever feel that way again—but there in that pub was the closest he had come since he left.

He still did not know the girl's name, nor did he care

to ask. The pint of ale he held spilled down his rolled-up tunic sleeves, exposing his tattoos against his sun-kissed skin.

The girl looked at the tattoos, her eyes trying to understand the clusters of flowers that flowed freely. He tried not to admire them, for rather, they served a purpose. Because of them, he would never forget who he was. They never let him lead a normal life. He was anything but normal.

He was extraordinary, no matter how much he ran from it.

He took a thick swig of the ale; the warm pleasure of the alcohol heating his belly. "Destiny is all," he cheered with the fellow people of Brinn, who had joined the knights in unison.

"It's quite a silly tune," the girl said, holding her ale steady in her hands. He suddenly felt quite unorderly in comparison.

The bard sang on behind him, *There once was a man from the Ten Kingdoms who lived with his sword and his eyes to the night. There once was a man from the First Kingdom who distanced himself from the destiny of all…*

"Destiny is all!" they cheered again, lifting their glasses and taking a swig in unison.

All drank but the girl.

"You don't believe in destiny?"

"I don't always know if that which is prophecy is to be celebrated."

"I try not to think of destiny often myself," he said without a filter.

"You don't celebrate it?" Her voice was clear, the question muddled.

"I find that the more I do, I run from it." He did not

28

know why he was answering her so candidly, but he did not care.

"You have something to run from?"

"Don't we all?" He purposefully laced his words with sarcasm, no matter the truth that they held.

"I feel as though when I'm not in control, I'm on a horse with no reins. I feel as though without the saddle and the tools I need, I'm at the mercy of another. And I cannot stand the feeling. I need to feel the wind in my hair on my own terms. I need to taste the sea air because I wanted to blaze down the beaches of the Second."

"You want to blaze down the beaches of the Second?" Randolph said, laughing at her fire.

"If I wish to, I'd wish to do it on my own terms."

"So, you're one who likes control." Randolph smirked, curling a tattooed finger along his jaw. He watched her eyes follow, wrecked as if this conversation terrified her.

Good. Destiny was not to be trifled with.

"It's the only way."

"I stopped trying to control destiny a long time ago." His voice was sheer ice.

"And how's it going for you?" Her violet eyes flashed with humor.

"Like I'm being jostled around on the saddle by a horse down the beaches of the Second, and I have no say in the matter," he said with a chuckle.

She smiled, the kindness explosive and enamoring. "I like you, sire…"

She did not finish her sentence, leaving his name to question. *My name*, Randolph thought to himself with a smile. *What is my name? Randolph, the head of the King's Legion? Or Randolph Eniar?*

"If we ever meet again, miss, I will learn your name as you learn mine," he said, winking as he put down his ale. "And it will be on your terms."

She crinkled her nose, deflecting the compliment, but acknowledging the boundaries Randolph had outlined.

"My father was a member of the Council here in Brinn," she said to herself. "He dreamt of becoming what you are."

Randolph nearly snorted, but kept it contained. "Your father wanted to be a Knight?"

She nodded. "He wanted to serve the bigger picture, fight for those who couldn't fight for themselves."

Randolph gaped. It was unusual for a member of a Council to want to be a part of the knights. The only people selected were either born into the position or wanted to escape their demons.

The girl touched his wrist and the rose that wrapped around it delicately. He nearly flinched at the connection, but held steadfast. Her touch was instinctual, and he was locked in by it. He could not pull away if he tried.

"Roses are one of my favorites," he managed to gasp out, remaining calm.

"I always admired them for their line of defenses," she said, her pointer finger leaving his wrist slowly. The electricity between them remained in the air. "What's it for?"

Death. "You'll be privy to that when you learn my name."

"On your own terms," she replied softly, her eyes blitzing with violet hues.

Suddenly, the boy with the same violet eyes bounced over. He touched the girl's shoulder with a familiarity that Randolph had not been witness to in some years. The boy looked a few years older than the girl, but his eyes were alight with a youth which could not be deemed to be anything but that of a child. His smile was wide and bright, offsetting the same black hair that the girl had. *This must be her brother.*

As if on cue, the boy said, "Having fun, sister?" He gestured with his eyebrows and a flashy smile.

Randolph took a swig of his ale, making sure to flash the cold disposition he often took when meeting new people.

"Dashing good, sir, if you wouldn't be so saddened to say good night to my dearest sister here. We have *training* in the morning." The boy seethed the word.

Randolph almost asked why he spoke of training in such a way. For him, training was a release. It was also an opportunity to get better every day. He did not know what type of training the girl would be doing, but regardless, he was swarmed with pride that the people of this kingdom had a thirst for survival.

They'd sure need it.

The girl turned to Randolph, a hand on her brother's shoulder as she said, "Until we meet again."

Randolph smiled before he could help himself, taking in one last look at the radiance of those violet eyes and midnight hair. "I can only pray to the Gods that if we do, it will be on your terms."

Randolph meandered to the top of the stairs of the tavern. His legs heavy with sleep and ale, he dragged them more the closer he got to his bedroom. His eyes closed without warning; his lids fighting to stay open against the heaviness so he could fall into his bed without harm. Despite the exhaustion, he smiled at the memory of the girl who reminded him of purpose. Of what it was like to have purpose.

Destiny was *not* all.

Randolph flopped onto his bed. He did not even care to throw a blanket over himself as he fell into sound sleep for the first time in three years.

FOUR

alton Saphirrus's evening jaunt around the castle was led by Cyril, for God's forbid if he were to enjoy a stroll by himself. He did not feel like escaping tonight. The escapades and consequences of the night before still weighed heavy on the side of his cheek, a courtesy of the hands of the King. The healers were been brought in after he had been whipped, but the phantom pain was still there. He had heard his father command them to heal him, "just enough."

Dalton definitely had had enough of all of this.

Cyril had spunk; Dalton would give him that. He knew the Thinkers were blessed with an unnaturally long lifespan, a gift that came with the package of prophecies and knowing all. Cyril seemed youthful in all ways but his appearance. Short with wrinkly hands and a bald head, he was the epitome of old. Dalton would never confess that to him, for he liked his head attached to his body. He would also never tell him, out of risking his own pride and vengeful persona, that he was so grateful tonight for his company. The frozen demons who haunted him seemed to be stronger the past few weeks, uncontrollable and sporadic.

As they strut down the hallway like brothers, it shocked him—no matter how many times he remembered—that Cyril was over one hundred years old. He had served Kings and Queens since the rule of Ciara and Cian, and had preserved the secrets of his family for two generations. He tried not to smile to himself at the thought of Cyril as a boy, for it was hard to imagine him as anything but a constant pain in his backside. However, there were instances where they would be speaking, Cyril would look at Dalton, and he almost saw the knowledge spinning behind his crystal blue eyes. There was a deep sadness too, that clouded him more frequently than Dalton thought anyone was aware.

It was rather dreary, Dalton thought, to know the future and be its voice.

"And why are we off to the Hall of Portraits, my dearest Cyril?" Dalton asked, the boredom in his voice forced just to play with him. He could not have been happier when Cyril appeared at the door to his chambers earlier that evening. He had demanded Dalton put down his book and come with him. However, for good measure, Dalton still put up a fight of laziness and indecency. *What was the point of being good when the world thought me so bad?*

Cyril smirked at him, that youthful persona coming out briefly as he continued to pound his feet against the white marble of the hallway. "Because boy, you need a reminding of who you are."

Dalton shook his head in response, not interested in becoming one of Cyril's latest pet projects, even if it meant he got to leave his chambers. He looked down at his feet, his golden shoes the personification of his position. The white marble floors, the personification of his power. The detail to them was so ornate, as if winter itself had kissed these very halls. Dalton hated how beautiful his home was. He hated how powerful he was.

With no warning, Cyril spun around to face him. He had caught Dalton gawking and then shoving away interest in the castle. He blinked twice. His white eyebrows turned into a frown as he looked the Prince up and down, then back to the hallway. "Did you know, boy, these very walls used to be black as night?"

Dalton could not hide the surprise on his face. The perfection of the white marble and detailing of the walls had permanence. It was everlasting. "When did it change?"

Sadness flashed in Cyril's gaze, so quick Dalton thought he imagined it. He turned around to continue walking toward the Hall of Portraits at the end of the corridor, but slowed his pace, as if he remembered that he was no longer in a rush. He sighed. "When Queen Ciara was crowned in my first lifetime, her inner darkness took hold of the castle."

Dalton interrupted him, "Because she murdered her father, the mad King."

Cyril nodded; devastation reappeared ever so briefly. "The darkness was not born of the incident; however, it was born within her. Her power to control the minds of those around her, personified in this darkness—this *fear*. The castle became infectious to the ruler of those days, for their power was so strong it would breach the walls and bend the will of the world."

A chill went down Dalton's spine as he tried to ignore his imagination—what it felt like to have all that power course through your veins. He shook his head; his white hair swooshed gently over his eyelashes before he moved it again. The gesture was almost cleansing to him. He could not think of regicide. Not now and not ever.

Cyril continued, "When Queen Ciara gave her life for her husband in the Great Battle, King Cian inherited that gift, as well as many others. But most importantly, for the sake of my point, he inherited the castle's allegiance."

He paused as they made their way down the hallway to the door, and Cyril shoved it open with all his might. It creaked slowly and opened up to unveil hundreds of portraits, Kings and Queens of Old who had shaped the destiny of the world. His gaze fixated on two portraits at the end. Dalton followed him, enamored about the factuality of the changing castle. *Imagine having that type of power.*

Even though he had seen their portraits before, they always took his breath away. Ciara appeared vacant, her green eyes a stone-cold fury filled with nothingness. Her red hair draped around her shoulders, framing her beautiful face in fire. Cian, on the other hand, looked much like Dalton as a boy. His hair was black as midnight, his eyes a crystal blue, full of light. He was the first King of Snow.

Dalton cleared his throat, trying once again to seem disinterested. It was no offense to Cyril, for he felt like deep down, he knew Dalton cherished his company, even whilst acting like an ungrateful bastard.

Dalton had had a hard day and did not feel like being weak.

Emotional.

Disgusting.

"Well, they look lovely as always, Cyril."

He frowned, placing his hand on Dalton's shoulder with a calming grasp. "He had trouble, you know," he started, not taking his eyes off Cian's portrait. "When his power first erupted, Cian had real trouble."

Dalton's jaw unhinged, for his history and the legends always made him seem like the master of the element. "He did?" Dalton asked.

"The first time his power erupted was so much like yours. He was faced with an impossible situation. He was at a crossroads. He could let Ciara die or he could embrace what lay within. It seems to be a thing for royals to unleash their power in a moment of great stress or life-deciding situations…"

"What happened?" Dalton asked, his disinterested persona slipping away like melted ice. He did not want to talk of five years ago.

Cyril smiled. "He unleashed himself and almost murdered Ciara in the process."

"I am sure she *loved* that," Dalton said, unable to keep himself from being an ass. He had heard of the Queen's raging persona and firecracker demeanor his entire life.

"If only you knew." Cyril chuckled, suddenly looking very far away. "I only wish… I only wish you could have met her, boy."

Dalton smiled, embracing that as his form of comfort toward Cyril when he got like this. "Let's go, old man. I think we have lingered long enough with your friends."

Cyril smiled back; his eyes clouded with grief as he exited with Dalton. They turned to walk down the Hall of Portraits once more. They glanced up and down the aisles as they went in silent prayer. Dalton stopped suddenly, his arm still clenched around Cyril's arm for support as he looked to his left. There she was—dark blue eyes like the first evening sky of winter, hair black as night like their forefathers, and a face much like his own.

Dalton's sister. Princess Carinthya.

His heart twinged in two. He forgot her portrait, as well as his own, was in there from when they were younger. From when she was still here. He missed her dearly, her death still a fresh imprint in his mind, for it had only been six years. The wound was still fresh if he pondered it for too long, so to cope, he rarely did such a thing. Dalton would not subject himself to pain if he did not have to.

It was Cyril's turn to be his guidance and light, as he seemed to melt away from his grief and embrace Dalton's.

"Let's go, son," he said, guiding him toward the door.

Dalton went, shaking Carinthya's memory off with every step as if she were a plague to his mind. It was not often that he let her cloud him, for it had been so many years of solitude since her death. He tried to push the plethora of memories away, the pain of losing her, and the pain of being locked away like vermin all too heavy for him to bear alone. He had begun to come to terms with it, but it did not mean that it did not hurt.

Cyril and Dalton walked back to his chambers, their breathing solemn and their comfort in one another apparent. He might have been assigned to the Saphirrus court for all those years out of debt to his King and Queen, but he had become Dalton's unofficial guardian. He was the man who led him out of the darkness and helped him quell his demons.

As they approached Dalton's grand white wooden door, he sighed. Dalton hated his chambers—this prison cell. He hated what it had done to him, made him weak and hidden. It made him shameful of who he was and the power he had. He envied King Cian, for he made the world his. Cian and Ciara used their powers to forge the world, rather than let their powers cage them in.

"Goodnight, my boy. Remember who you are, always."

Dalton nodded, unable to bear all these emotions at once. He stepped within his chambers quickly and let the doors slam behind him. He would apologize to Cyril for the abruptness of his departure eventually. He would understand. He always did.

He went over to his bed, unable to even will himself to get undressed. The four walls of his chambers did this to him; it suffocated. It quelled his inner fire. It put out his inner light.

He laid down and immediately closed his eyes, willing himself to sleep. *Ten... nine... eight... seven... six... five...* He counted the portraits on the ceiling above, the paintings of the greatest battles their world had ever known. *What it must have been like to...*

Without warning, he began to cough. His senses filled immediately with fire and soot, but as he walked around, there were no flames. He sat up, doubling over as he struggled to breathe. He tried yelling for Cyril, his guards, anyone who could and would help him, but he had no voice. His throat was raw, the burning sensation inescapable. He tried to run toward the door, but he caught himself by his dresser to look in the mirror. His face was flushed, cheeks burning with the heat of invisible fire.

What has happened to me?

He moved again toward the door, pulling as hard as he could. He felt exaggerated and ridiculous, but he was moving with all the force he had. His frozen power had evaporated from him. All that remained was this invisible chord pulling on his chest with no direction to follow.

He ran out into the hallway to see Gwendolyn—whether she was a nurse or a maid he had yet to deduce—coming down the hallway with hot tea. Upon seeing Dalton, she dropped the tea set, and it clattered with an explosive ringing that momentarily drowned out his incessant coughing. He heaved, vomiting from the force of the invisible smoke that clouded his lungs. Gwendolyn screamed, and he caught Cyril's name as he burst through his chamber doors and hobbled over to him, just as everything went black.

FIVE

harmaine coughed violently; smoke filled her lungs as she fought to taste fresh air. Her skin was hot; her vision clouded by the searing pain of the thick black smoke. Another cough racked her chest, and her hand covered her mouth. She stifled a scream as she fully came out of her stupor.

She crawled toward the doorway, her breath ragged. The heat of the flames prickled against her cheeks; her back doused in sweat as she tried to break free from the fire that threatened to swarm her. She squinted, barely making out an image, but she knew what it was. The blazing fire engulfed the bottom stairs, as well as the entire entryway.

Charmaine was trapped.

A hand that was not her own grasped at the ends of her curls, frantically searching for her shoulder blades. The hand was rugged, sweaty, and impatient. The deep rasps of coughing sounded in her ear as she tried to turn her head. The reprieve from the flames allowed her to see who had reached out a helping hand.

With a gasp, she threw her arms around James's soot-covered shirt. Whimpering in relief, throat raw from the fires below, she released her brother.

"We have to get out of here," he wheezed. Scooping her up in his arms, they headed back to her bedroom.

She could not speak; the flames took her power and her voice.

He stood her up, her feet grazing the floor as he steadied both of them. That was James, her anchor. His eyes were ablaze with fear, but his face never showed it.

"The window," he said, steadying her with his arm.

Charmaine's jaw dropped before another cough shook her forward. Her throat burned in agony, warning her not to breathe too deeply. With both of her hands in front of her, she steadied, giving her lungs a second to recover before hoisting herself into the frame of the window. Moonlight danced on the fires which raged around them from all sides, besieged by an invisible enemy.

James took her hand, his mouth thin with worry. "When you hit the ground, run as fast as you can. Don't turn back. Don't wait for me. I'll be right behind you."

"James," she gasped out, the burning of her throat unbearable as she moved her hand to touch it. Her eyes pleaded with him. They were a team. They went together. They always did.

"Get out of here, little sister," he said, that familiar smirk appearing on the side of his mouth.

He pushed her and she fell.

She flew through the air, a silent scream escaping her as she took no breath. Landing with a thud, her knees buckled with sharp pain. The adrenaline rushed to her veins. *Stay whole, stay together.* She tried to focus on her surroundings. She had lived here in the Ten Kingdoms for her entire life, yet at this moment, she did not recognize one piece of the town she knew.

Brinn.

It was gone.

All burned around her.

The fire that she escaped was not contained; rather, it followed her. The moon was covered in a fog of ash and smoke, the only light in the nighttime taken. She squinted as the horror of truth became visible to her eyes. Women ran and screamed, their lives in jeopardy. People—her people—coated in blood, defended the town with all they had. Bile rose in her throat, disgusted, as she realized who stood before her.

The mercenaries were here. They had come.

Ten Kingdoms save us all.

She scrambled to her feet as she pounded forward. She prayed that James was right behind her. Charmaine started toward the town square. Her nightgown dragged behind as she turned the corner of the street they lived on, past Sir Cyania's bake shop, past Tommy's house. Her feet were light, despite the smoke that clouded her lungs, determined to run from the wrath of the evil that plagued the continent.

Footsteps thundered behind her. *James.* Relief overtook her. She whipped her head around, only to see a large man with black teeth and black eyes, smirking as he pursued the chase. His teeth were mostly broken, pieces of them jagged and ruined. His garb was that of a midnight black, an armor to signify the invisible enemy they worked for so tirelessly.

"Hello," the monster said as her spine shook. "Are you who we're looking for?"

Charmaine screamed, terror boiling through her blood. Her arms pumped wildly as she made a break toward the center of Brinn. Her heavy legs dragged her down with each step, the smoke a poison to her lungs.

Think of your training.

She made decisions as she ran. *Right, left, right, right, and left.*

Her breath was labored, heavy, but she pushed on. *You will not take me too.*

She rounded a corner, and without warning, she slipped backward. She hit the ground with a sickening thud. Her vision went black; her coughing explosive as her stomach contracted. She rolled over and vomited on the cobblestones. The mercenary loomed over her, having caught up, and held a lock of her dark hair which he had used to yank her to her doom.

"You are the one we have been looking for," he whispered, his face looking at her with a lust she did not understand.

Who was he? Who did he work for?

Blood pooled on the back of her head as she laid on the cold ground. Her vision faded in and out. The screams of the women and children held her down. The cries of her fellow townspeople shackled her to all she knew of the world's cruelties. She looked to the left and right, searching for someone, *anyone* to save her.

Charmaine was going to die. He was going to kill her.

The man stepped toward her, tossing her black curls aside. Blood coated his hands, his face wicked. She closed her eyes as a scream erupted from her mouth. The mercenary loomed over her with interest, and she realized now what was happening to her.

She was fading, the familiar sensation of her power flickering. She lifted her hands to cover her face, relief washing over her only as she realized that she had not disappeared. For a brief moment, her power threatened to take her tonight.

The mercenary moved to open his mouth as a flash of silver danced across her vision, and the clang of metal met with flesh.

James.

She watched her brother take vengeance on everything the mercenaries had taken from their village. His sword pierced the side of the mercenary's head with haste, and blood sprayed across his shadowed face. *Striking once, two times, and three times.* He plunged his sword into the body of the betrayer. His violet eyes shone as he looked down at his sister, extending his hand as he wiped off the blood of the enemy.

The mercenary was dead.

James grunted as he hoisted her up. Charmaine pushed aside the twinge of pain in her leg. Her head was light, the blood loss evident from the force of being knocked down. She gritted her teeth, but managed to get to her feet with his help.

"We have to go," James said in one breath, his eyes glazed over in worry. He looked very far away.

She shifted her weight forward and took off again, struggling to keep up. The blood coated the back of her neck, dripping from the wound that had been created on her scalp.

Her injuries were too severe to keep running.

She was tired.

Tired of it all.

She slowed down, her breath erratic, a sensory cue to her brother that she would not make it. That she could not make it.

James whipped his head backward, his violet eyes latent with fear. He slowed and flanked her left as they continued to run. They rounded the corner of the town center again, bodies left to the fires as mercenaries made their way to the outskirts.

The mercenary's words played over and over in her mind, *"Are you who we are looking for?"*

She shuddered at the remembrance of the look in his dark eyes as he had said, *"You are the one we have been looking for."*

SIX

harmaine stood by her brother's side at the top of the ravine. The bottom of her nightgown was blackened, charred from the smoke as well as mud. Her midnight hair was plastered to the nape of her neck and James's fingers were covered in blood.

His jaw was set in a hard line, but his eyes were soft. "Do you think Tommy made it out?" he asked softly.

Charmaine sucked in a sharp breath. She thought of Tommy's red hair and green eyes, always inviting one on a scheme that would end in discipline with the townspeople. His kindness and fierce friendship. She could not imagine losing Tommy and he was not even hers to lose.

"If anyone made it out, it is Tommy Cheshire," Charmaine said, trying to sound confident. She tousled James's hair playfully and he half smiled. She could not ignore that his violet eyes remained plagued with worry.

"Chesh would have made it out. He would have survived." He repeated the statement as he turned away from the ravine toward the forest. It was the border to the Second Kingdom, about a mile from Brinn's town center.

"We have never crossed a border before," she said as James took a step forward.

"There's a first time for everything, Char," he said softly, holding out an encouraging hand.

They approached the edge of the ravine. The trees of the forest were larger; the forces of the foreign Kingdom seemed more powerful. They had lived in Brinn their whole lives, yet never had a reason to cross. She thought of the legends that their mother used to tell them of the Second Kingdom. The Kings of Old had risen the seas to fight off their enemies. Their powers brought life back to towns diminished by drought, the healing properties of their gifts. It all seemed so foreign for a King who had not had powers in decades.

"It is nature's way of providing balance," my mother said. "The Kings of Old, from all of the Kingdoms, used their power for evil, instead of good. For selfish reasons, instead of kind ones. This is nature creating a balance. Nature having the Kings pay for their sins. The Gods will rise again, dear one, and they will pick a King to have power. Maybe even many Kings. A King that will rise above the sins of his forefathers and pave the road for a world where those like you will not be outsiders, but rulers in your own right." Her mouth opened into a smile as her dimples became exposed. Her brown hair fell gently over her shoulder blades to her breasts, contrasting her beautiful yellow day dress.

"Mother, you are so pretty," I said, admiring her. "The Kings of Old would have fallen to your feet in worship. To your power."

She squatted down, her eyes soft as she touched the side of my cheek, closing her eyes and breathing in. "No, child, it is you they shall bow to in worship."

Charmaine shivered at the memory.

It is you they shall bow to in worship.

The breeze from the trees picked up and James

slowed. His protective instincts took over as he moved to stand in front of her. The hair on the back of her neck stood up as the winds began to howl.

"James, maybe we should stay in the First Kingdom," she said, apprehensive with the tree's sudden shift in demeanor.

Charmaine remembered the legends Tommy used to spoon-feed her and James about the trees that snatched children from Brinn who drifted too close to the border. *"That's what my Mother says,"* he would say, smirking as if he was in on a big secret.

James whirled around, his brotherly protection radiating. His bloody hands grasped her shoulders as he said harshly, "There is nothing for us here, Char. Mother is dead. Father is dead. Gods know where Tommy is, and the only thing *I* know is that Brinn is gone too. It's all gone."

Tears fell down his cheeks as he tried to take a deep breath. Charmaine was rendered speechless by the sight of her brother so affected. He never spoke of Mother. Not after what happened to her.

She grabbed his right hand, taking it off her shoulder, looking into his eyes softly as she said, "To the Second."

"To the Second Kingdom. The mercenaries would not dare go up against King Blarquenza," he replied, wiping a tear with his pointer finger.

The wind picked up as they approached the tree line. They were massive, towering over them like Gods. They creaked and cracked as the wind pushed them in different directions. The sound of the leaves bristling sent a shiver down her spine as though the trees were warning of the danger of going beyond Kingdom lines. Of leaving Brinn.

James took a step into the trees first, beckoning

Charmaine to come with him as the breeze suddenly halted. They entered the forest with quick steps, eager to be hidden by its legend. There was no clearing in sight, but the magic of the forest could be felt. The darkness that had appeared from the view of Brinn was no more. There was a light to this place, a beauty of greenery and a magic that radiated deep within. It smelled of roses and pine. Charmaine's nose tingled as she smiled.

James craned his head back, laughing softly as they continued onward. Her heart strained at the sound—*happiness*.

"I'm thinking of Tommy—if he knew the beauty of this," she said to herself, daring to bring him up again.

James smiled. "Tommy would have to treat us to ale and wine at the Dragon's Egg."

She laughed at the thought; simultaneously, her heart sank. "The Dragon's Egg. Gone too."

James frowned. "Mercenaries," he spat.

"Did you... did you hear what the one said to me before you—"

"Did he speak to you?" James asked, concern rising in his voice as he slowed to walk beside her.

"He made it seem as though he was looking for me," Charmaine said plainly, suddenly afraid of revealing too much. To know was a risk.

James eyes flashed a dark purple, his jaw set. "But why?" he asked.

"My ability has been a secret to all but family," she said softly, as she stepped carefully over a rather large tree root.

"To me and mother. She took it to the grave," he clarified. "There have been rumors these past months that Tommy and I'd frequent visits to the Egg. Rumors of magic stirring in the border towns, rumors of the King becoming... uncomfortable with the mercenaries' presence among the dissenters."

"And you are just mentioning this now?" she asked, trying to keep the anger out of her voice. "These rumors... what have they said?"

She heard the concern rise in his voice as he answered, "Fears of powers among the commoners. A purge from the mercenaries coming again—not by the King's Guard to remind us that practicing is illegal, but by the dissenters who believe people like you should not exist." James knew that Charmaine's power was her greatest weakness.

"Has it happened recently, Char?" James asked genuinely.

She swallowed. "When I jumped from my bedroom, I felt it coming on. The feeling... it was different though. I could control it. And when the mercenary loomed over me—"

"We need to get you training. For your own safety," he said point-blankly.

"James, we have been training." The thought never crossed her mind to be trained because of the King's disposition. The rumors stated that King Ronan was foul-tempered and hated magic more than anything. His cruelty was unmatched, a hatred for the gifts that once ran rampant among the royals of the First.

Yes, Charmaine herself was not royal, and she did not know why she had been given her gift by the Gods. But surely, the Gods had made mistakes before? People had magic who were not of the royal bloodline? Even if it was a part of history, unwritten and silenced by the Kings who wanted to stay in power, Charmaine would rather not find out. Her mother had always alluded to such, but never gave an explanation.

"Someone had to teach the Kings of Old to control their powers," James half-whispered to himself. "You know—"

"What?"

James had the same look on his face that he had when he figured out the strength or charisma of a new blade.

"They say the Prince of the First is a King of Old."

She blinked. "Mother's prophecy."

"Mother's seer abilities were… periodically correct. In some capacity." His eyes darkened. "But the prophecies she came up with, she reverently believed. She died for it."

"Is this more talk you heard at the Egg?" she asked, trying to ease into the conversation. Mother was always a point of discussion among men, especially superstitious ones. Not for James though, not since he lost her.

Since *they* lost her.

Their mother was a Cipher, a woman with the abilities of a Thinker, but she was never allowed to train as one in the Tenth Kingdom, due to her sex. She wanted to keep James talking about their mother as long as she could. She held her tongue as her mind tumbled into the depths of her budding anxiety.

"For once, this information was not just privy to the people at the Egg," he said as a chuckle escaped him. "I am serious, Charmaine. The Prince is apparently *chosen*."

"Jamie, I am sure you have heard the rumors that the Prince has not been seen by anyone really, since Princess Carinthya—" She stopped, unable to voice the brutality that the mercenaries had taken upon the Princess of the First Kingdom.

"Servants talk, Char, and they come home to their families where they divulge secrets they observe from the royals." He smirked; curiosity piqued across his face as he ducked under a branch.

"They talk of what? We do not even live near the castle. It is still an evening's ride away," she said as her own curiosity got the best of her.

"They talk of the Prince—those from Thallgan who come down to the likes of Brinn for cheaper goods. They speak of rooms freezing over ten times colder than winter itself. Of the King being specific about who sees him. Of him being locked in his room, private lessons on how to control his growing power." He spoke as though he lived it himself.

Despite his chilling words, she laughed, exhausted. The pain returned to her leg as the adrenaline from the escape wore off. "Do you really think this so?"

"This is serious, Char. They have tutors at the palace, Thinkers who know how to control their powers." James looked into her eyes, a sincerity so deep she almost crumbled.

"The Prince is not going to share his tutor with me if that's what your grand plan is," she said, masking the uncomfortable pins of pain that slammed into her knee with each step.

He punched her lightly on the shoulder. "I do not think we should head toward the castle. Shit, Char, I do not even know where the bloody thing is! I only think if we seek out a tutor, we know they exist."

"And? What good does a tutor do if we end up in the Second Kingdom? Do you think that King Blarquenza has magic too? Will he lend me his powerful friends out of the kindness of his heart?" she asked, adoring irritation for her brother's optimism laced throughout her questioning.

"Buzz off. If the Prince is truly who he is rumored to

be—the first King in centuries to have power—then he could end the mercenaries' terror on our lands. Across our Kingdom. Maybe he could even help us protect you. *How can a Prince with powers live under the rule of a man who bans abilities?*" he said, his voice breathless. "If they catch you, Char, if anyone finds out about your abilities—I cannot lose you."

"Does he terrify you? The idea of him?" she asked, afraid of the answer and afraid of the questions she could not ask.

"With a power like that, power like King Cian? He could destroy us all. Easily."

SEVEN

Charmaine awoke with her head against James's legs. They had stopped to rest in the middle of the night, broken by the defeat of losing all which they held dear. As she opened her eyes, she discerned more than just James hovering, concerned.

A purple robe came into her line of sight, draped with gold armor. She sat up quickly. The immediate rush of blood to her head gave her an instantaneous headache.

The Knighthood.

James grasped her hand tightly as a man crouched beside them. His eyes were dark blue; nose covered in dirt, a stark contrast to his immaculate uniform. His hair was light blond. His eyebrows were raised inquisitively, arched perfectly at the ends as if he were hand-painted by the Gods. His shoulders were slim for what she imagined to be a member of the Royal Court, with thin lips that looked like they would betray secrets.

"My lady." He dipped his head slightly in a bow. "My name is Lawton Thornwood of the King's Knighthood."

He was getting a read on her, she realized. To figure out who they were and why they were there. She would not give him the satisfaction; too much had gone wrong as of late.

She took a deep breath and steadied herself against James's body. Her eyes were still heavy with sleep as she focused to look awake as she faced Lawton. He did not appear unkind; the Knights of the Kingdom had a reputation that preceded them. They did the bidding of King Ronan, but they were fair and just. Their only fault was that they did not control the mercenaries; even they frequently fought against their tyranny. She thought back to hearing of Ronan's tour for his knights, out in the villages trying to catch the mercenaries before they struck.

And picking up the pieces if they were too late.

They did not pillage. They respected women, obeyed their King, and prayed for the salvation of their Kingdom. Her mind wandered to the knight of destiny, who had drifted into Brinn before the fire. Charmaine wondered if he was there. *Did Lawton Thornwood know him?*

Charmaine hoped they could trust him, as she trusted their legacy.

She pushed away the traumas of the past few hours— the walking, the running, and the heat of the flames that destroyed all that she knew.

Nodding in response to his greeting, James answered, "I am James Grimes of Brinn, sir. This is my sister, Charmaine Grimes of Brinn."

"Brinn?" Lawton asked, his eyes clouded by grief. He looked between them, noticing the blood encrusted on James's hands and the charcoal ends of her nightgown. "You survived." He seemed bewildered. "We… we determined this morning there were *no* survivors."

"Well, here we are. Sorry to disappoint," James said, his familiar smirk appearing across his face, despite the gravity. This was her brother, the man she knew. The terror in his eyes last night at the thought of losing her—losing everything—would haunt her forever.

Lawton returned a similar smile; his eyes darted between the two of them in wonder. "I do not wish to be intrusive on your details. You must return to my encampment with me," he said, worry clouding his eyes.

"We were not followed, sir. If that was what you were wondering," Charmaine said, speaking for the first time. She would not lose an opportunity to protect her family. *To protect James.*

Lawton looked at her intently. He approached cautiously, as if she might reject him. If he were anyone but a knight, she would consider the gesture improper, a gesture of courtship. Something was different about Lawton, though. He seemed sincere.

"I am only worried about the horrors you two have experienced. War waged against an invisible enemy is no war for the likes of men, women, and children." He extended a hand to help her up.

Pulling herself to a stand, she grunted with effort. She did not need to look at her leg to determine that it would be black and blue. The impact of last night left its mark.

"Are there any others?" James asked hopefully as they walked toward the camp.

"We found not one alive, Sir James. I am deeply sorry."

She squeezed James's hand. *Tommy. Their townsfolk. Everything.* Looking at James's face, he offered a weak smile. The fire in his violet eyes that glimmered before was dulled.

They walked onward, approaching the crest of a hill

shaded further by trees. She looked at James as he mouthed, "Back to the First."

She nodded in reply. These were the King's Knights, after all. *But why had Lawton been in Second Kingdom territory?*

"Sir Lawton, please pardon my forwardness," Charmaine said plainly, straining on her leg to keep up with him. She hated feeling so weak.

He turned around, a smirk appearing on his face as if he enjoyed all that was improper. "Please, be more forward," he shot back, once again turning to focus on the descent of the hill in front of them back toward the border of the First Kingdom.

She could not help returning the smirk. She bit her lip nervously as she blurted, "What brings you to the woods?"

James whipped his head in her direction, playing parent with her directness. She shrugged her shoulders in reply.

Lawton threw back his head and laughed, almost tripping over a root as they finished descending the hill. "I like you."

He continued, "We were looking for survivors. If you thought I was doing something suspect, within reason of course, but incorrect. We went back to Brinn when the fires started. We salvaged all that we could—clothing, food, weapons, and things we could bring with us to give refugees—as we continued our mission. Our Knight's coalition leader, our head to say it formally, suggested that if anyone ran, they would have hopefully run for these woods. The mercenaries wouldn't dare follow in such a magic-encompassed land. They wouldn't have been able to stand the invisible powers that fill the very air here. We decided to split up per our head's request and I happened to find two very sleepy siblings."

"So, you have been to Brinn before?" Charmaine said.

"Well, I guess we have your head to thank for finding us," James chided at the same time.

"You can tell him yourself, Sir James. I am sure he will love the ego boost," Lawton replied lazily, but not without a look in Charmaine's direction, acknowledging what she now knew.

She had met these knights before. He gestured to the break in the trees below. He seemed to relax more as they walked, as if the formalities fell off him with every step.

In front of them were four vibrant purple tents with gold detailing. As they got closer, she noticed they were snowflakes, delicately falling to the bottom of the tent. They were beautiful, made to demonstrate the wealth of the Kingdom, and the men who lived inside them.

She noted the tent in the center. *The head's tent.*

As they approached the purple tents, Lawton yelled, "Rand! Pen! Laoch! Come out, come out, wherever you are!"

James laughed. "Are you calling dogs or your king's men?"

"Both," Lawton said, grinning.

"Lawton?" Charmaine heard a man's voice, as the front tapestries of the large middle tent rattled.

The man standing in front of her was breathtaking. His skin was tanned from the sun, his brown eyes warm and inviting. His hair was a light brown, amber flecks shining in his gaze. He was tall, a purple tunic tight around the swell of the muscular arms. His jaw was set as he looked between James and Charmaine, unsure of their disposition. As he lifted a hand to run it through his honey-coated hair, Charmaine stifled a gasp. His hands and arms were covered by the most intricate flower tattoos. Roses, lavender, baby's breath, and endless vines decorated his arms in an embrace of beauty.

She had seen this man before.

Spoken to him.

At the Dragon's Egg, not but two nights ago. This was the knight of destiny.

"Lawton…" he said, exasperation evident in his voice.

"Rand, it isn't what you think. They're from Brinn," Lawton said. His appearance shifted from the young man they had met to the knight he claimed to be.

Randolph paused, running another hand through his hair. "Survivors?"

"I found them in the woods. Asleep. They are the *only* survivors." Lawton walked in front of them protectively, shielding his new friends from any more trauma.

Did he think Randolph would turn us away?

"Do they have names?" Rand asked, gesturing to them with his flowered hands. A smirk appeared on his face. He enjoyed messing with Lawton.

We never told each other our names.

"Sir James and Miss Charmaine Grimes, Sir Randolph."

"You'll be privy to that when you learn my name," he had said.

Randolph. This was Randolph. *Then why did he have those tattoos?*

"And as the head of the legion, Sir Lawton, what do you suppose my decision should be regarding Sir James and Miss Grimes?" he asked, his eyes playful, but his voice stern.

Charmaine could see it took everything in Lawton not to roll his eyes. "Sir, we are about to depart for the castle tomorrow. I only think it is fair to bring Sir James and Miss

Grimes with us, to testify against the mercenary attacks."

James stepped forward before Randolph could answer. "You want to take us to the King?" he said, his eyes clouded with concern.

Charmaine's stomach dropped. The King. *What if I can't control my ability? What will happen to me? What will happen to James?*

Her mind tumbled into despair when faced with the different scenarios that could get her enslaved to the King's servitude. His prejudices were known across the continent. The belief that only the royals are to hold powers of Old. If she were caught, it would be a fate worse than death.

"Justice," Randolph said, looking at them both. He panned to Lawton, taking two steps closer as he extended a tattooed hand to pat him on the shoulder. "Well done, brother." He said it kindly; a dimple appeared on the side of his face.

"Justice for whom?" Charmaine asked before she could stop herself.

Randolph turned, his eyes wide as if he had forgotten she was there to begin with. *That they knew one another.* She twirled her hair with her finger slowly, avoiding direct eye contact to prevent her pale skin flushing a bright red. She was self-conscious with her burned nightgown.

"I want justice for the people of the First," Randolph said sternly. He paused, surveying her body language. "If you are comfortable."

On your own terms.

His voice had a kindness to it she did not expect of a head of the King's Guard, but it was on par with the man he had been at the pub. He seemed determined to right the wrongs of those over whom he had no control.

She replied, "I am okay with it." She looked at James.

"For Tommy." She inched closer to put a hand on his shoulder, steadying herself as much as he was steadying her.

"Very well," Randolph said as he retreated toward his tent. He looked over his shoulder as a hand of roses pushed the opening to the tent aside. "Lawton, show them to their tents. We ride at dawn."

The tent that Lawton directed them to was small, fit for one man. They would be sharing. It was decorated simply. A straw bed with a few blankets and pillows decorated the head, while a chair existed in the corner with a side table for any work to be done. But there was no work to be done. It had been burned to the ground with the rest of Brinn. They had nothing.

"I hope these accommodations are comforting for you."

"It's more than we have," James said.

"We will ride at dawn," Lawton said, reiterating Randolph, looking around the tent as if he were inspecting it. "Perc and Laoch will be back soon, our other comrades for our escapades."

James smirked as exhaustion hit Charmaine like a wave. She had no inclination for food or water. She just wanted to rest. To have sleep find her and wipe away the nightmares for the next few hours. To distract her from the fear of what was to come.

James looked at her as she sat on the straw, her leg's fatigue spreading fast to all corners of her body.

"We will ride at dawn," he repeated, gesturing softly for Lawton to exit the tent.

"Sleep well."

EIGHT

ue to his extenuating house arrest, Dalton Saphirrus had gotten rather good at sneaking out of the castle. It was his favorite game. Something about ditching his manservants and eluding Cyril thrilled Dalton's blood. Just because he was to be kept under lock and key did not mean he could not unleash himself from the cell.

Well, it did, but nobody had to find out.

Except sometimes they did, and that was the end to his fun as he knew it.

Dalton laughed like a madman as he picked the lock to his chambers; the familiar groan of the massive wooden door a comfort in the last five years. The heavy doors gave way to the world which he dreamt of once again rejoining; the gateway to his prior life, but also the entrance to a new one.

The doors gave him hope.

He pushed harder. If he moved slowly, the groan was worse. It was like ripping the bandage off a wound which was not fully healed, stinging and burning.

He stepped through the crevice and blew air out of his

mouth. His lips tingled with the sensation of winter, a declaration of his heritage and bloodline seeping into the air. His icy declaration of power plunged toward the door's hinges, freezing them just enough that if they were to close, a forgiving groan would slow the passage of time. If he moved quickly, the door would shut fully by dawn, with him sound asleep inside.

He smirked like the Prince he used to be as he twirled and danced down the hallway. He was silent in the night, not interested in awakening anyone and having to explain what in the Ten Kingdoms he was doing outside his chambers.

Dalton laughed. The last time he was caught was luckily not by Cyril or Athelred, rather by a maiden. He recalled she had red hair that draped down her back, her breasts rather exposed by her nightgown as she tried to flirt with him, despite no knowledge of who he was. It was refreshing as it was irritating—to feel normal again.

"I have yet to see you around the castle," she said.

"If you had seen me around the castle, you definitely would have remembered me." He smirked, for there was no way she could have missed the crown which would have been cemented atop his head if his father ever let him return to his normal life.

She leaned against the door; her eyes heavy with desire as they lingered a little too long on his lips. He licked them just to mess with her. His eyes surely twinkled with the fun of the game they played.

Dalton laughed himself into a fit the next day when he heard Cyril outside his chambers, yelling about the Cipher from the Fifth who had somehow seen him out and about the prior night.

Of course, he denied anything of truthful substance.

He was more focused on the fact that a Cipher, a woman who could claim Thinker rights, was in the First Kingdom. Cyril scolded him for asking dangerous questions, to which Dalton reminded him to no avail, according to his father, he was the most dangerous thing in this castle.

"Therefore, I have nothing to fear," Dalton said, pretending to be bored, but really more so irritated that there were things in the castle happening that he was not aware of. For the first time, he realized that his position seemed to rock his sense of what the First Kingdom was, and how it played a part in the world they lived in.

Cyril smiled at him, his eyes flaming with irritation, but also another emotion Dalton couldn't place. "You have everything to fear, boy."

The madness of Dalton's situation became more apparent the more he snuck out. He did nothing wrong, other than being the pathetic son of a King who was determined to make a mockery of his son's life.

He walked the halls with his head high, his fingers interlaced behind his back, as though he greeted crowds and waved to suitors. He bowed to doors as if he was meeting the Kings and Queens of other Kingdoms. He smiled as if he were smiling to his sister from afar, playing a secret game like they once did many years ago.

Sneaking out to play Prince, what a joke.

Slammed with the memory of the other night, pain throbbed in his throat as he remembered what it was like to choke on air. Cyril had been mad with rage and worry. The look on his face reminded Dalton that Cyril cared deeply for him.

Dalton was a pain in Cyril's backside, but it was not without affection.

A door swung open. The familiar creak of the wood

shook him to his core. He was taken back to being locked out of his own chambers, forced to reckon with the decision of escaping. He breathed, shoving the memory of the whip against his back that first time. His bloodcurdling screams replayed in his head perfectly, harmonizing in agony as he had sobbed through each round of the abuse.

He threw himself against the wall in response to the noise. The wounds that had almost healed from his most recent escape were rough and itchy against the silk of his dark tunic. He took a sharp breath. His eyes fluttered shut in response to the irritation of his scabs.

He stopped breathing entirely as he waited for the body to turn from the doors that were closing shut. He refused to look, refused to pay tribute to them. He knew he had to strike while he had the element of surprise.

"Three, two, one…" he whispered as he twitched the tips of his fingers. His eyes fluttered open as he stared in the opposite direction of the open door. The familiar cool air whisked around his fingers in a passionate embrace.

Calling on his power somehow felt like performing a dance: the push and pull dragging him to a deeper understanding of the twists and turns of raw magic. It swirled faster in his blood, the frozen sensation unbearable now as he called on all that was primal.

He flipped his head to the side, and at the same time, unleashed all the pent-up energy.

Fear.

Happiness.

Sadness.

Pain.

It exploded out of him in an array of frozen tundra.

His fingers closed together as he pulled back on all that he had let go.

Come back to me, come back to me, come back to me.

The light of his snow died as he refocused on the scene before him. He was exhausted, the unfamiliar bounds of his energy tested. Dalton silently cursed. He would have loved the opportunity to exercise his power beyond small bursts with Cyril. He wanted the chance to dance with his power and see where he would bottom out.

If there even was a bottom to the limits of his gift.

He blinked twice as the world returned to night around him, and he immediately withheld a howling laugh.

From the waist up was Cyril; his eyes blazed in fury. His white tunic was laced with snowflakes, and from the waist down, he had been frozen to the marble wall of the castle. A block of ice cauterized around his legs, entrapping him and preventing his release.

His voice was laced with a rage Dalton had never heard come from Cyril. "Did I do something to offend you, my Prince?"

"Dearest Cyril, I thought you were a murderer in the night!" Dalton unlatched a dagger from his belt to chip away at what he had done.

Cyril wiggled uncomfortably. "Have you been practicing?"

"My target practice? Seriously, Cyril, you almost get blasted to smithereens with my snow, and you think I have been practicing? We are lucky I have not been, and that my aim is shit. Thank the Ten Kingdoms that it was only your legs…"

"My boy, it isn't to fret over," Cyril said as he lifted a leg and broke free of the ice. "I am rather impressed with you."

"Impressed that I didn't almost kill you by accident?" he asked, his voice latent with sarcasm.

"Impressed that you *haven't* been practicing."

was King Cian, over a century ago, but a ruler had not had such power since.

She remembered James telling her of the Prince and the swirling rumors. *To be a Prince and have the power of the First...*

Hearing a horse behind him, Randolph craned his head to see who it was. His face softened when he realized it was Charmaine.

"Were you expecting someone else?" she asked.

"I am glad you are not who I suspected." He glanced backward at Lawton, who was taking the final bites of his apple. "If it were, I would have shoved you off your high horse." He chuckled, the dimple once again appearing at the corner of his mouth.

They slowed as they looked upon the front of the castle for the first time. The gates were gold at first glance, a pale blue hue which complimented the white stones that fortified the castle's exterior. A massive, white door seemed to glimmer, outlined in a marble so white it seemed to be part of a glass lake. There were three towers that sat atop the monstrosity of its structure. The tops of them were a light blue, covered with blue and white stained-glass windows.

"It's..." Charmaine said, stunned at the opulence.

"It is," Randolph replied, taking his sword and inserting the tip into what she assumed was a keyhole. Twisting the blade, the gates opened as they stepped through the threshold to King Ronan's domain.

ELEVEN

ismounting from their horses, they were escorted by the palace guards to the throne room to meet the King. The servants took their belongings, anything the Knights had brought with them or collected in Brinn.

As Charmaine walked through the castle halls, she realized that only stiffness remained with her leg. It was as if the wound had healed itself along the ride. Passing through the castle walls was the medicine.

The blood roared in Charmaine's ears. Fear stirred within her, elevated with every step. She was entering the palace of King Ronan, who executed men and women without a fair trial for magic.

And she had magic.

It had been days since she last almost shifted.

Turned invisible. Blinked out of existence.

That did not mean it could not happen again. Charmaine took deep breaths through her nose and out of her mouth as they walked along the hallway.

Focus.

The halls were grand, lined with gold and pearls as

decorations on the walls. The marble flooring was magnificent. Instead of swirls of natural stone, the flooring had accents of a winter blue. She focused on that blue, letting it consume her with its serenity and beauty.

I will not shift.

She gritted her back teeth against one another as they approached the grandest of doors. The door was also gold, covered with similar decoration to that of the hallway walls. Depictions of Kings, Queens, Princes, and Princesses: a homage to the lineage and prestige of the First Kingdom. She was mesmerized by the rich history that this door portrayed, but also the symbol of wealth King Ronan perpetuated by living in this environment.

Her own inferiority gazed back at her.

She grinded her teeth again, harder, fear taking hold. With a crack of her neck to the side, she reminded herself that she was the one who had power. She needed to start believing that more.

The guards opened the door, revealing a throne room worthy of the dynasty, and atop a staircase of no more than ten steps, stood the King and Queen. Their hair was black as night, their skin a flawless porcelain. Their eyes were a deep blue she had never seen before, the power of their lineage living within.

Queen Aine had a beautiful face. Her features were soft, kind even. Her long black hair looked like silk, pulled neatly behind her head in a braid. Her eyes were highlighted with a blue dust, heightening their intensity. Her lips were covered with a blue lipstick. The Queen of the First Kingdom looked like all that her title commanded.

King Ronan was nothing short of handsome. His eyes blazed with a fire Charmaine did not think possible for being so blue. His lips were thin, pursed with a displeasure she only assumed could come from his own lack of magic. His eyes had dark circles under them, almost appearing bruised compared to the rest of his beautiful skin. Despite looking tired, he was alive with a persona worthy of the true King of the First.

This was the man who imprisoned those he deemed unworthy of their gifts from the Gods, who hated anyone with the powers that had been gifted.

James's presence loomed behind her, standing close enough to protect her, should something go wrong.

If she lost control.

This was the first test.

They bowed as a collective unit, stopping before the first of the ten steps, gazing up at their superiority.

Randolph spoke. No one else dared to breathe. "Your Majesty. I bring with you grave news regarding Brinn." He did not fear the King, it seemed. For Randolph, this was business.

The King continued to listen, giving no indication that he was set to reply.

Randolph continued, "Your Majesty, Brinn was attacked two nights ago. Pillaged by mercenaries."

The King's shadows under his eyes darkened as he sat in his chair.

It was Queen Aine who spoke. "Mercenaries? Are you sure? There hasn't been an attack since the border of the Third in the summer." Her eyes were grave, her expression sad.

She cared?

"I am, your Majesty. These are the only two survivors. We have brought them with us today, to speak about their experiences. They are willing." Randolph stepped backward, allowing James and Charmaine to step forward.

"How old is the knight?"

"Nineteen. He joined when he was sixteen. Ronan promoted him after two years."

"Why?"

"Wait till you see that man with a blade," he whispered.

"How old was Carinthya when she went missing?" Charmaine asked pointedly, changing the subject. *Anything to avoid discussing my obvious attraction to Randolph that Lawton so keenly detected.*

"My, my. So many questions," he said, looking bored. "She was sixteen." He gestured to the picture. "I think I said that already, did I not?"

Her jaw hung open. "She was sixteen? The Queen let her go?"

Lawton shrugged. "One, I never said Aine was a good mother. I only told you she's more ruthless than she appears. A woman of many talents. And two, I did say Carinthya was a free spirit. Dalton and his parents—maybe a few servants—those are the only ones who would remember her today. There are so many quick visitors here." He lightly touched the portrait of Carinthya's face with his index finger. "There wasn't much stopping her from what I remember. A legend with a knife, talented in all facets. But she had a knack for exploration, for being what she wanted versus what was expected of her."

When he pulled away, he was smiling. Craning his head, he looked at Charmaine. Half rolling his eyes he said, "I know you have another question. Just ask it."

"Have you met him?" she asked in a whisper.

Recognition lit up Lawton's eyes as he smirked; his eyes alight with mischief. He replied, "I haven't seen him since he much looked like this." He gestured to the picture. "Ronan always kept a tight leash on him, not difficult to imagine given the end of his sister. And Ronan himself. You saw him earlier, pleasant man."

"There are rumors—" she started, ignoring Lawton being Lawton.

"There are always rumors, Charmaine. It is what you choose to believe as fact from fiction that matters," he interrupted.

"There are rumors of his power."

"Oh really?" he asked, nonchalantly running a hand through his waves.

"James told me that the rumors were from the castle servants. The cold air, the frozen objects—" She stopped herself as he paced in front of the painting. "What is it, Lawton?"

He glanced at the picture one last time, getting a last look. "We should go. I think we've overstayed our welcome with the Snow siblings."

⊕

She found James after, awaiting in her designated chambers. He sat at the foot of her silk sheets, his eyes glistening with a purple daze. He seemed entranced by the whole palace, the ferocity in which it stood.

"Jamie, this place—" she whispered, afraid the walls would hear of her admittance to it and tell its inhabitants.

He stood, hopping off the bed with grace. He shook his head, knowing what she meant without an explanation. That is how he and Charmaine were. They spoke without speaking. They were two halves of a whole, bonded by their secrets and by their reality.

"Charmaine, you look rattled," he said. There was no warm embrace in his voice; rather, it was a fear that encapsulated it.

Randolph's mouth parted slightly, "That is my King. Your father."

"I never did care for family much," he said.

"Well, I did," Randolph pushed. *Was I trying to be executed? He was a Prince! My Prince.*

"You and I both know that isn't true, Eniar," Dalton said as he meandered down the dark hallway. As he entered the light, the white marble seemed to glisten in his approach.

Randolph thought it must have been the trick of the light. His hands balled up at his sides. He fought slamming them into the wall; frustration and disgust taking over.

How in the Ten Kingdoms did he learn my last name?

FOURTEEN

t had been two days since Charmaine and Lawton visited the chamber of paintings. They returned again today and Charmaine was just as haunted the second time she saw Carinthya's painting as she had been the first.

He grunted, drawing her attention back to him. "It might be best, Charmaine, if we keep our escapades our little secret. Especially the content of our discussions and the visit with the world's most famous siblings."

Charmaine nodded in reply, pretending she heard whatever it was Lawton had said. "Indeed, Sir Lawton," she said mindlessly.

Lawton faked being scared, pretending to shiver with a dramatic expression upon his face. "That is my name and title. Oh, how you wound me Miss Grimes."

She closed the door behind her. Her chamber was one of the most beautifully decorated rooms she had ever been in. In the three days since she arrived, she had yet to overcome that feeling of the wind being knocked out of her upon seeing the beauty of every room. There was a vibrancy of colors—the rich purples, stark teals, and pungent greens engulfed every room in a beautiful chaos. The materials of the furniture and decorations were outlandish. They were gold, velvet, and silk. The richness of the room was both beautiful and suffocating.

Her bed was that of royal proportions. The silk on it was a deep purple, matching her eyes, as well as James's. She touched them, the delicacy overcoming her sense of touch.

Charmaine walked toward the desk in the corner. The chair accompanying it looked much like a throne itself, teal and gold decorations turning it Godly. She had no work to do, but somehow wished that she did so she could use it properly. The velvet that sat upon its seat was plush, daring those only worthy to sit on it.

The door to her chambers suddenly opened with a loud creaking, and in walked James, dressed in a new garb similar to that of Randolph. His black tunic deepened the gaze of his purple eyes, his hair looking less wild. His pants were those of the guard.

As if to answer her thoughts, he gestured to them, muttering, "Randolph."

"You look good, brother," she said, cheekily smiling at his new dressing.

"How was your walk with Lawton?" he asked, surveying the room in all its glory.

I went to the gallery again. I saw the portraits of Princess Carinthya and Prince Dalton. The rumors from the Egg are rumored true beyond its walls. The Kings of Old are rumored to have returned. She took a deep breath, instead replying, "It is nice to make friends."

James looked at her with a gentle smile. "Are you nervous? Do you think we should not have come? Continued on the run in the woods?"

"It is a little late for that, Jamie," she said, striding toward the stained-glass window next to the grand desk.

"Char, I am serious," he said as he took her arm.

"I think this is right. Being here. I cannot help but feeling like… like it is good. Like we are needed somehow, to right the wrongs of what happened to our people," she said, trying to sound strong, even though it was taking everything in her not to be terrified. "If the King were to find out of my abilities… even if Lawton did today while we were alone… Who knows who we can trust? We do not know when, or even if, I will change again. There is no direction, no pattern. But you know as well as I that the last few years it has picked up in frequency. I do not want us to get complacent and then all hell breaks loose, and we lose our heads."

His mouth twitched, fighting a smile. "I definitely want to keep my head, as I do think it would not suit you if you did not have one."

She nearly landed a blow to his shoulder.

"I think we should trust Randolph," he said after he swatted her arm away.

"The head of the Knight's Guard? Legionary to the King himself? That is the last person I would pick Jamie. You cannot be serious," she spat harsher than she intended.

There was something speculative about him. He had an angst behind his persona that left her breathless, yet confused. She could not get a read on him.

Yet, the night that she had met him for the first time seemed to haunt her, for he had been kind and welcoming.

But now that she was at the castle, he had barely seen her, for he was sworn to duty.

Her mind had not turned off since she arrived.

"While you were with Lawton, I was with him, Char.

Ever so briefly, it seems, but before he left to go to his council meeting. He seems... different than the rest. Where Lawton is playing the world around him like a fiddle, Randolph is fighting for the rights of the King's subjects. He only wanted us to come here, of our own accord, to appeal to the King. To draw him out of his complacency with the mercenaries attacking towns, instead of attacking him. To bring peace, for once, to these lands." He took a deep breath, not breaking eye contact.

"Char," he said, "do you trust me?"

"I have not heard you talk about anything this passionately since you and Tommy saved up enough to buy yourselves new swords from Smith."

"I feel as safe with Randolph as I do with a blade in my hand, I assure you," James said.

Charmaine smiled up at him, willing the conversation to shift yet again to anything but Randolph. "What are we do to with ourselves for the next fortnight? When are the lords to come to the Kingdom of Snow? When are we to give our testimony?"

"Many questions, sister. For one, we are to do what we please that is safe. Two, the lords are to come in one day. Randolph confirmed with the King himself that they will arrive at Winter Solstice. We are to give our testimony then."

"I swear you and Lawton are more siblings than we," she said, laughing and gesturing to his demeanor.

James flashed her a smile as he rolled up his purple sleeves. "I am off to find something to occupy my time," he said, turning around and skipping toward her chamber doors.

"Be good, Jamie," she said, a smile encroaching against her will.

James was infectious. He always had been. He turned around once he had a hand on the door handle, waiting to pull it. His eyes clouded with concern as he said, "Please try to stay visible."

Charmaine was not sure what Gods she specifically prayed to, or if any existed at all. The Gods' power died with that of the Kings of Old, according to the continent's history. The Gods went to sleep and so did their power—the gift to the true Kings and Queens to wield to protect their people. But now, apparently, a royal had the power again. So, what did that mean for the Gods?

She sat in her chambers now, wrapped in the purple silk that lined her bed. A full day had passed since her brother visited her last. She had also been introduced to her chamber maid, a gesture she deemed wholly unnecessary, but Randolph said was a 'Gesture of kindness from the King and Queen.'

That was the only interaction she had had with Randolph over the past two days, and it happened earlier this morning. Charmaine felt as though she was avoiding Randolph, unintentionally.

He introduced Gwendolyn to Charmaine, her new chamber-maiden. The girl, Gwendolyn, was incredibly kind. Her blonde hair was vibrant. Her voice was cheery and her blue eyes were bright. She needed her company, for the two days she had been there were mostly driven by fear.

James seemed rather inclined to spend all his time with Randolph. She sighed, curling the silk around her legs in a comforting embrace. She needed her brother more than he was ever to understand.

Her skin was ragged against the serenity of the bedding. The luxurious purple made her skin look like that of velvet porcelain, if there was such a thing. She did not know how long she lay there for, pushing aside the fears that had plagued her mind all day in the courtyard with Lawton. The openness outside of the castle walls felt freeing, whereas the masses of people felt suffocating.

Tonight. Tonight was the Winter Solstice.

Almost on cue, there was a knock at her door. Without waiting for a reply, the door swung open, and James skipped through it, merry in his gesture as if he were laying siege to the Fourth Kingdom, like King Deaglán centuries before. Gwendolyn followed behind him, her straight blonde hair neatly tied behind her head in a braid.

Gwendolyn noted her posture, wary of Charmaine and James. Charmaine tried to reassure her upon their introduction that there was no need for formalities, but she continued to call her "Miss Grimes" and James "Master James." He got a kick out of it.

"Wakey-wakey, sister dearest. I come bearing gifts," James said, his smile wide across his face.

He took a deep breath, his hair unkempt as he ran a hand through it, as if it were to do anything to fix it. Gwendolyn walked behind him, in her hands a ball of black tulle and black flowers. Charmaine looked at her, confused.

"Jamie..." she said, as Gwendolyn laid the dress on the bed in front of her.

The girl's eyes were bright with emotion. *Kindness? Happiness?* She could not place it.

She gasped. Her hands flew to her face in wonder. It was the most beautiful gown she had ever seen. The intricacy of the flowers that decorated the petals were so detailed she squinted to get a better look. The bodice of the dress was nearly opaque.

"Jamie, how did you—" she asked, unable to finish her sentence.

"I have been… looking around. There was a dressmaker in the courtyard yesterday, appealing to the ladies from the court. I told him of you, and he made this."

He made a noise of surprise as Charmaine nearly jumped into his arms. The hug took him off his feet as he fell to the floor with her atop him. He threw his head back and laughed, *really laughed.*

"JAMES," she shouted, tears threatening to fall from her eyes as she stood up again, extending a hand to help him.

"CHAR!" he half shouted in reply, playfully mocking, touching the corners of her eyes lightly.

"What did you sell?" There was no way he could have afforded this luxury by himself.

"My sword," he said hesitantly.

Her heart dropped in her chest. "James… I cannot accept this," she said, turning around at the words.

The sword he got from the Smith with Tommy.

Gone.

He stepped closer to her, and his eyes glistened with emotion. "You will, and you must. We have endured too much to have our joy taken away." He gestured to the dress now lying on the teal bedroom chair.

She forced a smile, trying to forget the information James had told her, turning her gaze to Gwendolyn, who gave her a nod of affirmation. She took a deep breath before returning her gaze.

"I will be back to escort my sister to the solstice," James said, heading toward the door.

Gwendolyn glanced at him as he strode past her. Her eyes contained an emotion she could not define.

The door closed behind them with a gentle click. She walked over to the gown again, admiring its feminine beauty.

"May I help you?" Gwendolyn asked, her eyes looking downward.

"Please, Gwendolyn," she said.

Together, they reworked the curls of Charmaine's hair to a refined version. With the front strands pinned back, her face became alight, no longer shadowed by the darkness of her features.

Gwendolyn lined her eyelids with a green pigment, the shimmering glitter offsetting the vibrancy of her violet eyes. Her lips were left untouched, as well as her cheeks. Taking a step back as they finished, her mouth went agape.

The dress was anything but modest. The roses were dramatically placed on the bodice, as well as the waistline. Where there were no petals, the fabric seemed to dissipate, leaving very little to the imagination. A skintight black material hit the line of her groin, enveloped to the floor by a black tulle. A slit in the tulle strode up her leg, allowing her to expose more skin than she ever had before when she moved.

Charmaine felt beautiful.

"Just lovely," Gwendolyn said, proud of her work.

Charmaine smiled at her, feeling regal and powerful. "I am forever indebted to you for your skills, Gwendolyn."

She blushed, but said no more.

❦

James looked dazzling. He wore black garb decorated similarly to hers. The tunic had black rose petals at the collar, looking as if the prose of power had dawned on him. His pants were a black leather, donned with boots to match. His hair was the usual tousled mess, but it did not seem to matter.

Together, they were a matching pair.

Charmaine felt exposed as they walked down the hall toward the throne room where the festivities would occur. Her heels clicked against the marble floor, consistent with her feet landing in strides as they made their way down the white hall. The blue and white stained-glass windows illuminated the passage with a blue tint, bringing the castle to frozen life.

She took a deep breath before entering the room where they agreed to do the King's bidding.

There were hundreds of people in the throne room.

Immediately, Charmaine was overwhelmed.

"Breathe," James said as he pushed further into the crowd upon spotting Randolph and Lawton.

Lawton, upon laying eyes on her, dropped his jaw. Randolph's brown eyes went wide, his tan skin darkening in a flush.

Charmaine stifled a snort at their expressions.

"My, my, do you have any idea how you look tonight?" Lawton said, touching the roses on her bodice.

"Better than you," she said, gesturing to his Knight's uniform. The light blue tunic and white pants were ceremonial, decorated lightly with gold detailing.

"Claws do not go with your gown, I am afraid," Lawton said with a smirk, raising a glass of wine in a fake cheer.

Randolph looked between the both of them, his eyes burning with an emotion he could not read. He also held a glass of wine. His skin was flushed with the heat of the drink. "Charmaine," he said, stepping forward, his tattoos almost completely covered, except for his hands in his ceremonial gear.

"You are a rare beauty tonight." He lightly touched her hand, kissing it softly as he raised it to his lips.

Her cheeks heated as he lowered his head. She could also smell the drink on him now, noticing the red that had begun to stain his lips.

Charmaine did not need to look to feel Lawton and James's smirks behind her back. She silently wished that someone would get her a glass of wine.

"What are the festivities of the evening, gentlemen?" Lawton asked, breaking the silence of the four of them.

Randolph stiffened, uncomfortable with what she assumed was classified information. "There are the traditional ceremonial things, you know. Winter's dancing, feasting, drinking..."

"Any introductions this evening we should be looking out for?" Lawton asked, his eyes almost turning demonic with the promise of pissing Randolph off.

It worked. Snapping his head in Lawton's direction, he spat, "How could you possibly—"

Interrupting them, the King and Queen emerged from the front of the throne room. They wore colors similar to that of their Guard, symbolic in their unity. Queen Aine was in a blue gown, delicately conservative. Her makeup was light, her hair done in a familiar pulled back fashion. The crown on her head tonight had blue jewels atop it, sitting perfectly against her dark hair. King Ronan wore a white tunic, shielded by a white cape, which hit the floor below him. His pants were a light blue, matching that of his crown. He looked more alive tonight, more whole.

King Ronan stepped forward. His voice boomed

across the room as everyone seamlessly fell to the ground in a bow. "My loyal subjects, lords, nobles, and fellow rulers of the Four Kingdoms. Welcome to the Snow Solstice," he said, his eyes ablaze with a blue fire. "Tonight, we shall adorn old traditions and new. Tonight, we shall celebrate the joy that is our Kingdom. We shall celebrate our peace, as well as our misgivings. We shall display our power for the world to see."

Those around clapped lightly as they rose to meet his gaze as a crowd.

"All, I have someone for you to meet. Someone who has finally returned to our life here at court, an acceptance I have long awaited," he said, his eyes brighter than before. His lips curled into a wicked smile.

Suddenly, whispering started among the crowd.

"Who?" Charmaine heard a woman ask beside her.

She felt Lawton's smirk next to her as he whispered into her ear, "I knew it."

"Knew what?" Charmaine asked him, barely a whisper.

Look, he mouthed.

The crowd parted as a wintery chill overtook the throne room. The door that she had just walked through blew open with a howling wind as a young man with white hair sauntered in.

II

THE BOY WITH THE CROWN

FIFTEEN

Prince Dalton of the First Kingdom entered the room in a blaze of winter wonder.

James had told Charmaine that the servants told tales of the King's desire to keep the Prince's abilities a secret. They had felt the frozen tundra, witnessed the power of snow. Lawton half-confirmed it himself with his expression—the Prince was on a trajectory to change the Ten Kingdoms by legend alone. Nobody had seen him since he was fifteen—five years ago. The rumors swirled around Charmaine's head like a tornado.

If only I could reach out and pluck the truths out of air to separate the lies.

Charmaine willed her face to remain neutral. Standing where she was with Randolph, Lawton, and James, she saw nothing but gold and dazzling blue gems. The top of his white jacket was barely visible among the robust character of his crown. With every step, it seemed to grow brighter, dazzling as he moved toward his destiny.

All she heard was the Prince's footsteps.

Click, click, click, click…

Randolph was perfectly still. His gaze focused on the trajectory of the crown.

Surely, he has met Prince Dalton before?

His fists were balled at his sides, his jaw set.

Lawton smirked, squinting to get a better read on the man that had so much mystery to him.

Dalton approached the ten-step staircase to greet his mother and father on the throne, and the whole room leaned forward to get a visual. Queen Aine did not move a muscle. His father reached his arms outward, reaching for a hug.

"My son." He beamed. "The Prince of Snow."

No noise erupted from the crowd for everyone was starstruck. King Ronan's dark blue eyes scanned the room, lacking all empathy that had been there a moment prior.

It was clear to Charmaine that he was the one. Dalton was not just the Prince of the First Kingdom, for he was the Prince of Snow.

"Bow down," King Ronan commanded no one in particular, yet the room collapsed in unison. The power of the king seized hold of the room as everyone went down on one knee, holding their heads low.

"You may rise," he commanded after a moment.

"Prince Dalton Naoise Saphirrus of the First Kingdom," Queen Aine announced.

Dalton turned and Charmaine blinked twice, snapping a permanent memory. She imagined this moment to be painted frozen in time for all eternity—to be gawked at by women and men for thousands of years to come. It would replace the image in the gallery of the boy who was destined for the throne, for this was the man to sit upon it.

The power coming from Prince Dalton seethed. Charmaine could almost reach out and touch it.

Thick dark eyebrows and hair white as snow, the Prince was the depiction of a winter's blessing. He was so different from the portrait in the gallery, his dark features replaced by frozen ones. A straight nose, other than a slight bump in the middle as the most minor of imperfections, dazzled with freckles long-since kissed by the sun. His eyes, deep blue, as beautiful as the gems that sat atop and embedded in his golden crown. He was rather thin, compared to the hard muscles that Randolph had, but it made him look ethereal. It did not diminish him. He walked with purpose, no uncertainty as he turned to survey the crowd.

He was beautiful.

All eyes were on him.

And he looked like he enjoyed it.

A slight smirk appeared on his mouth, allowing a dimple to appear on his white cheek. He was almost colorless, but there was nothing lifeless to him. The white of his hair looked almost normal; he carried it with such grace.

Charmaine bit her lip, double-checking to make sure she was not dumb with shock. This was one of the most powerful people in the world, just two years older than her, future commander to the First Kingdom and blessed with King Cian's power.

⸬

As the evening progressed, Randolph could not stop thinking about Charmaine's violet eyes. She had a strength to her that was silent, unmatched by anyone else he had encountered. The way she moved was graceful, honestly too graceful for that of a commoner from the likes of the First. There was something angelic about the look in her eyes. They burned with life when she was not aware.

Randolph had forgotten most of the things he had

learned in the Seventh Kingdom, and had been taught many other things since arriving in the First three years ago. He did remember how to read people: their wants, their desires, and their strengths. However, he always struggled with going deeper. *What were they hiding? Did they possess power?*

The Prince of the First Kingdom undoubtedly carried with him unknown gifts. It had taken Randolph half an hour following the council meeting to warm up again. Dalton's icy prowess had bombarded him.

How dare he call him Eniar.

He touched the flowers that inked his skin—a permanent reminder of his sins—and pushed down the fire built within him.

Charmaine was innocent and kind; that much he could read. Her inner power flickered casually beneath her skin. Randolph smelled it radiating off of her. He did not know what it was, nor if he was correct in his assumptions. There had been no signs of it when he first met her, but he also had been so overwhelmed by the town and the tour. His senses had been dulled for so many years. He was bound to miss a thing or two. He was not sure if she was aware, and he could not find the clues that normally chimed the signals. She had no arrogance to her, no blatant confidence. If anything, she was nervous, unsure, and focused on staying alive. His instincts roared in his head as he tried to breathe through the methodology.

She seemed to rely on her brother, but her brother also seemed to rely on her. They were a duo, with black hair and violet eyes, different pieces of the same craft. Randolph envied James for having that person, someone to love endlessly. It had been so long since he had had family.

There was something about her that Randolph felt

like he needed to protect, a fragility that needed to be guarded. He swore to himself that he would check in on her frequently, to make sure no harm came to her during her tenure at the castle.

Randolph cursed himself silently, for his mind would not shut off.

He should have seen this coming. Dalton's return to the political spectrum should have clued him in to the fact that he was to return to the other aspects of his birthright. The way that the world froze up at him without him unleashing his power—it was mesmerizing as it was sickening. He was a King through and through. It took everything in Randolph not to bow before him just now.

But Randolph liked his head attached to his body, and he noted how Ronan surveyed the crowd.

There had been rumors for years about his swirling powers, a gift not one person alive had seen since the days of King Cian and Queen Ciara. However, these rumors were dredged up by those who made up stories regarding the Prince to begin with.

When he became of transition age, the King and Queen persisted to hold him back, while everyone assumed that it was for reasons regarding the death of his sister.

As soon as the ceremony finished and the proper introductions were made, Randolph fled back to his chambers. He made a quick stop to brief Lawton on his departure and let him know that he would be back momentarily.

Lawton would take care of it. His mind whirled at the insanity of it all. *The white hair, the grief that clouded his eyes speaking of Charmaine and James, the look he gave his father upon hearing what he needed to hear...*

Ronan had to be up to something.

Randolph took a big swig of his red wine jug seconds after entering his chambers, not bothering with a glass tonight.

The Prince's warning pulsated through his veins. Unexpected terror flowed through his heart. The King was just as littered with sins as he was, and those with sins could not be trusted.

Charmaine noticed that Randolph had disappeared immediately after the ceremony, only to return with a few glasses of wine and a lighter air to him. She wanted to ask him where he had gone off to, but something about the way his amber eyes now shone gold forbid her from doing so.

"The born ruler," Randolph cheered to nobody in particular. He took a swig from his wine glass, not even blinking as he gulped.

She followed suit.

"Oh, he is dazzling. But where is his black hair?" Lawton whispered.

She elbowed him lightly, afraid the sound of her hitting his bedazzled jacket would create such a noise that would draw attention to them.

"Easy," James whispered behind them. A slight breeze pushed a few of her black curls over her shoulder. She turned around and, with a jolt, realized that Lawton disappeared, vanished from the throne room. Randolph looked around pointedly, taking another swig of his wine when he realized Lawton was no longer behind him.

Blinking to clear her mind, Charmaine returned her focus to the party, where King Ronan and Queen Aine spoke to the crowd as if they did not just reintroduce their son to the world.

Dalton was perched before them, looking uncomfortable and impossibly bored. The wonder and power that had appeared in his body language as he walked before the crowd was no longer present.

Charmaine wanted to laugh. Despite being a perpetrator of this regime, nothing about him seemed cruel. He had the whole Kingdom's eyes on him right now, yet he did not seem to care.

"Would you care for a dance?" Randolph asked. His eyes glistened with the crackle of darkness as he fought to quell whatever was making him so upset.

Charmaine bowed, her curls falling forward, as she took his hand and followed him to the dance floor.

SIXTEEN

andolph brought his hand to the side of Charmaine's waist slowly, checking for her consent as he rested his calloused hand against the seam of her dress.

He should not have returned to his chambers only to return to this solstice festivity. He was still feeling the effects. His brain thudded against his skull. The bright lights of the room were like acid to his eyes, and the only thing that seemed to be the cure for his agony was more wine.

Temporarily.

Determination flowed through Randolph's heart, as well as pure confusion. Ronan *hated* magic. He hated that people had the opportunity to best those without it, so he villainized it. He made it different not because it was a natural gift given by the Gods, but because it made the individual wielder stand out. It made the individual more powerful than he; therefore, he wanted them destroyed.

Randolph hated that they had moved so far away from the values as the First Kingdom. When he joined the kingdom, he prided himself on how they used to be revered, due to the powers that existed within the realm. Their most famous histories were cultivated by those with unimaginable powers. King Cian and Queen Ciara utilized their gifts to forge a new world for the people, a world that they, Ronan, had torn down.

The power that radiated off of Dalton gave Randolph a headache.

No, you idiot, it was definitely all the wine.

He was too stunned when he entered the chambers to even notice, but *now*, watching him waltz around and drink wine with the nobles, it was impossible to ignore.

He *was* power.

"Randolph?" a small voice asked, breaking his focus regarding the Prince.

Randolph cleared his throat and readied his eyes at the same time. He needed to be more present. The matter of the Prince did not concern him. He was assigned to the King last he checked. For now, that would be a good enough cause to rally his mind together again.

Get it together, Rand.

"How are you enjoying the winter solstice?" Randolph asked Charmaine, smiling cheekily.

This girl was truly lovely, in every shape of the word. He tried to ignore the dress that she was wearing tonight, the way that she looked so uncomfortable when she walked into the throne room, but the way she had adjusted... The fear scent disappeared off of her as she acclimated to the environment.

No longer would this girl from Brinn be weak and helpless. Randolph smelled the winds changing around her. The violet in her eyes more honed and powerful.

However, he could not shake that feeling of power

radiating off of her. *What did she possess? And how was she to wield it?*

Don't worry about it now. Focus on the moment.

She looked up at him, her eyes full of light tonight. "It is everything a girl from Brinn has ever heard. The lights, the ornamental showings, the beauty of everyone here... It is all a worthy celebration to our Prince being reunited with us."

He stiffened, her words dangerous this close to the King. If anyone heard her suggesting that the Prince was to be favored to rule... Randolph blocked out the thought.

Focus on the moment, Rand, focus on the moment.

She tilted her head to the side. Either she had no idea what she had said or she did not care.

Randolph did not know what he found most endearing: oblivion or treason.

Ten Kingdoms, what was wrong with him today?

"I would hardly call you just a girl from Brinn, Charmaine." She stiffened slightly at his words. Maybe it was the wine talking, or the way that he felt around her—relaxed—but he reeled it in. "I did not mean to overstep."

She shook her head, her black curls bouncing. "No, no, it is not that. I am not used to all this attention."

"Court is very *attentive*," he played, trying to make her smile.

"That it seems." She paused. "Do you like it here?"

It took everything in him not to bark a laugh. "I have been a resident of the King's Guard for three years, and despite the flaws of this court, it has become home to me."

"How did you join the King's Guard?" she asked, her dark eyebrows raised in inquisition.

Murder. Vengeance. Sadness. Betrayal. "I needed a job."

The side of her mouth quirked up, and Randolph

knew there was not a chance in this world that she believed he told her the truth.

"I hope it pays well," she murmured, so low that he almost did not catch it.

He nearly snorted, but refused to break this mask he had adorned since running into her again. He had unveiled too much of his real persona in the tavern before. He had been who he wanted to be, rather than who he was.

He could not afford to do that again, not here. Not with this much at risk.

Randolph and Charmaine twirled endlessly. The chiffon of her gown filled the space between them. Her chest rose slightly in order to catch her breath. Randolph normally despised dancing and avoided it at all costs, but being with this girl was like the first kiss of winter. She seemed rather shy, but had tendencies to be bold. She was ravishing and a breath of fresh air in this stuffy court. The sparks of power seemed to fly around her the more they spun. Whatever it was that she contained was wild and free, untamed. *Did she not have any training?*

Randolph wondered how he could ask her as they continued to dance. He was sure part of her quietness had to do with the fact that she was bloody terrified to be in the same room as Ronan.

Ten Kingdoms, even the same room as me.

Even though he barely knew her, Randolph wanted to tell her that it was okay.

Except it was not okay.

And he would not lie.

Ronan was unquestionably a monster. A disaster, as was the kingdom he served. The rulers of the Ten Kingdoms had powers for centuries, given by the Gods to keep their people safe. However, since the dawn of Ciara's reign, the bloodlines had been realigned, as had the God's hearts. They were no longer kind, no longer fond of saving the people from misfortune.

Randolph guessed that the Gods were angry. *Were* being the key word. They had not seen a King or Queen with the blessed powers in over a century.

So, why now? Why Dalton?

Randolph looked at the beautiful girl dancing with him. Her smile was subtle and bashful. It was as if the very experience of joy was one that she felt she should not have.

Survivor's guilt.

He knew the feeling.

"Would you like to get some more wine?" she asked, leaning so close to him that he could feel her hot breath against his neck.

The last thing I need. Yet, he agreed.

Gods help me, he pleaded, knowing well that if the Gods were mad at anyone, it was him.

They walked over to the servants silently, her keeping pace with him with relaxed ease. Randolph grabbed a full glass of red for himself, out of mere self-deprecation and loathing. It was so full to the brim that it spilled over, so he moved it to his lips to take a generous gulp. Charmaine reached for a less aggressive glass, filled with only a few ounces as she laughed at his inability to control himself.

As he moved the glass away from his mouth, he engaged in conversation when a white figure stepped into his line of vision.

Randolph went gray, thrown off by *his* boldness tonight. His face was as ethereal as it had been the prior night—his white hair like a fresh powder of snow on a frigid winter morning. His long fingers were like icicles, holding a large flute of champagne. He smiled at Randolph, as if greeting an old friend.

Prince Dalton of the First.

Dalton looked at Charmaine with interest. His eyes traveled up and down the bodice of her dress as if drinking in every inch of the fine stitching. The contrast between them was stark—the Prince with the frozen powers on display and the girl who was hiding everything. A mirror of one another yet their undoing.

Dalton took a gentle sip of his champagne flute, before extending his hand to Charmaine's in a casual greeting.

"Sir Randolph, why don't you introduce me to your friend? It is quite rude to leave a *Prince* without an introduction to such an exquisite beauty." He spat the word like it was a curse, but his eyes never left Charmaine.

Randolph lifted the wine glass to his mouth once again, finishing its contents in one dramatic gulp. "Miss Charmaine Grimes, meet the Prince of Snow."

SEVENTEEN

harmaine's black chiffon gown enveloped the ballroom in a darkness that the continent had not seen since the dawn of Queen Ciara.

The bodice left little to the imagination; the nearly opaque material the only barrier between her skin and the crushed black rose petals that ordained the dress. Her lower half was covered by skintight black chiffon, her waist and groin covered by a matching ensemble to the bodice. Her legs were visible underneath the tulle skirt. She moved surprisingly gracefully in the black heels James had procured for her—a matching piece that he afforded with the sale of his sword.

The Charmaine that was dancing in the King's castle was reborn from the ashes, the Charmaine of the past lost to the chaos of fire.

The ballroom offset every physical attribute she had. The white walls, marble floors, and snow-covered trees that decked the perimeter of the room had a heightened ambiance contrasted to the depth of her physical darkness. Charmaine's long, black curls and borderline scandalous dress exacerbated the hate for the mercenaries who had overtaken her soul.

This court was not what she had expected.

Randolph's kindness to her, least of all, had been one of the more shocking points of her evening thus far. They danced, spinning like carefree children. He spoke freely, friendship budding between them like the flowers which decorated his hands.

She only hoped that the hand he extended for friendship was not a farce.

And then she spotted *him* from across the ballroom. His white cloak, identical to that of his predecessor. His arrogance was flaunted, cool ambition blitzing off him like a snowstorm. Dalton wore the crown tonight, a reminder of the future of Snow. A chill ran down her spine, her shoulders shivering slightly as she shook off the cold.

The room, for how chilled it looked, was brought to life by those who entered it. She recognized the real-life versions of the many portraits she had seen with James in the town square as children. The leaders of the kingdoms. Their children. Their friends. For all she was concerned, famous individuals who sacrificed their own mortality for glory. Men, women, and children from all walks of life. All colors, all shapes, all sizes, and all ages.

The Kingdom of Snow on display.

Without warning, her breath before her became a cloud of white air, dissolving before her very eyes as she tried to focus. A voice, collected as it was calm, spoke so clearly behind her. "Sir Randolph, why don't you introduce me to your friend? It is quite rude to leave a Prince without an introduction to such an exquisite beauty."

Randolph's demeanor changed. Whatever he had been hiding from her took over as he said, "Miss Charmaine Grimes, meet the Prince of Snow."

And then he took a sip of his wine.

Click, click, click. Shoes sounded, pronounced and powerful. She looked down, afraid of seeing who had just addressed her as *my lady*. They were covered in gems the same color as *his* crown. The same colors as *his* eyes.

But she already knew who it was—Prince Dalton of the House Saphirrus, Heir to the First Kingdom's Throne and supposed second-coming of King Cian.

She lifted her head to meet his gaze, noting that Randolph was backing away, a defeated and venomous look in his eyes.

She met Dalton's gaze slowly, concentrating on the ambiance around her, so she did not make a fool of herself. She nearly stumbled, silently cursing herself, for he was more striking up close. His features and coloring were harsher than she anticipated. His eyes a deeper blue, clouded by long black eyelashes. The Prince had freckles sprinkled across his face, star-kissed instead of sun-kissed. His long fingers scratched across his right collarbone, the gesture adding to his informal presence. He locked his eyes with her own, extending a hand forward. This hand was covered in an array of blue jeweled rings, while the other held a flute of champagne.

"Care for a dance?" he purred. A side smile appeared, creating a dimple at the corner of his pink lips. His fingers twitched, extended as he awaited Charmaine's reply. An invitation.

She was struck by the offer. Without thought, she extended her jewel-less fingers forward.

An acceptance.

His long fingers embraced hers and the touch was ice cold. The temperature had her gasping for air as if she had jumped into ice cold water. He rubbed his icy rings against her finger, her soul yanked in different directions, trying to make sense of whatever power it was that he had.

She looked back at Randolph, asking for permission to leave. The Prince keyed in on this, waiting for her with a smirk on his face as if he were part of a big secret. Randolph nodded in assurance before walking toward the beckoning King. However, the approval did not reach his eyes.

With one glance back and an attempt at reassuring him with a smile, Charmaine turned toward the dance floor. Dalton held her hand as they walked.

They turned to face one another, releasing her hand. He lifted it in front of his eyes and Charmaine lifted her own, holding it mere centimeters away.

She had to play the part of the girl who was not terrified.

She had to play the part of the girl who did not fear this young man's father more than she feared death itself.

Their hands held steadfast and they began the dance. He threw the champagne flute to the side and did not even blink when the glass shattered behind them.

Walking around one another, she realized how tall the prince was. Randolph was tall as well, but the Prince had a disposition to him that enveloped his entire persona. He was larger than life. His blue gaze affixed on her hand as they danced and turned. They twinkled with a wonder that had her speechless. They spun as one, dancing as the singing of the violin continued to fill the room with its grace.

Sweat grazed her brow, pressure building as a part of this dance with the future king. The cold of the room melted away as the music picked up faster and faster.

He smiled at her, genuinely, speaking of the meaning of the Snow Solstice and what the event meant for the history of the Kingdom. "It was my grandfather, King Cian, who deemed this a celebration. Or rather, it was his wife Ciara, the Queen of Fury, who wanted to celebrate his power on an annual basis. A celebration of power, the Gods' divinity reincarnated in men themselves." His eyes flickered to different parts of the room as if he were unsettled.

Not for one minute did Charmaine think that he believed even a word he said. He seemed detached with his eyes, but his voice stayed level.

Sure, he knew his history, but did he relish his heritage?

"The Snow Solstice is such a lovely event for all the aristocracy. It's a shame the common people aren't able to come into the castle and enjoy it the same. The dancing, the food, the admiration from the powerful—it's really just a big show of all the things the Kingdom has to show off. The celebration started by King Cian in the dawn of the Snow Ages, a celebration of his power and the power of everyone else." He looked directly at her this time, clearly tired of hearing himself speak and begging for reprieve.

She nodded in reply, believing that this celebration was nothing more than a demonstration of power. He was not wrong that it was meant for the aristocracy.

Charmaine snorted at the thought of Tommy and James running amok in this ballroom with the other members of Brinn. Their simple clothes and minds focused on the problems of their village, rather than the power that ran through their veins. This was a place for Kings and Queens, not commoners, by design.

Dalton, however, did not seem shallow in his expression of the significance of this day. He seemed matter-of-fact, trying to seem neutral, but also in defiance of the problems the Kingdom suffered from under his father's rule.

"King Cian, you said, wanted this day to be for the

people?" Charmaine asked quietly, knowing well in proximity to the King that this was a dangerous conversation to be had. "And do you enjoy the day, Prince Dalton?" she asked, curiosity overtaking her before he had a chance to answer her already forward question.

He almost stopped dancing, clearly shocked, but regained his footing with casual grace. "I have not experienced this day in five years," he said softly, almost sadly. He ignored her first question pointedly, but she saw it lingering in his eyes. *Was he willing to break the rules? To defy this establishment?*

"But it is celebrated annually?"

He smiled, a cruelty appearing in his eyes. "Yes."

She left it at that, realizing that he had been open regarding his imprisonment. It was not a secret, for nobody had seen him, and rumors had spread throughout the Kingdom. It was un-Princely to discuss such a thing with a commoner, let alone a woman.

Especially someone he had just asked to dance and knew nothing about.

Prince Dalton flashed a slight grin and the freckles across his nose wrinkled. Curtsying, the Prince extended his frozen fingers yet again. She took them without hesitation. Once again, the jolt of his frozen skin took her breath away.

Why was he so cold? Were all of the Snow Royals a frozen embodiment of power?

"Do you want to accompany me for a walk?" he asked as he led her away from the dance floor that had erupted with a slower tune.

"A walk sounds wonderful."

They began to exit the ballroom. The looks that followed filled her heart with such a power that she had never experienced before. Mouths agape, eyes following the chiffon trail of her dress as it swept the marble beneath it. She stood taller.

"True power is fickle. It is so dependent on titles and a demonstration of force." He turned his head slightly, flashing another simple grin.

Just then a servant boy with red hair walked by sheepishly with a tray of wine. The Prince extended his arm swiftly, muttering the boy's name, she realized, and plucked a glass from the edge so seamlessly that she doubted the boy even noticed he took one. Dalton took a sip, smiling as his cheeks blushed for a second when the heat of the wine entered him.

"Is that not who has the power though, my Prince? Those who have titles and demonstrate strength?" She tilted her head to the side, curiosity getting the best of her.

Dalton's grin expanded across his pale features. He handed the glass of wine to a man behind him, not even glancing back at him. The man looked perplexed, even angered for a second. Upon seeing who handed it to him, he backed up, his eyes wide at the realization. He bowed to Dalton's back as they continued to walk along the length of the throne room.

"Yes, Miss Grimes, I suppose, by the definition of the word." He moved closer to her, his breath an icy chill so close to her ear. The smell of peppermint and berries suddenly concealed all her senses as he whispered, "But the way you changed the atmosphere of the room by dancing with me? That was a display of true power."

He walked with his hands in his pockets, casual. His blue eyes were afire with some constant amusement. He kept glancing over at her as they walked, as if he was not sure what to say or do.

"Do you need anything? More wine, perhaps?"

"No, I am quite fine," she said, taken aback by all that he was. "Is it not you I should be asking if I may retrieve something?"

He burst into laughter. His hands flew from his pockets to run through his hair. "You would ask about me? What I need?" he asked breathlessly as if it was the funniest thing in the world.

"Yes?" she asked, confused by his own confusion. "You are the future King, and the way that you are—" She stopped herself as his face darkened, the humor leaving every aspect of him.

"The way that I am?" he asked quietly, his hand caught in the flowing of his white hair.

"The... t-the things that they s-speak of..." She managed to gasp it out, for the first time terrified of being alone with him.

He smiled with a cruelty only the Gods would know. He lifted out his elbow so she could grab his arm as they descended the stairs into the rose garden. "And what lovely things do the people have to say about me, might I ask? I would love to hear them. It has been a little bit since I have been privy to the gossip of the continent."

Charmaine found it hard to draw a full breath. Her eyes darted from left to right to find an escape route. Her training—the prep with the swords and invisibility prevention strategies—seemed to go out the window. *I can't do anything. I can't run...*

"You seem to be somewhat of a mystery, your Majesty. I didn't mean to bring up the rumors of common folk like me."

He held her gaze. The blue of his eyes brightened as they got closer to the grass below.

"Please, indulge me."

"There have been rumors of you being a true descendent of Cian and Ciara, in every sense of the word." She gulped.

He smiled, but his eyes darkened. "The realities of my... *situation* have always been a spectacle. My heritage and my physical appearance are conducive to rumors, Char."

Char. The way it rolled off his tongue without any thought had a heat rushing to her cheeks that she did not expect from the embodiment of frozen power.

He sighed dramatically, blowing a white curl that had fallen through his sapphire crown. "Honestly, I am glad to hear the rumors are as such. I would rather hear those closest to the truth than to lies."

"Is being Prince not just glamour?"

He took a deep breath, recentering himself. "It is far less beautiful than the world would make it seem. Believe it or not, I do not enjoy it."

❖

Dalton did not want to admit it, but the castle was unarguably stunning at night. The darkness obscured all that had been blessed with King Cian's power. The stars above twinkled on the grounds. The white and red roses of the famous Queen's Rose Garden were illuminated. The garden was square, bushels of roses so high that when they entered, they were encompassed in a maze of brash beauty.

Dalton inhaled the familiar aura, the only place in the whole castle which he felt was home.

Charmaine kept a firm hand on Dalton's arm as they walked slowly through the ballroom to the garden. She was unwavering and eager to understand what went on in his head.

As if she were Cyril. Nobody else dared to enter my mind.

At least, not in the last five years.

He plucked a red rose off the bush, careful not to be cut by the thorns. Extending a hand, Dalton offered it to her. "Roses are my favorite flower," he said as he looked at the beautiful flower affectionately.

She smiled, taking the red flower and tucking it behind his ear with one of the hundred pins Gwendolyn had put in her hair. He knew her maidservant was the girl who had found him in the hall that evening, choking on invisible smoke, because he had overheard her being assigned to a "Miss Grimes". He nearly asked if Gwendolyn had mentioned anything peculiar about him, but he did not want to encourage their interactions beyond what it was.

A Prince had no place entertaining a girl from Brinn, and he knew that.

But maybe that was precisely why he was doing it.

"Thank you, Prince Dalton," she said.

Dalton almost choked. The formality of the title suffocated him every time she said it. He wanted to beg her to call him Dalton, to forget the formalities of the First Kingdom and do what she pleased. He held back, though, trying to embrace who he was, trying to embrace who he needed to be to survive this place.

"I worship roses for their ferocity. They offer such a rare beauty for this world, but if you are hasty, rough, you will get pricked." Dalton smiled to himself, suddenly feeling very clever. He dramatically stroked the rose she had put behind his ear with his long fingers. "I always wanted to wear them in my hair."

Dalton smiled as he realized that she was doing

everything in her power not to laugh at his absurdities. "It is okay to laugh, you know. My father might not be much fun, but I am."

"I am sorry, Prince Dalton. I am not used to dabbling with Princes in gardens."

"I am not used to walking with girls I do not know in gardens, and yet here we are, a match made by the Gods."

Dalton did not miss the heat that flushed in her cheeks. He began to walk again. Answering an unspoken question, he said, "This is one of my favorite places in the world." It was none of her business, but he wanted to tell her, nonetheless.

"Thank you for bringing me for a walk."

"That party was daft," he answered dryly.

She snorted.

Ah ha! She does laugh.

"I do not believe it is proper of me to say indeed, your Highness."

"But if it were *proper*," he said, putting fake quotations around the word with his hands, "would you agree?"

"Absolutely," she said with a laugh.

It felt so good to laugh. To talk to *anyone*.

"Where do you come from again?" he asked, even though he knew it was Brinn. That was one of his many problems. He never forgot anything.

"Brinn," she said, shorter than he would have expected.

"Do you miss it?" he asked, turning suddenly to look at her.

Her eyes were filled with a deep sorrow that Dalton did not realize prior. She was polite, sure, but he saw other layers to her emotions. They were a window into her and hid nothing as she wrinkled her nose at the slight breeze.

She was asking such genuine questions, as if she was afraid of running out of time. Dalton's breath caught, both at the smell of the roses and her genuineness.

"I do not," she said. Final.

"No?" Dalton said with a chuckle. He could not help but laugh at the prospect of telling your home to buzz off.

"I do not have the... best memories of my home."

Dalton kinked his head to the left, arching an eyebrow as if to tell her that he was not going to let up.

Avoiding more direct questions, she got the cue and elaborated, "My mother was murdered when I was quite young. My father died of sickness, as did a lot of others while we lived there. The—"

His inquisitive posture turned violent. Dalton's fists clenched at his side. His voice filled with nothing but hatred as he spit out, "Mercenaries?"

Her silence was all he needed to know it was true. They had been to her home and she had felt their wrath. Randolph had mentioned as such during the council meeting, but hearing it from the one who was affected set Dalton's blood afire with hatred.

Why had nobody fixed this yet? Why did the people of the First Kingdom live in such dire circumstance? This was a matter of safety and defending the realm. Had his father given up?

Dalton shifted, and his gaze of terror transformed to one of sadness. "I'm so sorry. It's the duty of the crown to take care of not just its kingdom, but those who live within it."

Her mouth parted slightly, part in horror he guessed, at his straightforward nature. He had undermined his father, the King, with one fell swoop of conversation. One breath. Ordinarily, he would have laughed at the attack on his father's court, but for some reason with Charmaine, he felt like he had betrayed some formative part of himself.

He came toward her, reaching his hand to stroke the top of the rose that she had attached to his head with grace. "I can only hope I will be a better King."

Even though, truly, he wanted no part in the crown. Not anymore. But for this moment, for this conversation, he wanted to be anything he could for this girl. A beacon, a moment of hope, even a friend; all of which sounded like avenues that he finally felt like he could be purposeful with.

And it had been so long since he had a purpose.

"You do not deny the rumors that surround you?"

He nodded to himself, an acknowledgement of the man he wanted to be. "I learned a long time ago it is best not to dim your light for others to try to shine."

"How did you manage? Your nerves must have gotten the best of you at some point. That crushing weight of being ostracized would have left me mad." She was projecting, but it did not stop her from uttering her truth.

He blinked, taken aback. "First of which, my nerves have never gotten the best of me. I am not even sure I have nerves. Second of which, I was not utterly alone. I had Cyril and my wits about me. I was able to escape on more than one occasion. And if I was unsuccessful, the strife of the struggle was enough to keep me looking forward to the next attempt. Yes, I felt the consequences, but I would not let it break me, because if it did, my father would win. I hate to lose, Charmaine Grimes. Skin heals. The mind heals. Power regenerates, or at least, I like to believe it does. I am not scared to be punished when I did nothing wrong."

"What would they do to you?" she asked.

"It does not matter because I lived to tell the tale." He smiled, crooked, but she saw that he was masking his pain.

"Do you ever speak without humor?" she questioned, exasperated.

"Darling, there is no fun in telling lies."

She opened her mouth to respond as the South Wing, where they had just walked from, exploded.

EIGHTEEN

harmaine and Dalton took off toward the castle, her pace matching his after she flung her heels to the side.

James. I have to find James.

Flashbacks littered her mind—scorching, choking, blindly crawling, and aimlessly wandering as she looked for her tether to this world. Her brother.

Dalton and Charmaine reached the threshold of the castle and familiar stars panned across her vision. She leaned up against the white stone exterior, deep breaths grounding her as she fought off the urge to succumb to her power.

We do not have time for this. I cannot go invisible, not now.

A delicate hand landed atop her shoulder, holding her upright as she breathed deeply, fighting off the urge to turn.

"Charmaine?" Dalton asked, ignoring the sounds of eruption from within his home.

She nodded her head, unconvincing, "Too much wine. Too daft of a party," she lied.

How was I joking at a time like this? Remember your training.

He cracked a smile, those freckles wrinkling again under his dark eyes. "Come on then," he said, dashing into the chaos.

She thrashed her head from side to side, frantic. "James!" She searched for the mop of dark hair everywhere. Her head pounded against the force of her secret power.

As she crossed into the castle, she saw them. Her chest caved in, constricted and riddled with crippling fear.

"Mercenaries." The word was a curse on her tongue. Their garb was different from the last time she saw them. They wore all red, draped in no luxuries but gallant swords. Their black leather pants, masked by red boots. Their faces painted red to mask their true identities.

Who did they work for? Who sent them? Where they did not burn, they attacked with brutal force. Swords unsheathed, they stabbed, blundered, and cut anything in their path. Frozen in place, if not by her impending change to invisibility, then by fear itself, Charmaine held her ground.

The Prince, alive on the battlefield in what was once his ballroom. He fought with the grace of not just a royal, but a warrior. He jumped, slashing the necks of two mercenaries in one flippant spin. He laughed, cackling maniacally as he inflicted pain upon those who cursed the legacy of this kingdom. Those who hindered the development of the world that his dynasty had pledged to build. Blood sprayed wildly, decorating his white hair as he continued running around the room, hunting for the evil that plagued his nation.

He made eye contact from across the battleground, bounding over bodies with a speed she did not think he was capable of for his exquisite fragility. His eyes darkened with an unreadable expression.

"Are you alright?" he asked loudly over the roar of the battle, walking toward the wall away from the chaos.

Charmaine almost giggled at the silliness of the question. Of course, she was not *alright*. "My brother," she managed to gasp out. Frozen in panic.

"We will find him, Char," he said, unsheathing his sword quickly. Before bounding off into the sea of red again, he turned, flashing a stupid grin as he said, "A daft party, no longer."

Despite the terror, she smiled. She had to do something. Anything. She whipped her head from side to side, searching for a weapon so she could join the chaos. She was no warrior, but she was a fighter.

Remember your training.

Across the room, her eyes landed on a dagger sticking out of the right eye of a dead mercenary. Removing it was better than he deserved, but she needed a weapon. Knights and mercenaries fought around her in pure adulterated chaos, but she saw an opening and she went for it.

Striding over barefoot, nearly slipping on the blood of her enemies, she reached the mercenary and ripped the sword out of his head. It was a beautiful weapon, the hilt dark and dangerous. Dangling from it were the most peculiar chains, decorated intricately with diamonds.

She held it tightly in her grip, cursing herself for not training like a warrior all her life. Now, when she needed it most, she wished she had been practicing like a warrior, instead of reading about them.

She took off like the Prince, letting him be her inspiration, wildly looking for any familiar face she could find. Strangely, nobody noticed nor came near.

She glided through the battlefield with newfound confidence. She slashed at men where she could, grinding her teeth as she quelled her screams. Her hair danced around her as she spun and struck out at her enemies. They crumpled around her slowly, but did not fall completely.

Before she realized it, she was headed toward the throne room. The siege had moved past the ballroom.

Of course, they're headed for the King. Where was Dalton?

She took off at a full run, headed for the wooden door that was strangely left ajar. Slowing to avoid slipping on the blood and battle carnage around her, she braced herself, unsure what she would find when she entered. The clanging of swords behind her sang, the rhythmical slashing and screaming a song in her soul. She whipped her head one last time, to make sure that she was not being followed, before she snuck in the cracked door.

The throne room's beauty this evening was more than a distant memory. Mercenaries lay scattered on the floor with Knights, blood running over the marble smoothly, coating it evenly.

On the throne sat King Ronan, his hand covering his chest, leaning forward. He looked so gray. Wounded, she noticed, seeing the blood covering his hand, spilling down his tunic. His head suffered a wound as well, his black hair clinging to his right temple. No emotion overcame her at seeing the King so defeated. He was not a King for her and her people.

In front of him stood James and Dalton, defending the injured King's last line of defense before his demise.

His throne.

His power.

Pride surged within her as did betrayal. Ronan was not on their side.

James swung wildly at the mercenaries before him as Dalton followed in pursuit. Both boys stark in contrast: James with his physical darkness and Dalton with his luminous beauty.

Where Dalton's fighting was the skill of a soon-to-be King—a warrior—James's skill was that of a mercenary. Hours of training and his deep love for swords shone as he maneuvered the weapon like a piece of art. A tool of destruction, but a beautiful one.

Remember your training.

Suddenly, from behind her, a mercenary opened the door. He was large, carrying a sword six times the size of her own. He wore a sort of crown of his own, a battered and rusted metal.

Was this the leader of the group?

Upon seeing the Prince and the wounded King, his black eyes managed to light up. She crouched against the wall, praying to the Gods that he did not see her and that she still had the element of surprise on her side.

"Stop! Please!" she shouted, slashing his calf with the blade of her dagger.

He stumbled, turning around growling at where she stood. Charmaine closed her eyes, hearing the grumbling get closer and closer.

"Over here, you slimy sack! We have a plethora of royals over here for your taking," she heard from across the room.

Dalton.

She cracked an eye open to see the mercenary running full speed at the Prince. A scream erupted from her throat as his charge sped up. His muscular build propelled him forward, a yell erupting from his mouth as he lifted his sword to strike.

The whole world seemed to go to hell at once.

Without warning, James stepped in front of Dalton, striking him backward. His thick, dark hair covered his eyes as he took the brute force of the mercenary's weapon. He screamed as the mercenary's sword connected with his shoulder and seared through it. Blood poured out of the wound as the mercenary retracted his weapon with speed she had never seen before, and lifted it again to go after the King.

Charmaine screamed again—bloody and full of hurt, and shattering the world.

As the mercenary lifted his sword a second time, he turned, as if seeing her standing there for the first time.

Did he not remember me from when I slashed him?

"How did you get in here, pretty girl?" he asked, his voice deep with prowess.

She almost vomited on the spot. He turned, ignoring her wounded brother completely as he stalked toward her. Her dress suddenly felt too sheer, her fear rooting her to the ground.

"You look…" he started before he stopped suddenly, taking no more steps. His eyes rolled back into his head and he stumbled forward, face planting to reveal a dagger lodged in the back of his head.

Chaos erupted around her as the battle seemed to stop. Mercenaries crumbled to the ground, their eyes rolling into the backs of their heads just as the one that lay before her. *They were linked,* she realized with shock. They were linked to their leader, the mercenary who wore the crown.

Prince Dalton stood behind him, covered in so much

blood that he looked like a painting. He nodded in her direction, mouthing, "You're safe," before turning to aid James.

"James." She breathed heavily as she dashed toward him, sliding over the blood that existed on the floor.

Kicking the mercenary as she stumbled to James, she noticed the fever already setting in his eyes. His blood poured all over, drenching her.

"James, please. James. Listen to me. Stay with me," she pleaded with him, her voice growing coarse with emotion.

Dalton called for guards, healers for James and the King.

"You saved me," King Ronan whispered, blood pooling on the side of his head as he looked upon her brother.

Dalton seethed as he sheathed his sword onto his belt. Hatred blitzed in his eyes, his mouth in a taut line.

"Char," James said, groaning in agony.

"Jamie."

"Char, you turned." He touched her face. Blood coated his fingers as he touched her cheek, smothering it red.

She felt Dalton's eyes burning into the back of her head, his concern for James turning to curiosity about her, no doubt.

She held his hand there, daring not to let go.

Had I changed and not noticed? Anxiety flared in her chest, but she shoved it down the best she could. *Later, later, later, later.*

"Char, do not leave me." He coughed, his color turning that of the King.

"I remembered my training," she said, trying to force a smile.

"I know," he said between gasps.

She felt a hand on her shoulder. Without looking, she knew it was a healer. Their presence calming, lavender overtaking her senses, forcing her to relax.

"You are going to be okay." She tried to sound confident as two healers picked him up, laying him down on the plank of wood to take him to the infirmary.

She walked behind him quickly, taking a trail of blood with her from the bottom of her once beautiful gown.

They turned out of the throne room toward the main room of the South Wing. The destruction and death that lay before her was jarring-bodies scattered everywhere. Mostly mercenaries.

They were linked. Dalton killed them all. Her stomach dropped, the strongest of them meant to be the assassin of King Ronan and the Prince.

This enemy could be vanquished.

Blood saturated her feet as she trailed James. Charmaine heard the healers whispering to him, their hands beginning to glow with their healing properties. Realization and disgust overtook her as she realized that magic was allowed for the healers because they directly benefited the King. They worked for him, so it was allowed.

They turned out of the South Wing and headed down the long open hallway toward the infirmary. The white stones of the castle exterior only heightened the massacre that had happened that evening. A fortress of winter power, destroyed by a plague of darkness, but protected by the King's living descendant.

She jumped, feeling a hand on her shoulder. She turned around and found herself staring into the eyes of Prince Dalton. "Your father," she stammered, realizing the look of pain on his face.

"My father is fine," he said, unnaturally cold in his tone. That look was there again, that irritation that she had seen before. "How is James?"

She stifled a laugh. "The future King wants to know about my brother?"

Hurt flashed across his eyes. "He did save my life," he said pointedly. "And he is your only remaining family."

Surprise overtook her harshness. He remembered what she had told him.

"I am not sure," she whispered. Tears flooded her eyes, slowly beginning to drip down her cheeks.

The Prince lifted his hand, wiping them away as they fell.

Exasperated, she whispered, "You do not need to wipe my tears, your Majesty."

A slight smile appeared across his battered face. The blood crusted from the battle stuck to his hair wildly, a stark contrast to the deep reds. She imagined the Prince as he was in the garden, immaculate and regal. His garb was worth more than all that Brinn had. His castle, a fortress of not just safety for the royals, but an example of their power. Charmaine thought of him with the champagne earlier— their dance, their walk in the garden—it could not all be for show. That crown he wore did not dictate him. It could not. This had to be him, the real him, standing in front of her right now.

She bit back tears, terror, and sadness of what would become of her by asking what she was about to. "Could you see me?"

"I have always seen you," he said reassuringly, although clearly confused by her question. Darkness lingered behind his deep blue eyes, as if his confusion was more about what he had heard rather than what he had seen.

She looked at him pointedly. "Could you see me... the entire time, after we left the garden?"

"Yes. I saw you as I am seeing you now," he said, his pupils diverting to behind her and beside them. As if he were paranoid. As if he were nervous? He reached forward, moving a curl from her forehead.

She dared to draw a breath, the intimacy of his body language reawakening her dulled senses. Her breath quickened at the realization that froze her blood, dragging her from the depths of her despair to the familiar thrumming of anxiety that pulsated in her veins. Whether Dalton understood her question or not was unclear to her, but the reality would not change.

The Prince could see her when she was invisible.

NINETEEN

"ell, that was a blast of fun, was it not, my old friend?" Dalton asked Cyril as they reentered his chambers.

Dalton's entire body pulsed with the sensation of battle. He had never felt what it was like to be in true combat before, not counting the times he escaped his chambers and fought off his father's Knights. The exhaustion crept through his bones, and his mind would not shut up.

Cyril snorted in response, but worry clouded his eyes. He had been in the Thinker's Chapel when the mercenaries invaded. When he emerged, he was livid and more determined than ever to find the culprit behind these attacks. For once, Dalton agreed with his father. They needed to act, and fast. Cyril hobbled from side to side with old age as he approached Dalton's desk, sitting atop it like he owned the place.

"Aren't you a little old to be sitting on top of furniture?" Dalton teased as he ran a hand through his white hair. His massive sapphire rings, his family rings, got caught on a few of his waves. He pulled them through aggressively until they were free of the tangled mess. One by one, he took them off and set them next to his bedside table.

Cyril's blue eyes shot through him like a spear, a wicked grin appearing on his face. "One hundred years ago, I was hand to the King, boy. You think I gave a damn about sitting on top of some furniture? I used to own this furniture. This castle? I used to help rule it with an iron fist."

Dalton laughed, his voice cracking through the room like a bolt of lightning. He relished pissing Cyril off. "There is no doubt, even in your old age, that you would still make one hell of a hand."

Cyril smiled at him, his usual kindness returning to his wrinkled face. "And you will make one hell of a King, boy."

Dalton sat down on the bed dramatically, unbuttoning the top of his tunic slightly for effect. "Do you ever miss the old world?" Dalton asked, not sure where the question had brewed from.

He laid down completely on his bed, unable to see Cyril from this angle, but he heard him stiffen.

"What makes you wonder?" There was a tinge of fear in his voice.

"The way you speak of your friendships, your role, and the world that Ciara and Cian created... It seems much better than this one, that's all." He blew a loose wave out of his face with a huff.

"Much better? My dear boy, if anything, it was worse. The Gods were angry. King Finn was a madman of the Gods' creation. There was no peace, rather no semblance of hope. Ciara was one of my best friends in the Ten Kingdoms, but she had a brutality to her that often devastated more than it healed. Cian, her counterpart, was the shining light, a diamond in the rough against the grain of mankind. They did not have a better world; they forged it with iron and blood and sweat and vengeance. Ciara murdered her way to the crown, her seat frankly undeserving of her. If she were not such a fantastic ruler and all the men on the council did not piss themselves around her like they did, she never would have risen to the throne."

"How could you possibly be fantastic, yet feared?" Dalton asked, more so for himself than the history lesson.

Cyril had been talking about Ciara and Cian since he was young, their presence one of the only things he remembered about his life that was pleasant. Cyril used to take trips with Dalton to their favorite places among the castle and Cyril would tell him stories about them. If anything, they felt like the family Dalton never knew.

"Ciara was fire and darkness. She was much like you, boy. I would have paid some coin to see you two go at it." He winked, readjusting himself slightly on top of the desk as if it were becoming too much for his joints to sit like that. "She ruled with fear, but never ruled with cruelty. She was harsh, but fair. Ambitious, but open-minded. She was an amazing ruler. I only wish that destiny had another plan for her."

Dalton paused, hesitating to continue at the note of Cyril's sadness returning to his voice. "You speak of them frankly now between us. Did you then?"

"Boy, I spoke to them more frankly than I speak to you." He chuckled slightly as if remembering more fondly now.

Dalton sat up at that. "Then Gods rest their bloody souls," he said, mimicking *cheers* with his hands.

Elena nearly rolled her eyes at the First Kingdom and their history with Thinkers.

This Thinker, in particular.

"What in the Ten Kingdoms does that even mean?" Elena asked, her mind whirling as she let the words of this foretold prophecy sink in.

"That was why he locked me up, you know," Dalton said, his eyes now very far away in their gaze. "He believes the King of Snow is me."

"How could it not be?" Elena asked quietly.

Ronan was no idiot, and the physical appearance of Dalton was a dead giveaway. Dalton was completely infected with his power, except for his eyebrows, which still remained the rich ebony that had been familiar since his childhood.

"'The death of his father.' He also believes it is me that will kill him."

Elena gasped. "Do you plan to?"

Cyril answered, "To even utter such a question is treason, Elena."

"No," Dalton said at the same time.

"Even after all *this*?!" she said, gesturing around his chambers. He did not answer her, as if it were too painful to discuss, so she pressed harder. "Who is the Violet Queen?"

"There are so many components to this that we have yet to unfold," Cyril said, his philosophical drivel reigniting among their conversation.

"I... I have not thought much on the prophecy," Dalton said. His mind, however, seemed to drift elsewhere again. Now his face flushed with a memory of some sort.

Elena grunted; her irritation lay bare within the confines of this room. "Enough of this." She saw how the

161

weight of this conversation and her returning to court was beginning to take its toll on Dalton. If she had ever been good at one thing, it was understanding what her friends needed.

He smiled at her gratefully in reply.

"Where should we be off to today, Prince of the First? Your best friend has returned to court, and given your return to society, I believe it best that we use that to our advantage this afternoon."

Elena extended her hand as they rose, determined to steady him where he needed to be steadied today and every day that she remained.

"To our advantage we go, Princess Elena."

TWENTY

ragged to the depths of her own darkest fears, Charmaine was unable to understand and comprehend exactly what had befallen her last night.

The Prince had seen her and openly admitted to it. She figured there was no way he could have genuinely understood her question, no way he would have just accepted her magic, despite having his own. If for some spectacular reason, he had understood her blurted out question and basic admittance to having magic, she hoped to the Gods that he would stay quiet. He lived with the consequences of having magic, so he would understand it better than anyone else.

If he even knew anything at all, that was.

As her thoughts wandered, James twisted and turned. The healers worked diligently to repair his wound. To keep him with her. She spent the night at her brother's side. She held his hand as she prayed to the Kings of Old not to take him.

Gwendolyn sat with her. The servant girl's eyes were wide in alarm. Her skin turned a sickly gray color as

Charmaine felt her jerk, her hands clasped over hers.

"Charmaine…" Gwendolyn whispered. Her cheeks filled with a deep red to replace the lifeless drain. Tears formed in the girl's eyes, her blush extending to revive her facial features of all colors.

"He is so kind," she said, gazing at James. "So kind."

Charmaine made it back to her chambers after being reassured that James would survive the night. Gwendolyn had been so shaken, repeating over and over the kindness that James exuded.

It almost brought tears to her eyes that her brother was capable of such an impact in such a short period of time. Not that she was surprised. Charmaine smiled to herself as exhaustion creeped through her bones. The tears had not stopped flowing the entire time that she was with him. Now she felt heavy from her sobs, the emotional aspect of it too much to bear.

It was no wonder the force of that explosion and the madness within the battle had caused her to shift. James had even known. It had been that obvious. Her mind went back to the Prince. She knew he saw *something*. Whether he would ever confront her about it, she didn't know for certain.

Charmaine could not put her finger on it, but the feeling stuck with her that even if he did know, it would not be the worst thing. He had a kindness and a brokenness to him that Charmaine couldn't put into words and reason. His soul seemed to be ignited by fire, despite how cold his physical body was. How he spoke of the world, the genuine sympathy for what had happened to her and James…

The feeling that she had being around him tonight was what scared her the most—her body seemingly at ease, the fear of changing for the first time really out of her mind—even given the company she kept. She felt grounded, safe.

And it terrified her.

Dalton lay in his bed. His green silk sheets covered him up to his neck. As if they could bury away his obligations, his destiny, and his thoughts.

He wanted to vomit.

The mercenaries had entered his home tonight. They killed members of the court. Although it was hours ago, the hot breath of his father was still on his cheek as he yelled their names at him.

"Sir Michael of the Second Kingdom, Lord Mackelvein of the Fourth Kingdom, Miss Pokinsky of the Town of Kent, Sector to the Tenth Kingdom… This is our obligation, Dalton. This is now our problem."

An attack on the home front was an atrocity Dalton assumed would happen sooner rather than later. He had only been free for what felt like a bloody minute and the Ten Kingdoms erupted into further chaos. His father's relationship with force was only enacted upon him and disciplining him. *This is now our problem.* Dalton tossed in his silk sheets, irritated. *As if it had not been before?*

He hated this room. He spent so much of his life there, locked away like a prisoner. The moments of joy were rare, encapsulated in his mind, and vaulted away. Dalton longed for the daytime when he could plot reasons to escape. A new portrait? Sure. To be briefed by his father on some bullshit version of the truth he wanted to hide

Dalton from? Absolutely. A little ceremony to demonstrate that he was alive and well, and that he was preparing to take the crown? Why not.

Dalton grunted at the memory of his father, just hours ago, before the party had even started. Ronan had told him of his grand plan to unveil Dalton to the world once again, this time demonstrating force and a united front.

"It is time now, Dalton. The Knights tell me the Mercenaries are picking up again, at a rapidity which we cannot track. We need to show them strength from the crown. We need to show them you."

Dalton attempted to grunt then too, a show of indignation. His father could not know that for five years his heart did backflips at the prospect of socialization. To be free for one evening, and hopefully many more once he had been exposed. Dalton laughed out loud at the word, *exposed*. Exposed for nothing other than what he was.

My father locks me up because he fears me so, and now is fine with installing me as his one true heir? How do these two personas coexist?

He howled at all the fears his father had of him, the cold that erupted out of his soul in a power so old that it terrified him. Made his father feel like he had no choice but to lock him up.

Dalton cackled that that fear and power was now the least of his father's worries.

In fact, if Dalton played his cards right, maybe one day, it would be his greatest asset.

The prospect was utterly hilarious to him.

When he would be King, he decided, he would not hide from the world what he was, who he was. His father's lack of tolerance, the inability to accept even the gifts from the Gods that sat directly in front of him, would never be felt by another in his society. All because his son was different. All because his son was better than him. Dalton did not want the job, but he did not see a way out of it. With Carinthya gone, it was him and only him.

Dalton thought of Cyril, and the day that he told his father of his fortune. How he went to the Thinkers in the Tenth Kingdom, prior to deciphering the prophecy Cyril received from the Gods themselves. Their resurrection pointed in revealing who he truly was.

"Your Majesty, if I may. This has gone on long enough. The poor boy hasn't been allowed to be anything other than a conduit of power. He needs training, sir, far more costly than those of control I can instill in him." Cyril looked at him lovingly, his eyes cherishing him as if he were a son of his own.

"Costly?" his father answered. "The only thing that is costly is his little talents. The displays. The servants we have to pay to keep quiet to not reveal this. It's a burden to us all, to play our cards when they matter most."

Cyril, a tiny old man, suddenly seemed very tall. Speaking with clarity, he said, "He is not some chess piece for you to move to checkmate your enemies, sire. He is your son. He is the future ruler of this Kingdom. He is, frankly, far more powerful than you or even I."

His father held his scepter so tightly that he thought it would burst, but Cyril continued. "I went to the Tenth Kingdom for you, sir. I spoke to the Thinkers. Dalton is the one true King. My vision is true, sire."

His father paled and sat down, his scepter falling to the floor in a plea to escape his now lifeless clutch. "Get. Out," he spat.

Dalton rolled over again, shifting the green silk off as he felt his breath, hot against the temperature of the room.

Focus on something else. Focus.

He got up and walked over to the window. His mind wandered aimlessly to her.

Throughout the chaos of the whole evening, she was a constant. When he saw her black curls from across the room, talking to Randolph, Dalton could not explain the draw. Physically, she was gorgeous. But her soul? There was something there which he had never encountered in a girl before, but he could not put his finger on it.

He had to fight the overwhelming urge to coat the entire throne room in ice just for looking at her in that dress.

Dalton snorted. Randolph certainly had noticed. He smiled to himself at the look on Randolph's face when he whisked her away with as little as a look, overtaken by a Prince. Her violet eyes were somehow inviting, even after being so rudely interrupted by him. The purple not cold, but intelligent. Curious. Her hands constantly twiddled against one another, as if she were nervous, afraid of losing control.

Somehow, Dalton felt as though they were one and the same.

But the draw he felt from her was of another nature, unlike anything he had ever felt before. Like a thorn in his side, he could not escape. It had been there for a few days now. Dalton assumed it was ever since she arrived at the castle. However, the thorn was not unpleasant, rather a reminder that she was there. That they could be close.

Dalton touched the window, tracing the stained-glass design of King Finn decimating a village with his pointer finger. As he removed his finger, it left a frost. A smile overtook his features as he imagined freezing King Finn in the image, forever rendering him unable to hurt anyone else.

He stood up. He needed to talk to her. He needed to find out more.

He grabbed his shirt buckle—the sword attached to it strapped across the front—in case the Knights figured he was an intruder in his own home and tried to run him through. He laughed at the prospect of the young, cocky knight they called Lawton doing anything other than gossiping.

Taking a deep breath, Dalton stepped toward the exit of his chambers. The exhilaration of the escape was always his favorite part of his antics. He didn't know why he was complacent for so long. There was much more to life than listening to the rules.

He popped his head outside the door with a loud creaking noise. He looked left and right, taking in his surroundings to make sure that none of the knights had decided to actually do their jobs this evening.

All clear.

He picked up the pace, noiselessly closing the door as he made a break for the wing that harbored the guest chambers.

His breath deepened. His heart threatened to rip through his chest as he gallivanted across his former home. This forsaken castle had been his home. It *had* been full of laughter and love. It *had* been full of life, something his father sucked from this place the moment he discovered who he was. Or rather, who the Gods promised he was to become.

Before he realized it, he was in front of her chambers. Following that invisible tug, he knew this was her door. He had arrived.

Dalton knocked twice, his nerves getting the best of

him. His mind quickly wandered to Cyril, always treating him like he was some God on the verge of cracking. If anything, he was a boy that needed to be cracked. Like right now, he would deserve it, not only for sneaking off, but for being outside of a common girl's chambers.

Somehow, he did not care.

He took a deep breath and honestly hoped Cyril murdered him when he returned to his chambers. She was not there, clearly, or she would have answered the door.

He put a hand to his hair, grabbing it until he could feel it pulling from the root of his head. He was surely going insane.

Suddenly, the chamber doors flew open, and there she stood.

Dalton tried to pull himself together, but failed. His state of disarray could not be fixed in a nanosecond. The heat that rose in his frozen body could not be squashed. His hands trembled before him, and he cursed himself for being the way he was.

What in the Ten Kingdoms was going on?

She was ravishing, just as she had been earlier this very evening. Her eyebrows were raised slightly in confusion, her purple eyes inquiring as to why the Prince was standing before her.

Fantastic question, he wanted to say in response to what she probably was thinking. Her mouth however, despite the swell of her eyes from crying, was raised in a slight smile.

Dalton smiled back.

"Good evening," he started, looking at her eyes with a sudden sadness in his own.

Cian save him. He really was insane. She was without a doubt crying over her brother and the horror she had just gone through, and now he was there like a fool.

She smiled even more brightly. Her black hair swept across her arm as she waved him inside her room. He paused slightly, never afraid of the rules, but afraid of the implications if he were to be caught. He breathed deeply before deciding to damn the Ten Kingdoms, and entered.

"What do I owe this pleasure, Dalton?" she asked, not without kindness in her voice.

"I…" Dalton stammered like a bastard. He was the Prince of the First Kingdom, future ruler of the Ten Kingdoms. *What did he owe this pleasure?* He envisioned the conversation in his head if he told the truth.

"I am following this invisible draw I have to you, and I cannot stop thinking about you for some reason, so I followed my instincts here. Sorry to disturb you, and I hope you have a wonderful evening."

Ten Kingdoms save him.

He took a deep breath. "I wanted to wish you a proper good night and to make sure you were alright."

Her mouth dropped open ever so slightly.

"No need to say anything. If you need anything," he started again. *Gods*, he thought to himself, *Cian is rolling in his grave at this conversation.* "If you need anything, please call Cyril. He would be happy to oblige."

And then he spun, and walked back to his chambers, that invisible tug yanking harder as he left her behind.

TWENTY-ONE

EIGHT YEARS AGO

The girl erupted into nothingness.

It had started with a glass of wine she was bringing to her mother. She was only ten years old. The desire to always please and be exact stifled her steps.

"Darling, might you bring me a cup?" her mother asked kindly, beginning to remove her boots from a long day working in the stores of Brinn.

The girl listened, eager to please the woman whom she so admired. The girl's mother's black hair was pinned up that night, not a strand out of place. The girl was suddenly self-conscious, her own hair a tumble of curls and waves, which she could not control. She was inadequate, a fire burning beneath her skin as she wished to prove herself. To do the bidding of her mother so perfectly that she would no longer feel less than. She was not perfect. It was not her mother who made her feel less than. The girl did that of her own accord.

The girl walked over the counter of their small home, the bottle of wine on the counter. She picked up a glass from the bottom of the cabinet closest to her. She did not want to risk clanging the glasses and appearing like she could not handle the simplest of tasks for her mother.

She had to be perfect, and to be perfect, she had to do it right.

The girl poured the glass slowly as her mother chatted about her day. She spoke of the usual prophecies and those whom she frequently saw in the town square. She mentioned the weather, but the girl was now too focused to answer. She poured the perfect glass of red wine, no splashes or drops of the rose-colored liquid anywhere for her to be caught in a mistake.

She turned slowly, her mouth beaming with a smile, announcing her triumph silently to the world.

And then the glass tumbled from her hand, as if her fingers had given out.

The girl looked down at her hands to see the faint outline of the curvature of her appendages. Her breathing was erratic. Seeing what was happening darkened her vision to near nothingness. She wanted to call out and scream, but her mother was already at her side, coaxing her softly and covering her mouth with her hand. The girl's arms were beginning to have the same sensation—a tingling as if being brushed by a feather by her brother— as if a part of some grand scheme or joke. However, her heart pounded in her chest, despite that innate response to call out her brother's name.

"It is okay, baby girl. I have you. I have you," her mother whispered, desperation creeping into her voice as the girl's mind went black and she drifted from sight.

TWENTY-TWO

harmaine practically begged Gwendolyn to bring forth a pot of tea to her chambers the next morning. Gwendolyn was hesitant to leave her to her own devices, clearly afraid of leaving Charmaine after the horrors of the night prior.

Charmaine demanded, kindly, of course, that the tea was the remedy for all her problems and gave Gwendolyn her best puppy dog face. She scurried off, promising to be back in a moment.

She knew damn well that tea would not fix Charmaine's problems, but it was an excuse to come back to a friend. Neither of them seemed to have that at the castle, Gwendolyn in particular. Charmaine knew the pain of being alone all too well. Sure, she had James, but she would always have James, so that did not really count for her.

He was her brother, after all.

The burning of Brinn haunted Charmaine as she wrapped herself in the black silk robe that had been brought to her chambers last night. She had debated falling asleep, tossing and turning, when *he* knocked ever so lightly on her door.

Her cheeks heated, that ever so silent knock that ensured she was absolutely not going to sleep.

What in the name of the Ten Kingdoms was Prince Dalton doing wandering about the castle last night without an escort?

Instead of the impropriety haunting her—a Prince coming to her chambers in the middle of the night to check on her—she could not help but smile. He had to be mad. Maybe even reckless? She knew he had been kept under lock and key for five years, but that did not mean that he was free to do as he pleased now. She did not get much out of him during the ball, or even when she spoke to him last night. *Twice.*

But what she had deciphered from their conversations was that he was a complete and utter mess.

And she was dying to see him again.

In those moments last night, no matter how scared she was, she was alive. Regardless of the trauma that they endured—her and Dalton—she was addicted to his relentlessness. He acted like being locked away was the worst way to cope with the gravity of the attack.

They had been attacked.

She clutched her arms tightly to her chest, her hands rubbing for warmth as much as comfort. Her memories were paralyzing, the constriction in her chest gripping as she came to terms with being recognized by two mercenaries now.

One time was a mistake, but two times was a coincidence.

She did not want to know if there would be a third time, nor what it would bring.

Charmaine remembered that as a child in Brinn, her mother told them stories of the Kings and Queens of Old.

She would tell tales of them fighting with the Gods and making peace with them. However, in all her stories, one thing always remained true: the castle of the First Kingdom remained untouched. It was a fortress, one which held all the realm's power and protégées of destiny. To see it attacked last night was more frightening than most thought.

And last night was frightening.

Charmaine's chamber doors squeaked open, interrupting her thoughts of her past life. Gwendolyn came through with a pot of hot tea, her big blue eyes genuine and kind. Charmaine wondered where she was from and how she ended up serving King Ronan and the royal family.

If she wanted to make Gwendolyn her friend, she wanted to know more about her.

"Here you go, miss," she said softly, putting the tea down. She poured a cup and offered it to her, which she took graciously. "Is there anything else?"

"Can you sit with me? I very much wish not to be alone this morning," she said quietly.

She nodded, her gray eyes teeming with emotion. "You must have had quite the fright."

"My brother is going to be okay, so I fear the worst is over."

"One can only hope, miss." Gwendolyn did not sound convinced.

"How long have you been working here, Gwendolyn?" Charmaine asked.

"Three years, ma'am, since I was sixteen." Her posture seemed to straighten, sitting a little bit higher speaking of herself.

Charmaine admired that, a hardworking woman.

"How do you take to it? Do you have any friends here at the castle?"

"I mostly work in the Prince's quarters, serving tea and tending to the bed sheets in the castle. I have had friends here at work before, but no longer." Her posture seemed to sag a little at the mention of the Prince, but Charmaine pushed onward, determined to learn as much as she could about the castle.

"And you enjoy it?"

Gwendolyn paused for a second, her hands running through her blonde hair. *Was she nervous?* "I am able to send the money back to my family in Hammen, so I do not mind that and the warm bed, miss."

"So, you are also from the First Kingdom. I am, well, *was* from Brinn. And the Royals are kind to you?" She could not help from asking.

Gwendolyn's voice lowered, as if she were afraid of the walls listening. "I do not interact with the King and Queen, miss, but I was permitted to work here due to being a citizen of the First. They do not accept outsiders from other Kingdoms as workers in the castle."

That was something that Charmaine did not know. Surprised, she asked, "But you assist the Prince?"

"Yes." She could tell that Gwendolyn was not saying something, holding back.

She went for it. "What is he like?"

"Mischievous," she said bluntly, then covered her hand with her mouth as if she should not have spoken her truth.

Charmaine laughed, kind of surprised by her answer. "It is okay, Gwendolyn. It is not as if you told me he was something vile." Charmaine was rather relieved, shocked even, that mischievousness was a defining characteristic of his.

"There is just… not much… information about him, miss. My friend Athelred used to serve him sometimes, but ever since the Prince's latest shenanigans… Well, miss, he has been under close watch and guard by Cyril. Us servants are not allowed to escort him."

"Please, call me Charmaine. Whatever do you mean?"

"He had been… in training and schooling… for many years. The last five? He formally returned to life at court not a few days ago, about when Sir Randolph returned to the castle."

Charmaine's eyebrows furrowed together.

He had been away all these years?

"You may laugh at his mischievous nature, but those who are assigned to him, minus Cyril, can feel the consequences if they do not follow Ronan's expectations."

Charmaine winced. "You had not seen him before then?"

"Never in public."

"Is he not without kindness?" She thought of him last night, standing outside her chambers with his flushed cheeks and telling her to call on Cyril.

Was it all just a game to him then? It did not seem like it in the courtyard. She also pondered his appearances in public. The verbiage that Gwendolyn used suggested that she had seen him before, but not in a court scenario.

"He has never been unkind to me, swindling perhaps, conniving in the name of good fun, but never unkind." Gwendolyn bit the bottom of her lip, running her hands through her hair again impatiently.

Charmaine did that thing again where she spoke without consequences. She blurted, "What are you hiding from me? What don't you want me to know, Gwen?"

Gwendolyn grabbed a cup of tea, her eyes flashing with an emotion that Charmaine knew all too well. Fear. *But who was she so afraid of?*

Bringing the cup to her lips, she took a small sip of the lavender concoction. She put the cup down with a tiny *ding* and leaned forward. "The Prince has... abilities, Charmaine. Ones that if they were to be discussed freely, I believe the King would have our heads."

Charmaine could not help but answer, her voice low. "So, it is true then? What all of the legends have come to pass? Cian's powers have returned... Gwendolyn, he basically admitted all this to me last night."

"You must be careful of that information," Gwendolyn warned, her lips pursed.

"But isn't it obvious? The chills, the white hair..."

"Yes, but you do not know the King. If you did... you would tread lightly with the Prince."

Charmaine grabbed the teacup in front of her and took a small sip as Gwendolyn said, almost too quietly for her to hear, "I would not tread at all."

She nearly spit out her tea.

"Gwendolyn!" she said, feeling like a child.

"I saw you in the garden with him, right before the explosion. Also... your dance."

"What about the dance?" Charmaine asked, self-conscious that she had made a spectacle of herself unwillingly.

"It was so—forgive me—*intense.* Him stealing you away from Sir Randolph, no matter how casually, was a sign of disrespect. You are both lucky to have evaded the King in that moment."

"What if he had seen?"

Charmaine did not want to know the answer, but not knowing would kill her slowly. The King was known for his temper and inability to accept those with magic, but Dalton was his son. And he was the crowned Prince. Surely, that counted for something.

Gwendolyn walked over to Charmaine's chamber doors quickly and yanked, checking to make certain that they were truly locked. She scurried back over to Charmaine and sat directly next to her. Her gray eyes flamed with intensity and worry, as she took Charmaine's hands in her own.

"I am only going to say this once, so please listen. The King has a reputation, yes? Well, whatever you have heard, envision worse. Yes, he is a tyrant, but what he does to the Prince…"

Her eyes flooded with tears, but she did not break eye contact. She breathed in deeply, gathering the strength to continue. Her chest rose slowly as she exhaled a breath, her hands not once letting go of Charmaine's. "The Prince is lucky to be alive most nights. As a servant, I cannot intervene… but what I saw a few nights before you all arrived… the blood… and the screaming… He hadn't done anything wrong. The Kings and Queens of Old must have been watching over him… and Cyril… I don't think Cyril could survive if they took the Prince from him."

For once, Charmaine did not want more details. She understood Gwendolyn's message enough.

The King was not to be underestimated, and he would do anything he had to in order to keep his power.

Panic swept through her veins and ignited her into a frenzy. She had changed unwillingly *and* unknowingly last night. It could not happen again. It would not happen again.

"I will never speak of it again," Charmaine said, walking with Gwendolyn toward the doors.

She touched the door handle, her blonde hair swept behind her as she looked back at Charmaine. "Tread lightly, for it is a dangerous path you are thinking of walking. I will not lose another friend to the wrath of the King."

TWENTY-THREE

he throne room was decorated with the ambiance of a snowstorm. Flurries fell from within the castle walls, adorning the throne room in grace. Icicles coated the ceiling. The golden lanterns of the room ignited an ethereal glare among the walls.

She looked down at herself, her dress crafted by the Gods. The white lace was decorated intricately as though snowflakes themselves had landed on the fabric and burned their mark through it. Her hands were covered in gloves, which she noted had the same detailing. The bodice all the way down to her feet was fitted, but not suffocating. She felt the weight of solid gold atop her head, interwoven between locks of her raven black hair. It was heavy, but it felt comfortable, as though it was natural to wear such a garment.

She tore her attention away from her dress as she surveyed the room more closely. She had not yet noticed the rows of people with a divisional aisle between them. They seemed to notice her at the same time, gasping and wiping their tears with handkerchiefs as they looked upon her.

"She's here."

"She looks so beautiful."

"All Hail the Queen!"

The whispers carried over the crowd to where she stood. She held a bouquet of roses in her hands, which now had snowflakes from the ceiling kissing them with winter's touch. She smiled cordially as she walked forward, an invisible force tugging her toward the front of the throne room.

She looked down at the roses as she went, using them as a constant among this newfound chaos.

As she approached the grand staircase, she saw none other than Dalton standing before her, except it did not look like him at all. His white hair was now more raven black than her own. His eyelashes were a beautiful array of darkness. His freckles were less noticeable now, given that his skin was no longer porcelain, but sun-kissed. Tears fell down her face in pure unadulterated joy, realizing that his cheeks were fuller, more beautiful, and more full of life than the Prince she had known. His hand was extended to her own, his smile genuine.

She took it.

⊞

Charmaine awoke and rolled over. She rubbed her eyes and willed herself to sleep again.

⊞

Her mother sat beside her, her oracle orb in her palm. The glow of the rock swirled with the vibrancy of her reading. The exemplified Thinker powers she was unable to manifest held her to the only form of expression she could enact. Her mother was a Cipher, and she had unimaginable untapped power.

And risked everything while exuding it.

"Charmaine, grab my hand," she whispered as she began to strain. It was as if the power was too much tonight. The reading took over, due to the nature of the vision.

"Charmaine!" she gasped, her head falling back as her

183

breathing became ragged.

But she could not move. She could not scream. She could not do anything.

"Char—" she started, a desperate scream forming on her lips, but she heard no more.

Sweat glistened on Charmaine's forehead, her chest and back soaked, as agony pulsed through her throbbing head.

She reached for a glass of water, chugging it ferociously as she tried to make sense of what had just happened.

It was a dream.

It was only a dream.

She laid back down, grogginess still in reach. She readjusted her head on the silks of her bed, but she still felt the whispering winds of Dalton's power and the darkness of her mother's memory as she drifted into a deep slumber once more.

TWENTY-FOUR

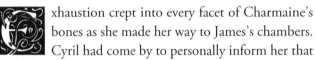xhaustion crept into every facet of Charmaine's bones as she made her way to James's chambers. Cyril had come by to personally inform her that her brother was on the mend to recovery, after two nights in the infirmary. He told her that James had requested to be moved from the infirmary back to his own private quarters. Charmaine tried to hide her tears of relief, but Cyril only smiled and told her that he would walk with her if she would like.

She declined, for she was determined to make her way through this castle without a helping hand.

She threw on a yellow silk gown, provided to her by Gwendolyn earlier in the morning. The bodice was loose fitting, draped across her chest casually. The skirt was long, just hitting her ankles to expose the short gold heels she wore. Her hair was unbound, tumbling down her back wildly.

Charmaine had no desire to entertain the glamours of the night prior, but Gwendolyn insisted that it was proper.

She had chosen to leave her new dagger from the battle underneath the pillow on her bed, after a few minutes of convincing herself that she was safe and she did not need it.

Before she realized it, she arrived at James's chambers after a short walk down the hall. She pushed on the heavy door with gusto, grunting with effort. The battle had really taken it out of her, mentally and physically. She entered with haste, not caring to turn around and gently close the grand door.

"Jame—" she started, her mouth closing abruptly as she saw the woman seated at the end of his bed.

She was the most beautiful woman Charmaine had ever seen. Her skin was a dark brown, her hair a deep auburn like a raging fire. Glistening with curiosity, her eyes danced with protectiveness. Painted red, her lips curved into a wicked smile. Her black dress was high at the neckline, nearly coming up to her ears. The lace adorned with patterns of flowers and leaves, the sheer sections in between leaving little to the imagination. The design flowed all the way to her hands and down to her feet, her long pointed fingernails poking out from the holes that the fabric gave way to at her wrists.

The girl looked Charmaine up and down, no doubt taking in her simply fitted dress and unbound hair. Despite Charmaine's rather unworthy dress around someone dressed like a queen, the girl genuinely smiled at her.

"You must be the sister," she said, looking back at James with affection.

He flashed a grin, his violet eyes filled with lust and longing.

"Yes?" Charmaine replied, somehow now unsure of herself. "I'm sorry, I didn't mean to interrupt."

"No, you did not. I was on my way out." She stood

up, not leaving James's focus as she made her way toward the door.

Charmaine noticed for the first time that there was a crown of rubies atop her head, so dainty that it seemed to blend perfectly into her red hair.

"Thank you for everything, Princess," James called as she continued to walk toward the door, without giving him a second glance back.

She paused slightly, her hands steady as she grabbed the golden handle to his chambers. She opened it easily, contrasting so with Charmaine's own difficulty earlier.

Charmaine turned around as she heard the *click* of the door, and approached James's bed. She kneeled at his bedside. His eyes were lined with silver, looking at Charmaine with true joy across his face.

And clarity.

"Why did you do that?" Charmaine asked, pain slashing through her voice as she reimagined James taking the brute of the mercenary's weapon.

"For you, for… Our world does not stand a chance if it is overrun by mercenaries." His voice was vengeful.

"I think the world would be better off if Ronan had died." Charmaine could taste the bitterness in her mouth as she said such cruelties. She knew it was treason, yet she did not care.

"Charmaine, you can't say things like that."

"But I thought it then, James, and I do now. If Dalton were to ascend to the throne…"

He lifted a hand as if to pause her. "If Dalton were to ascend to the throne, it would be at the hands of the mercenaries and whoever controls them. He would constantly be living in the shadow of a memory, the infamy that his father has created with such brutality and hatred."

Charmaine was taken aback by his tone. "So, you saved him?"

"I saved them *both*."

Charmaine pondered the words for a moment before asking, "Who was that in here earlier?"

"Princess Elena of the Fourth Kingdom." His voice wavered now, the collected nature he had displayed when she was in there gone.

"What? Are you friends now? How in the name of the Ten Kingdoms did you get her to visit you in your chambers?" Charmaine could barely keep the hysterics out of her voice.

"She healed me." Finality.

"She what?" She could not keep the confusion out of her voice.

He spoke of her like he *knew her*, and Charmaine knew for damn sure that she was not a member of the village of Brinn.

"She... has powers. I promised not to tell anyone but you, Charmaine. She is at risk here too."

Charmaine's blood boiled. "We all think that the Prince has powers, but nobody has seen it, James. Nobody has felt the power that everyone, including the King, seems to believe we should be *celebrating*."

She spat the word out of her own frustration. If Dalton truly did have power, which he essentially admitted to her in the rose garden, he would be the only member of the Kingdom who was *allowed* to have such a thing. He would not live in fear that he would face the consequences if he were to be one of the common folk. He would be safe.

"It is not a celebration. It is an execution."

"Whatever do you mean?" Charmaine's irritation was at the forefront of her voice, yet she did not care.

"This charade, Elena says—"

She had had enough, interrupting him like an impertinent child. "Elena? You are on a first name basis with the Princess of the Fourth?! JAMES! What happened to being inconspicuous? We are supposed to have a low profile, out of fear of exposure. If he finds out who I am... if he finds out who our mother was..."

Before Charmaine could stop him, James held her hands, sitting up without any sign of injury. "She healed me, Char. She *healed* me."

He lifted the top of his tunic, showing the spot of the injury. Charmaine gasped, for the sight of the injury was truly no longer there. "Nobody is going to find out about us because I know it. I can't explain what happened when Elena touched me, but I *know it*."

"You act as though she is your savior, but you just met her. It is a bit concerning, Jamie," she whispered, disbelief blinding her from reason.

"She is my salvation, and she will be yours too." The word was a plea, begging her to understand. As if he were trying to understand it himself. "Just trust me. There are other things at work here, and I feel it best if I lean into them."

What had she done when she healed him?

He placed a soft hand on her left cheek. "You will understand in time, I promise, little sister."

Charmaine blinked twice and before she could think, she said, "I miss her."

His mouth turned upward into a soft smile; his eyes filled with emotion. "I miss her too."

"We watched her burn, James." Tears dripped down her face at the admittance. The horror of reliving the execution of her mother swarmed her. She normally did not feel much of anything when speaking of her mother, but unannounced like this, the emotions always overwhelmed her.

"And she will be the last we watch do so."

"How can we know that for certain?" She wiped her nose with her finger, laughing to herself at the indecency of the act. "James, the mercenary in the ballroom… He was looking for me. Just as the mercenary had been in Brinn. What are the chances of another mercenary entirely looking for a girl with the power to go invisible?"

"We cannot live as if the next spectacle is imminent. Nothing is certain. We have to fight, Charmaine. We have to fight to stay alive every moment of the day, especially as we make a life here. But I believe here is where we need to be."

"Right under the nose of the King that would have my head or make me his servant?"

"He will never expect something so extraordinary from someone he deems unworthy," James said with a smirk. "And I know you of all people are worthy of the Gods' gifts. I don't know why they picked you, though. Their plans have never been clear. Not even Mother could see that part of destiny."

"I want to go home," Charmaine whispered.

James's voice was firm and a steady fire burned beneath his gaze. "There is no home. Not anymore. There is only life and what we choose to do with it in the time that we have."

TWENTY-FIVE

Despite exhaustion, Dalton sparred all morning. His back was ridden with sweat, running down his torso. His brows furrowed, and concentration kept his mind from wandering to things it should not.

People it should not.

The heat of the day was uncharacteristic for the First Kingdom. His power had no inclinations to rectify the brutality of the temperatures. The heat signified the arrival of Elena, who always seemed to bring with her the changes of the wind. He could almost hear Cyril's incessant voice, surveying what this would cost him with Dalton's father for not maintaining his frozen image he had been so eager to cultivate.

"You need to be careful, boy," he had said earlier as he got dressed for training.

Dalton snorted at him and proceeded to throw a shoe at his head. In good fun, of course. He fell back on the bed, laughter escaping his lungs with a childish buoyancy.

He was so tired after a long night of wreaking havoc with Elena, so he was yawning nonstop before that moment. After giving Cyril the characteristic slip in the library, they proceeded to steal a cart full of tomatoes and pelt them at the castle walls beneath the garden.

Thick as thieves, they went about their harmless fun given that they tested their brute strength and powers after being coerced with some wine. She threw a tomato and then shot water after it, small enough not to freeze the gardens around them, but large enough to slice the tomato before it hit the wall. Elena doubled over, her breath ragged as she tried to keep in her hysterics. Dalton kept his lips pursed, almost in tears at her ridiculous reaction.

Ten Kingdoms, it felt so good to laugh.

Out of the many admirable qualities that Elena had, Dalton had to hand it to her that she was more powerful than he was. Sure, he had the famous power that Cian had. But Elena had *two gifts*. Cyril always said that it made sense that she could manipulate water and heal, but they were not mutually exclusive. She could not turn anything to ice. That was Dalton's specialty, and he would be near livid if she took away the one thing that made him special.

After a few swigs from the bottle, Dalton tested his raw power. Holding the tomato in his right hand, he breathed in and out, testing the control he knew he did not have. His jaw clenched, his teeth grinding together. Elena's cheering notified him that he had done it. When he opened his eyes, the tomato was solid as a rock, frozen and crystallized to a winter's perfection. Tears welled up in his eyes as he threw it with all his might, watching it shatter instantly upon impact to the wall.

He smiled to himself before turning to his beautiful friend, thanking her for the reminder that magic was beautiful and raw.

Dalton had not seen his father yet that day. So much

for needing him to cultivate an image of power given by the Gods. If anything, his forsaken gifts were a curse. If he was not to be parading his power around like he was Queen Ciara ripping out the hearts of men, he was to be locked away like a maiden in a tower.

His father had no rhyme or reason for any of the behavior he expressed since Dalton was a boy beyond the fact that he was his sole heir now, and that Ronan had no magic.

Dalton tried not to think about what his lineage meant for him. All members of the First thought of the Kings and Queens of Old consistently, the stories that they had been told as children forever engrained in the way that they thought and believed. However, there was something to be said about being bitter for not having such attributes. The way that his father crooned his name after James had saved him, taking quite the injury to go with it, derailed Dalton more than he would like to admit.

Charmaine definitely saw his expression too.

Cian save him, who hadn't?

He could not have been more erratic if he tried. That man made him absolutely manic, driven with a maddening desire to—

Dalton moved to dry off his face with a towel, cutting off his treasonous thoughts before he could get carried away in fantasy. He would give anything to be powerless. As he smashed his face into the white towel, damp with the smells of roses and lavender, a voice rose behind him. It was cut-throat and antagonizing.

"Training hard, again, Your Majesty?"

Dalton slowly removed the towel from his face, carefully and strategically wiping his neck with its remains too. His hands held onto the towel in a fist.

Put on the mask, put on the mask, put on the mask.

Dalton slid the cool arrogance over his features, his gestures becoming more fluid and his Princely swagger returning as if trying on an old shoe.

"Yes, Randolph. One does not get stronger by courting pretty girls and drinking wine."

Dalton did not need to turn around to know he had struck a chord. He did, however, need to turn around if he were to drive it home.

"How is my dear friend, Charmaine? I was to visit her earlier, but got derailed by Cyril." Dalton grinned, the towel dropping into the pail of water reserved for the dirty cloths.

Randolph nearly imploded with rage. His green eyes flared, nearly driving Dalton to embrace this mask permanently.

He had seen Randolph that night at the ball with her, prancing around as if she were his discovery and a prize to be won. It made Dalton sick to see her be put on display as his father did to him, but to mask it in protecting her and bringing her to a safer place. He knew about Ronan's command that Charmaine and James were to remain wards of the court until they testified on the mercenaries' brutality. He believed it was a step in the direction to make that truth available to the people of the First, but not at the cost of their trauma. She was better off rotting in the likes of her town burnt to ash than she was frolicking among the walls of this castle.

"And how are you today? I heard you gave your father quite the fright the other night, disappearing from your chambers." The tone in Randolph's voice was enough to send Dalton rabid.

Randolph had also mastered the craft of being a royal bastard, in name.

"Well matched," Dalton said, leaving it at that with a smirk.

He did not dare reveal he had wandered off to Charmaine's chambers to speak with her, for he did not want to spread rumors among the knights. She was pure and he wanted to keep her that way. For her sake. For her survival against this wretched society.

Randolph snorted as Dalton grabbed a new towel, dabbing it underneath his eyes dramatically as Randolph moved to grab one himself.

"Do you hate me so?" Dalton asked quietly. He stepped closer to wipe off his own sweat, presumably from training hard as a stallion too.

Randolph's mouth parted in confusion. "Did you not think I would ask such a question?" Dalton asked, pushing. Dalton easily could have invoked the, "*I am your Prince*" crap, but even the likes of Randolph deserved more than that.

"I do not know what to make of you, your Majesty."

Dalton almost laughed, thinking back to Charmaine when she nearly said the same thing the other night. After a short pause, he mused, "I think the rest of the world is with you."

Randolph's eyes flashed toward Dalton again, latent with amusement.

Could I befriend this son of a bitch?

"I do not mean to disrespect, your *Majesty*."

"Sure, you do, but go on." Dalton smirked, his arrogance escaping more freely than his raw power ever had. He could not bring himself to reign it in, however, not that he was really trying to.

"I do not mean to disrespect, your Majesty, but I feel as though the world hasn't had a proper greeting of you. We, the world, are not sure what to make of you because the world does not know you. And these rumors—"

"If anything is to be hidden, be sure that it is not my doing. I have nothing to hide, nothing to be ashamed of. I never have and I never will."

Randolph's eyes flashed in rage at the pointed targeting. He looked Dalton up and down, tossing the rag-now damp with his own sweat-into the water with the rest of them.

"Then it seems as though we will be seeing one another more frequently."

Dalton flashed a smile with teeth this time, his charm shining as brightly as his crown had at the ball. "I was not planning on being locked away again."

Randolph's eyebrow quirked up, stunned by Dalton's directness and his absolute disrespect toward his father flying out of his mouth as easily as poetry. Randolph bowed slightly after blinking for a few seconds, then turned to head back to wherever he had snaked in from.

"Oh! Before you go," Dalton said, deciding he was not finished yet. "Make sure to say hello to Char for me."

Randolph went beet red, his eyes flickering with rage. The audacity of Dalton to call her by her given name, and his nickname at that, was truly unabashed. If the roles were reversed, Dalton knew he deserved to be punched. He was hellbent on firing up his father from every direction.

Let him make it personal.

Let him rage.

Let him think that the Prince was a monster and unworthy of the crown.

Dalton did not want it anyway.

✠

TWENTY-SIX

lena Leclair wandered the passageways of the Hall of Portraits without a semblance of direction or desire.

There were not many parts of the castle she actually enjoyed. She had been there a few times throughout her childhood, when her mother was still interested in creating alliances with other Kingdoms. The castle was beautiful— a marvel to all who came to visit the First Kingdom and pay homage to Queen Ciara and King Cian's memory— but there was something haunted about it as well. Elena could not put her finger on it, but she always got the sense that the castle was alive. That it had a spirit. And that spirit was wracked by the current state of the world—chaos.

She had stepped out of the carriage the first time she and her mother arrived, the King and Queen of the First dressed in their traditional white garb ready to greet them. Elena and Queen Maria attempted to present a powerful front, the physical embodiment of that which made their regime so famous.

But it was the children of the First Kingdom who caught the eye of her mother.

The girl, Carinthya, as Elena later learned, exuded regality. Elena remembered her long black hair had been pinned up with diamonds, giving her the appearance of being dusted with the first snowfall. She had an intensity in her gaze that almost took Elena's breath away. She was sharp and fierce.

That was all Elena could remember of her, even now, for she had only met her the one time before she was snatched away.

Dalton remained a part of the fiercest of memories, despite pushing away much of her childhood. He had worn white garb similar to that of his family. Atop his head was a white crown, dazzling as it was ferocious. He was as radiant as the sun was against a fresh snowfall. He was blinding—truly something, standing up with his family with a smirk on his mouth, his dark blue eyes alight with mischief.

She knew she would like him from the moment she laid eyes on him.

As she approached the foursome with caution, her mother warned her of the dynasty's heritage with magic. The magic that plagued these lands no more, the King of the First Kingdom's obsession with securing his magic-less regime.

"Why does he care if people have magic?" I asked my mother, too hushed for anyone to hear.

"He is bitter that he was not one of the chosen." Mother sounded equally bitter, for she had no power either.

"How do you get chosen?"

"The Gods decide who is worthy."

"Who was the last to be worthy?"

"King Cian of the First was the last to be worthy of such a power, but it died with him."

"What is the power, Mama?"

"You name the course of winter and that is what route the power shall take."

"But King Cian was not Royal," I said, feeling proud of myself for knowing the Ten Kingdoms' history.

"The Gods deemed him worthy. That's all that matters."

Elena had no idea that Dalton would be the one to control the power of the Gods. She figured if anything it would be Carinthya, with her sharp wits and strong demeanor.

He had bowed to her then, but never took his eyes off of her. Little did he know, now she was to bow before him.

Elena paused at his portrait as she walked, mesmerized by how he was frozen in time as the boy that lived life to his fullest. He was normal then, for the standards of a Royal.

Sneaky disposition bloomed within his eyes. The artist had captured it perfectly. The man she had known since her arrival had that within him. She knew it. It was buried, but not lost. She also knew that no matter how hard he tried to put on the facade, something was offkilter within him. He was no longer that boy, even though pieces of him had not changed at all.

She continued past his portrait, gazing aimlessly at the different royals whose regimes had somehow gotten them to this point. The point where a mad King once again ruled these lands, his iron fist responsible for so much cruelty and fear. Her mother's own kingdom was far from perfect, but at least people were not persecuted for being who they were.

With one final glance at the portraits around her, Elena turned around to continue toward the door. She had spent enough time thinking about this room and the people who decorated these walls.

It was a good distraction from who she was trying *not* to think about.

Pulsing and unstoppable, her power had been completely out of control. Weakness and irritation flowed through her aimlessly, unable to fight off the urge to use her gifts, given her exhaustion from traveling.

To save.

Her feet whisked her to the infirmary and paused at the foot of the bed of a young man with violet eyes. His black hair was elegantly swept across his brow, his face tense with pain.

Elena saw roses on his bedside table with a note from someone named Charmaine. She leaned at the side of his bed on her knees. The feeling that overtook her was strong beyond her wildest imagination.

She felt love, strength, purity, and hope looking upon the face of this sleeping man. He exuded a beauty beyond recognition, even with his shoulder ripped open. His battle wound called to her magic.

"How did this happen to you, darling?" she whispered, touching the side of his face with her long fingers before she even realized what she was doing.

His eyes fluttered open with exhaustion. His mouth parted slightly upon seeing her and that was when she saw it. Flashing between them, she was crushed with memories and moments.

I saw a wedding, me in all black and this man looking at me with adoration. I saw a battle, this man screaming my name, pained with excruciating loss—my death. I saw a child, dark skin with a crown upon his head.

When she came back, the young man was trying to sit up, sweat grazing his brow. But he never took his eyes off her as he did so.

She breathed out a name, but she was not even sure how she knew it. "James," she said.

"Elena," he said.

Elena was going to throw up. The memories were so vivid that it caved in her chest.

"Did you see that?" she asked, her hands shaking as she tried to back away from him.

He nodded in reply, his face grim with the pain of the memories. Without knowing what she was doing, her hands reached for his as they shook uncontrollably. He grimaced, making a hissing noise as her magic went to work.

She wanted to apologize for touching him, for inflicting her magic upon him without consent, but it was too late. She wrenched her hands from his, almost flying backward with the force of it to stop. She looked at the site of his wound as she breathed in deeply to see that it had not completely healed, but almost.

I should not be doing magic here.

She shook away the memory of the moment now as she exited the Hall of Mirrors. Her head still spun and her body still drained from the healing powers.

How could I have been so stupid?

She was there for her mother, and for Dalton as much as she could be. She would be no use to anyone if Ronan chopped off her head. She cursed herself again silently, looking down at her hands which had not stopped trembling since she healed James.

Resetting her shoulders with a deep breath, she entered the grand hallway, putting on the same mask that Dalton wore, as she finally began to understand its purpose.

TWENTY-SEVEN

andolph trudged his way through the castle grounds. Sweat continued to pool against his back and neck from the training he just put his body through. But that internal fire was all thanks to the crowned Prince.

Char.

Smoke nearly came out of his nostrils.

What was he playing at? Or was he really that much of a menace to society?

Randolph thundered through the entrance to the castle, glancing upon his men as he passed them.

"Sire," they greeted Randolph with kind smiles on their faces, despite the way he grunted like an animal as he passed by.

What was wrong with me?

Dalton was his future King, but the stench of magic that radiated off him and the way it altered his physical appearance... Randolph did not know why he chose to chance himself against him with his brute testosterone and fiery temper. As if encouraging that behavior ever solved a damn problem.

And he did have a problem.

He despised the Prince's persona. The way that he was arrogant with that casual swagger that seemed to propel him, or his blatant disregard for his father's rules... Randolph did not know what infuriated him more.

Randolph once wished for nothing but his own father's cruel demise. Yet as time had gone on, Randolph wished to give it all back. The cruelty, the quest for power, the death...

It was all too much for him to bear against the weight of his servitude.

He pinched the bridge of his nose as he pushed on, wishing that the pressure he felt between his fingers would alleviate some of the pain. He could never turn it off, the swirling and the temperance which set him off.

He was not sure who he was anymore, and he was beginning to think that was a bad thing.

A slight breeze blew past his right cheek, and as he turned, a hand landed on his shoulder, dragging him by the tunic toward his chambers.

"What has your knickers in a tussle?" Lawton said.

Slimy arrogance radiated off of him as well. And he hated it.

He made a mental note to never introduce Lawton and Dalton, or he simply might have to take himself to the gallows.

"Now is *not* the time." He put on what he imagined to be his King voice. One which could not be tested.

Of course, Lawton pushed anyway. "What? Prince got your tongue?"

Randolph whipped his head around, but continued to walk toward the end of the white hallway. "How is it that you possibly know everything?"

"Now, if I knew everything, the world would have a lot less problems."

"No, if you knew everything, the world would be the same because you wouldn't reveal *shit*." Bristling and slipping, Randolph did not care how unprofessional he sounded. Royal irritation built in his veins, flowing throughout his blood, and it demanded to be exuded.

Lawton was a lot of things, but he could take the brute force of Randolph's demons.

Lawton laughed, his volume inappropriate for their location. A few heads turned in Randolph's direction, surveying what had them so riled up. Nosy brutes.

"You are the least discreet person in the First Kingdom," Randolph snarled.

"And you are the grumpiest."

He balled his fists at his side.

Breathe deeply. One... two... three...

Randolph opened the door to his chambers, searching rather frantically for a bucket of water to douse over his head.

"This has already been so eventful that I forgot why I popped in," Lawton drawled, trying to seem bored.

Spotting the bucket, Randolph strode toward it. Damn the clothes. He would change his outfit after he brought himself back to reality. Randolph lifted the bucket hastily as the ice-cold water purified the world around him. It took his breath away, but being frozen always seemed to center him.

"Oh! I remember now!" Lawton said, completely ignoring Randolph and his bucket. "That's it. There is a council meeting soon. A surprise one too. The King wants us all there."

Randolph did not pause as he went over to his dresser,

fumbling for a plain tunic. His leather pants were fine, somehow unaffected by his harsh training session and the near bath.

"Oh, and what is the topic of today's meeting?" Randolph asked, pretending to be amused.

Lawton was always the bearer of council meetings to Randolph. If not him, then it was Cyril when he was not on hound duty for the Prince's undeniably consistent house arrest.

"*Magic*," he said softly, as if the walls would tell the King he simply said it.

Randolph turned his head as he put on a green tunic, chucking his wet one onto the floor. "Magic?"

"You know, that thing Ronan despises above all else? That thing I think we can all assume the Prince has?"

So, he felt it too.

"We do not know for certain," he said, trying to sound confident.

Lawton chuckled. His hand slid to his knee impatiently as he tapped his leg incessantly. "You do not believe that, come on."

"I do not know what to believe anymore," Randolph admitted.

"He even *looks* like Cian did when his power first erupted. The bastard is the embodiment of snow, ice, and fury. Look at the way he struts about this castle as if he owns it. He is a living, breathing, reincarnate of our long-gone King. Randolph, the powers are *back*."

"I have not seen him do one thing, Lawton. No ice, no frozen bodies. If anything, the Prince is a firecracker, blazing through this place as if he has never seen it before." An innate coldness had seeped in during the council meeting, but that was hardly Lawton's business.

Nothing was ever Lawton's business.

Lawton paused. The look on his face that told Randolph he knew too much, but he did not want to reveal it.

"What is it, boy?" Randolph hissed, losing his cap on his temper.

He blinked. "I do not think he has seen much of anything before."

The confusion on Randolph's face must have been apparent because Lawton sat up straighter, confirming his suspicion.

"What do you know?" he asked.

I was not planning on being locked away again.

"Ten Kingdoms," Randolph said, his hand going to his face as he stormed out of his chambers.

TWENTY-EIGHT

yril had been acting so strangely this morning that Dalton almost approached him about it. He was unable to focus on much of anything and continually *shooed* him from corner to corner of his chambers as he helped Dalton decide on a suitable council outfit.

"Is this really necessary? The bastards know what I look like."

"The bastards do know what you look like, but I need you to look presentable." Cyril's tone was curt.

"Why does it matter? It is not as if I am King, anyway," Dalton fired back at him.

"No, but you have a lot to make up for since you are no longer the Prince in hiding." His tone was unnaturally cold.

"And whose fault is it that I was even in hiding to begin with? Maybe I should dress like a commoner, a peasant even, just to mess with good ole Daddy."

Cyril tried to hit him with a tray after that, a plethora of curse words following as he pursued Dalton around his chambers as if he were an impetuous child.

Striding into the council chambers moments later, Dalton wiped off his smile. Cyril's violence always brought him a level of joy.

As the grand white doors were thrust open, Dalton nearly lost his footing at the sight of Randolph, Lawton, and James joining the usual councilmen. It seemed as if James had miraculously recovered, or rather, his wound had been patched up by the Gods.

Dalton swore silently.

Elena. Is that where she wandered off to after our escapades?

Dalton put up his mask, smirking as he nodded in their direction before sitting down.

"Gentlemen," his father said, striding in as he moved his chair into the overly large table.

Everyone bowed their heads in reply.

"Thank you for attending this meeting on such short notice. I have very important business that we must discuss, with action that must be taken immediately."

"What is the rush, your Majesty?" Randolph asked.

Dalton's father flashed Randolph a deadly smile, his eyes almost black. There was a feral nature to the way he was acting, as if he was full of his own power and was about to unleash it upon them all.

"I have discovered *magic*."

Everyone went silent.

Lawton turned a sickly green. Randolph was breathing rhythmically, but his eyes betrayed his emotionless nature. Even James was unable to hide, true fear stricken on his face.

Fear impaled Dalton, not for himself, but for Elena.

He knew Elena had magic, but he could not believe

she would be stupid enough to heal a guest of the court, no matter how grave it was.

Dalton could not bear to think about what his father would do if he knew Charmaine had some magical connection to himself. Whatever capacity it was in, Dalton was not sure, but the feeling of its draw was constant since he left her last night. She had been acting so strangely after the battle too. It was not anything he recognized then, but there was something that seemed to shift about her. Her focus became whether or not Dalton could see her, which he did not understand at all. She was hyper-focused on what he had observed, to which he had nothing to report.

But the fear in her eyes had been genuine, and that was enough for him to think of her. He made a motion to stand up and say something idiotic, maybe to calm the room or wipe that happiness off his father's face. As he made a move to do so, Randolph stood up faster, causing Dalton to sit down with a *thud*.

"In what capacity, sire?" His voice was that of his highest prestige.

Ronan was furious. "Does it matter? I found the girl holding the object of which we speak. She is guilty of harboring the forbidden and I demand to know where she got it. She was also carrying a potion, one which is often connected with magic. Lily root is not toxic to humans without the indulgence of foul play. The girl did not divulge any information, so as the law stands, it does not matter if the object is hers or not. Aiding and abetting *magic* is illegal, and she will die for it."

Dalton was suddenly unsure whose face was the most concerning shade of white in the room.

"Who is the girl?" he demanded, his voice ice-cold as his power began to stir.

A forbidden object?

His mind kept darting to Charmaine and that knife she had procured during the battle. Or at least he assumed she had procured it, for the jewels attached to it were so grand he doubted they came from the likes of Brinn.

He was going to be sick.

The temperature of the room dropped, his fingers sticking to the table that he grabbed with a ferocious nature.

His father's gaze upon him was filled with total fury, plotting war against his heir.

"*Look at me!*" Dalton wanted to shout. "*Look at me and my magic, you coward!*"

Dalton sneered at him as he sneered back. Two Kings thrust into a struggle for power, even though one did not want the crown.

"Bring her in," Ronan said, coldly gesturing to the door.

The doors swung open with force and two guards barreled through with a mop of once beautiful blonde hair and a skinny girl with cuts all over her body. They threw her forward and she landed on her hands and knees with a *crunch*. She whimpered quietly as if she wanted to cry, but had nothing left to let out.

The servant girl who served Charmaine was before them all.

Gwendolyn.

Dalton immediately looked to James, whose violet gaze was now murderous. Even Randolph looked enraged, but his shoulders relaxed. Lawton too. Whether the four of them acknowledged it or not, Dalton could guess they were glad it was not Charmaine that knelt before them.

The knife that Charmaine had taken clattered to the

floor, its shining jewels and chain mail ornamentals clanging loudly on the marble floor. Sick satisfaction befell Dalton that he had figured that was the object in question.

His father held out a finger, pointing to it as if it was the most disgusting thing in the world. He looked at the knife as if it was a viper ready to strike.

How could you let something such as magic take such a hold? How have you let it take your heart and turn it black?

"Listen."

And so, they did. Their ears peeled as they all craned their heads to the side to listen to whatever his father demanded they hear.

Randolph shot him a look that Dalton could only deem meant, *"What in the Ten Kingdoms is going on?"*

Dalton shook his head at him, as if replying, *"What makes you think I knew anything about this?"*

Gwendolyn continued to whimper on the floor as his father's personal Thinker entered the room. Eben, as he was called, only made rare appearances. He was as cruel as he was cunning. He spent the majority of his time in the library, reading and studying the Old Gods and Kings. He served very few purposes and rarely shared the prophecies that entered his head.

Bitterness blossomed with him gazing upon Eben, who he had not seen since his father unleashed his fury on him all those years ago once he discovered the prophecy. It had been Cyril who told Eben to wait until they knew more, but he had been unable to stop him, for even Eben was Cyril's elder.

Dalton snapped back to reality, looking at Eben with disgust like his father looked at the dagger.

His father licked his lips impatiently, the room still blazing with dropping temperature. Everyone held their breath, though, either unaware or unwilling to acknowledge the little bit of power Dalton was letting escape.

Eben began to hum. It was very soft. His gray eyes focused emotionlessly on the dagger. Without warning, a light blue smoke drifted up from the weapon. It shimmered slightly, the smoke rising and twirling as if it were in a dance.

Dalton found himself smiling, his eyes lining with silver at the beauty of the magic before him. The blue smoke had an aura of grace, kindness, and happiness. There was no malice here, no opportunity for sadness and anger.

Ronan's eyes pulsated with hatred, feral rage manifesting as a snarl on his face.

This was not beauty to him, for it was only madness.

"You see?!" he shouted uncontrollably. "This danger poses work from the Old Gods, sent to destroy the likes of men without the infection that some would deem a gift! And she is the one who had this weapon of mass destruction."

He pointed a finger at Gwendolyn, whose simple face was bruised and cut up, assaulted for her actions.

Dalton spoke before he could manage to filter. "Father, she is just a girl." He was begging and he did not know why.

Was it fear that this could have been him if he were not the heir?

Ronan spun. His hand connected with Dalton's face as he landed a blow. The other men in the room gasped, shocked that their King would strike his heir.

Dalton wished that Ronan would kill him, so they could truly see the cruelty within.

Being locked up for five years was mercy. Death would have been a more definite punishment.

"How dare you defy *me*." His voice was riddled with

violence. He did not even sound like Ronan. Dalton could not pinpoint who this monster really was.

"You? Father, you *know* who I am." Dalton did not know why he replied. He had wasted his breath on his King one too many times. It was as hopeless as his redemption.

"And I am disgraced by it. You live because I allow you to live. You live because one day you might be proven useful to me."

"I hate you." Dalton seethed.

He wiped his hand along his now swollen bottom lip. He fought for control of his power, anything he could use against him. However, it evaded him. The force of his fist disarmed him and his hatred dulled his gifts.

He was powerless.

Ronan walked up to Gwendolyn. His jeweled boot kicked her with force as she continued to lay on her knees. She cried out in pain, the sound of her ribs cracking against the strike irrefutable.

"She dies tonight."

III

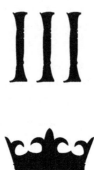

THE MAD KING

TWENTY-NINE

hat crimes has this girl committed? Holding a God's forsaken dagger? We do not even know who it belongs to."

"She was found with this dagger, which my dogs have discovered, reeking of *magic*." The King's adamance had Dalton's fists clenched at his side. Icicles sprouted from his fingertips.

"But she is only a child! A humble serving girl! A member of *our* royal household!" Dalton shouted, turning raw with emotion that he did not want to have. Showing emotion to his father was weakness, but he could not stop himself from caring.

"You are too! And you will burn with her if you dare defy me again. You are lucky it is not your head on the block."

Randolph heard Dalton and his father as he exited from the council chambers. They were battling for control. The whole room had all nearly shit themselves when Dalton's power flared. His father, the monster, did not flinch, nor did he acknowledge the power that seethed before him.

Here was a man who was about to execute a girl for

simply being found with an object of magic, but would not acknowledge the power that his son so freely demonstrated. Randolph admired the young Prince for how he had stood up against him and lashed out at the disgust of the moment.

Randolph could not hide—as he knew the rest of them could not—the joy that Charmaine was not before them in that position. James had grasped the table so hard his fingers turned purple. True anguish had gone through him at the thought of losing his sister. Randolph had even seen Lawton turn green in the moment.

That girl had a hold on them, whether they asked for it or not.

Suddenly, they were ushered to the courtyard, where those who were not a part of the council meeting would be privy to the savagery of the King.

Randolph whipped his head from side to side as James was doing, looking for Charmaine. *Where was she?*

This was going to be bad.

Really bad.

Commotion and confused ripped through the castle dwellers as they poured into the confines the courtyard. These members of court had no idea the level of monstrosity that ruled over this Kingdom. This moment was to be defining, one that nobody would forget.

But hopefully, together, they could move past it somehow.

James darted to the left of the crowd. Randolph followed aimlessly, assuming he was headed directly for his sister. They pushed past ladies and lords, who were as confused as he had felt moments before the King revealed his plans for an execution.

"James!" he yelped as he meandered through the crowd.

James seemed entranced, however, his focus narrowed in on someone Randolph could not yet see. He tried grabbing for his shoulder, but he evaded him completely.

And then Randolph saw who James reached for.

It knocked the wind out of him, for he had not been certain that it was her until he blinked twice. His chest constricted, the pressure freezing up his lungs.

Princess Elena of the Fourth Kingdom embraced James with a worried glance in his direction.

What in the Ten Kingdoms was going on?

Her brown eyes connected with his, and Randolph saw only raw emotion. Her eyes pleaded with him to let it go, not to ask questions. Randolph did not know Elena specifically, but had enjoyed her company on more than one occasion. She was full of life: loved hard, but did not fall into trust fast. In order for this *thing* between her and James Grimes to have flourished at all, there had to have been other forces at work.

Their embrace was full of familiarity and something else Randolph could not put his finger on. *Desire? Truth?* He tried to avert his eyes, but could not stop staring at the two of them, so close as James whispered in her ear. She continued to hold eye contact with Randolph, wordlessly swearing him to secrecy.

How were they so close? How did they know one another?

He bowed his head among the chaos of the courtyard, a silent promise that he would do this for her.

Wordlessly, he turned around, trying to pretend that he had not seen a thing.

The screaming match between Dalton and his father lasted a few more moments than Dalton was comfortable with.

His rage was unsettling. He had hated this man his entire life, but never had he been unsettled by him. Before today, he could never say his skin crawled with animosity. He was disabled, his power momentarily disbanded. He was helpless. *Again.*

Dalton never got the chance to fight back, and the moment that it counted, he was broken. He was weak. He was defeated.

His father hit him, and with it, destroyed his greatest gift. Once again, his power was like a curse.

He dragged Dalton by the nape of his tunic out to the courtyard. The pain of the motion was nothing compared to the strain in Dalton's heart.

An innocent girl was about to die and he could do nothing to stop it.

They stepped out into the courtyard and the crowd parted before his father. He scanned his eyes for members of the council room who knew what was about to happen. He wanted to scream and shout the truth of the moment, but could not find the words.

Without power, he realized for the first time, he was nothing.

He was empty.

"Ladies and gentlemen," his father purred. "Today we found a weakness among us. Today the Gods tried to infiltrate the great society we have built. Today we sniffed out *magic.*"

The crowd murmured among themselves. The disease his father had cultivated—this hatred of magic simply because it was different—it was infectious. These people believed it because they did not know differently.

Dalton spotted Elena among the crowd, standing unnaturally close to James Grimes.

Are you kidding me?

She met Dalton's gaze, unwavering and full of sadness. He must have told her briefly before they got out there.

You have to stop this, her eyes seemed to say.

I cannot, he tried to relay back to her.

Her eyes rimmed with silver, overtaken with emotion. This was over before it started.

There was no way to stop Ronan.

"And today," his father said, looking out among his people. "Today she will die for it."

The crowd split again as Gwendolyn was dragged out of the castle by her arms. Her legs held limp and scraped the cobblestones. The life had already been drained out of them. Dalton could not find the words to describe how broken she looked. He had seen her going to Charmaine's chambers just the other evening. Her beautiful blonde hair bounced behind her; her smile and kindness enveloped her whole persona.

The girl before him was just another vanquished by his father's madness.

The crowd murmured again, taking in the sight of the servant girl. And then Dalton saw her. Somehow, Lawton was the one to find her. He held her arm firmly, afraid she would run toward Gwendolyn. Her black hair was dark as midnight against the pale flush of her skin. Her violet eyes, always so full of life and curiosity, were dark. Solemn. Her lips quivered and her hands nervously sat at her mouth.

Charmaine was to watch her serving girl die.

The guards brought her to the middle of the circle that seemed to be created by those watching. The courtyard was silent, save for the heavy breathing of his father. As if he could not get enough of this madness, this moment. He was rabid.

How could the people not see this?

"Any last words, girl?" he said, kneeling down toward Gwendolyn as she tried to lift her head.

A firm hand grabbed his shoulder, dragging him backward with a force he knew all too well. *Cyril.* He looked back at him, his eyes full of a grief he had only seen from him when talking about the deaths of the King and Queen of Old.

Gwendolyn lifted her head to Dalton's father with whatever strength had not been beaten out of her. Looking directly in his eyes, she inhaled sharply, gathering courage.

The voice that spoke was not that of the serving girl, but that of a woman. Power was laced throughout every word. The effect caused his father to fall backward as she belted out, "*THE KING OF SNOW IS COMING. THE KING OF SNOW IS COMING. THE KING OF SNOW IS COMING.*"

A knight tried to run up to her, to stop her repeating. He turned toward his father who was trying to stand. The look on his face was absolutely murderous, with a blatant fear that raged within his eyes.

Dalton turned to Cyril as he did so. His eyes brimmed with tears as he sobbed uncontrollably. His hands were folded over his heart. Dalton made a move to stand closer to him, to hold him upright. He was trying to say something, but the voice of power silenced everyone as she chanted.

His father lifted his sword. His hands trembled uncontrollably. The voice inside Gwendolyn continued to shout. The woman was not deterred in the face of death.

Dalton shut his eyes as his father brought his weapon

down on Gwendolyn's neck, silencing her forever.

Dalton left the courtyard as quickly as he could, not making eye contact with anyone as he brought Cyril with him to his chambers. Dalton considered carrying the old man, but he did not want to draw attention. He was silent, his eyes bright red from the tears that had slid down his face since the voice started.

They entered his chambers hastily and he closed the door, guiding Cyril gently to his bed.

"Lay down, Cyril," he commanded.

Cyril looked at Dalton with kindness, reaching for his handkerchief.

"Dalton..." he started.

Dalton remained silent for once, as Cyril gathered himself.

"It was her," Cyril said after a moment.

"Who?" Dalton asked.

"It was *her*. All this bloody time, I thought she was gone forever. One hundred years, Kingdoms be damned, I waited for a sign. Something or *anything*. That... that *woman*!" He was yelling now, his incurable sadness turning to blatant rage.

Despite the horror of the situation, he felt the urge to laugh. "Who is the woman?" he asked.

"CIARA!" Cyril was laughing hysterically now, dabbing his eyes with his cloth as he continued to lose a complete sense of reality.

"Ciara?"

"I would know that voice anywhere, boy. One hundred years, she remained silent. I figured she had achieved peace, but all this time she waited. Never once did she give Cian a moment of clarity, of closure, and today she shows up in front of your father to profess your power? Genius! That genius fucking—"

Dalton's jaw hung open. Cyril was pacing now, repeating to himself the words Gwendolyn—no, Ciara—had screamed.

"The King of Snow is coming," he said quietly to himself, feeling woozy at hearing the dreaded prophecy again.

Cyril looked at him, his eyes full of light. His face somehow looked younger, as if hearing the voice of his forgotten friend had cured him of his decaying body.

"No, boy, the King of Snow is already here."

THIRTY

o matter how many pints Lawton and Randolph consumed, the voice that rattled the stars continued to blare in their heads.

The King of Snow is coming.

Randolph put down the pint with haste, and the foam overflowed down his arms. He was a barbarian in this tavern, drinking himself into oblivion with his only comrade. Randolph pinched the bridge of his nose with his ornately decorated fingers, letting go of the hell they had been put through lately.

He had tried to explain to Lawton earlier that he did not drink often, but the acts of today drove him to the pub in the village below the castle. The people within these walls were refreshingly normal. They were simplistic, and there was nothing wrong with that. If anything, simplicity was beautiful. The people of the First Kingdom, who were not witnesses to the violence that Randolph had become overexposed to, were blessed.

His heart ached for the loss of the pretty servant girl, and for Charmaine, who lost someone she could have had as an ally. *A friend, even.* But that voice crept into his head, ethereal and commanding. Randolph heard the power behind every word. Its incessant repeating was enough to drive one mad if it were not so terrifying.

The King of Snow is coming.

Randolph had not seen Dalton after the King murdered the girl. Lawton had dragged Charmaine away toward her chambers. Randolph tried to go with them, but the effort was futile. Lawton told him when he finally managed to part the crowd that she did not want to see anyone, and that it was best if they left her alone to grieve.

Randolph understood that more than anyone would ever know.

Lawton then dragged him by the arm and took him to The Beloved King, the dingy pub beneath the hill on which the castle sat.

"She's going to be fine," Lawton muttered as he pounded the rest of his ale.

Randolph growled in response, and sadness turned to frustration. "Nobody should have to be privy to such a display of intolerance. The way that Ronan handled that was—" He looked up. Lawton's eyebrows were raised as if waiting for him to drop knowledge that he somehow did not already have. "The way Ronan handled that was not the equivalent of the man who helped me become who I am today."

"You know something?" Lawton's eyebrows quirked up further.

Randolph was not sure how that was possible. The young knight had a way about him that was expressive and irritating. However, he knew everything. It was his reputation. And men were always partial to the truth of their reputations.

"And you don't? How the tables have turned."

Randolph sat back, his arms crossing over his broad chest.

"I don't know as much as you think," Lawton whispered, irritation laced through his words like smoke rising from a fire.

"I highly doubt that," Randolph said into his pint. "Do you know how the mercenaries keep getting into the castle? Oh, worldly one."

Lawton blushed, but his eyes flashed dangerously. "I am not worldly, first of all. I was born in the First Kingdom and only went to the Second Kingdom that one time. Second, no. I do not know why you think I have the answers to everything."

"You normally do."

"If I knew, Randolph, that would be quite the secret to harvest, and you know I like to share the wealth."

Randolph snorted. Lawton did not tend to keep secrets for long. "I would hope so. It is driving me mad. How did they get in without the sword? And what are they doing here? Invading us like that is bold. We cannot even figure out who the blasted person in control is."

"Does Ronan have any leads?" Lawton raised an eyebrow in question.

"Ronan is mistrusting. I think he fears slipping up above all else. He does not like relinquishing control."

"I hate to break it to him, but I would consider your Kingdom being invaded by mercenaries to definitely be a disaster."

"Thanks, Lawton, that is incredibly helpful feedback. I will be sure to let him know." He nearly splashed his ale at Lawton's face.

"I, too, do not understand. I don't know who they are, or what they are looking for, besides messing with the King."

"What makes you think their goal is to mess with the King?" Randolph's voice was lethal. *Could it really be that simple?*

"You said it yourself, my liege. Ronan loves to be in control. When the mercenaries attack, even a village as insignificant on the world stage like Brinn, it shows he has lost the thing he values the most."

Randolph huffed a laugh, disbelief overtaking him. "You might be a genius. What an oddity."

"What peculiarity I noticed was James Grimes standing unnaturally close to the Princess of the Fourth," Lawton snarled in response, clearly irritated from Randolph's poking, and picked up his ale again. "One would think that something... happened."

"Spit it out, Lawton." Randolph sat forward in his seat, his knuckles turning white on the handle of his brass pint.

"I do not know much of anything. It seems like since the battle I have lost my touch." He lifted up his arm to take a swig from his pint.

As he did so, a gust of wind blew in from the open door to the pub and Randolph's senses shifted. It always started sweet, as if he were breathing in a field of flowers, but then it turned burnt against his nose. It flared and demanded to be seen, the stench unavoidable against his childhood lessons.

Magic.

He breathed deeply, ignoring the urge to fight and seek it out. He had not been exposed to magic like this since he was a boy, never having such a reaction besides those in his training sessions with the Thinkers. The Prince clearly had magic, but Randolph never had his senses awoken like this before.

How did he not sense it before? Was he that out of touch with who he used to be?

He stared at Lawton intently and whispered so low it was a miracle Lawton heard him, "*You have magic.*"

Lawton's face paled, more sickly in color than when he thought Charmaine was the one Ronan had planned to execute. He tried to adjust and look natural, but for once, he was unable to play it cool.

"Please." Lawton was speechless, and it was all he managed to gasp out.

"What is it?" A simple question fueled to give complicated answers.

"I can... *jump*. I can jump from place to place." His eyes were wide with fear, and Randolph understood it, he really did.

All the times that Lawton would appear, a slight breeze over his shoulder before he realized he was there at all, struck him like a sword in battle struck its opponent. Lawton always had information at his disposal. It was not because he had heard it from another, it was because *he* had heard it.

"What are you going to do?" Lawton's lips quivered. His eyes glistened against the dim lights of the tavern.

Randolph paused, thinking for a moment.

"I am not going to do anything," Randolph said, rubbing the flower tattoos on his hands. "Enough blood has been spilt over magic today."

Lawton visibly sagged in his seat, the light reentering his eyes with relief. "Thank you," he breathed.

Randolph nodded, mentally agreeing to keep another secret of magic that existed within these walls.

Cian save us.

He took a massive swig of his ale before signaling to

the owner of the pub that he needed another round. "Do not thank me until this is over."

"Do you think it will ever be over?" Lawton said, his charm slowly seeping back into his aura.

Randolph chuckled, pushing away the dark memories of his past. He had been running for so long that he did not ever think he would be *here* today, serving and trying to do better. He figured he would be in his family crypt by now, rotting for all that he had sinned. He would have deserved all of it.

"Honestly, I do not know," he told Lawton.

"To the King of Snow." Lawton took the new pint to his lips, his eyes flickering with a peace that Randolph could identify, but had never known.

"Long may he reign. And may the Gods keep the magical from harm."

THIRTY-ONE

lena told James Grimes to return to his chambers and leave her the hell alone. Despite her insistence that she was alright, he did not listen.

He showed up at her chambers moments after departing. He stammered, flushed when she nearly shut the door in his face. He explained to her, holding the door ajar with his boot, that he noticed the execution had rattled her and he wanted to check on her welfare.

Dumb boy. Dumber excuse.

The plague that Ronan had unleashed in the castle caught up with her as she ushered him through the door. Bile rose in her throat without warning, her hand flying to her mouth in embarrassment.

James did not care. He put his hand on her back and coaxed her to bed. Elena could not explain what this *thing* was between them. She was used to having answers, and without them, she was not sure who she was.

The memories of their life together rattled her to her core. There was so much death and suffering.

She did not know how she knew it, but she knew she was in pain.

The memory of the child flashed through her mind too, more than she cared to admit. The brown eyes, dark hair, and dark skin of the child... The image haunted her. He was beautiful. She knew him too, and knew the pain of loving him, without ever meeting him.

Elena sat up in the bed without warning and looked at James. His face was all shadows and sadness, and she was certain it mirrored her own.

She was pissed at Dalton, and it was another root of her anguish.

An internal fire erupted in her heart when she dwelled on Dalton being sequestered all these years. It was unnecessary, but she was pissed at him. But this is what she did, throw blame where blame was not due. She knew it was not fair, but life was not fair. His circumstances had never been fair. Did he deserve to be judged for it? Things that were out of his control? Elena put her fist to her temple, the pressure relieving some of her headache.

Even if it was not fair, a part of her resented him, nonetheless. He had the power of Cian, for the sake of the Ten Kingdoms! And he did not use it, not even a *drop*.

Ronan was out of control. Her body physically lurched at the sight of him after he destroyed that girl and the voice that erupted from her.

Elena wanted Dalton to fight back more, not with words, but with whatever he had inside of him.

"I do not know you at all," Elena whispered, unsure how to handle a situation such as this. She was overwhelmed on all fronts, and conversation with James was the only avenue open for her to take.

She was a Queen to be, but she did not have the crown. The crown came with answers, power, and the ability to make decisions. As a Princess, one bowed.

James quirked up the side of his mouth with a smirk. "I do not either, but I am here."

"We should discuss what happened the other night." The thudding within her chest was not rhythmic, but unhinged. Blessed by the Gods she may be, but divine she did not feel.

"And what exactly do you have to discuss?" The curiosity in his eyes was vast. His tone illuminated the ferocity of the question.

Was he irritated?

"What we saw—"

"Has anything ever happened like that before? To you?" He was shaking his head, his black hair wild and uncontrollable as it swept over his eyes.

"Never. I have never had that type of... *connection*." Elena paused on the word, unsure how to phrase what she was feeling.

"Did it scare you?"

"Yes," she said before she could stop herself. It scared the Princess out of her, making her a little girl again.

"It did not scare me."

"Why?"

"Because you do not scare me."

Elena laughed out loud, high-pitched and manic. "You do not scare me either, but that does not mean I am not afraid."

"What are you afraid of?"

The truth spilled out of her as if she had no control, "Failure. My mother. Destiny. Thinkers."

"That is quite a bit to unpack." His mouth was still quirked up, as if he were enjoying this conversation. As if he were enjoying *her*. "Failure?"

"Failing my Kingdom. My mission."

"Which is?" He made a gesture with his hands, as if pushing to elaborate.

"To secure my realm and make peace with the First," she said matter-of-factly. A diplomatic answer for a Princess.

"That is a good one."

She smirked back at him. Maybe this made sense, after all.

"Your mother?" he asked again, pushing her to answer. To talk about *it*.

"If you met the Queen of the Fourth, you would not require an explanation."

"If she is anything like the King of the First, I understand."

Elena rolled her eyes. "All royals are more or less the same."

"You are not the same."

"Destiny frightens me most of all," she whispered.

"And the Thinkers?"

"Well, they provide the destiny. Bring it forth to the attention of Kings and Queens, so rather they go hand in hand."

"Do you believe... what we saw... was our destiny?"

The memories replayed in her head. The wedding. Life. "Ten Kingdoms, I hope not."

"So, what if it is? Are we to ignore that we were given something? We were given this vision for a reason, Gods-dammed or Gods-incarnate." His voice wavered, emotion taking hold.

"The Gods do not play in the favor of mortals." She clenched her jaw, unsure why she was arguing. She did not know this boy.

Yet, she did.

"The Gods brought me to you. I would think otherwise."

"You do not know me at all," she spat, harsher than she anticipated.

"And neither do you know me, but here I am."

"Here you are."

She made a move to get up, and he grabbed her hand without a word. His eyes never left hers as he helped her off the bed.

"What do you need?" he asked quietly.

"Wine," she said, moving toward the desk.

"The answer to all problems," James replied wistfully, his eyes flashing with amusement.

She poured each of them a hefty glass of the red wine, cold within chalices. She brought it to her lips as he brought it to his. He paused slightly, his violet eyes alight with kindness she had never seen before.

"To conquering our fears," he said, raising his glass to tap hers with a *clink*.

"To embracing destiny," she replied instinctively, only knowing, Gods-be-damned that was what they were doing.

THIRTY-TWO

Dalton decided that after a day of sulking around the castle he was due for an escapade.

Cyril was probably by all accounts, and by default, his only friend. Elena did not count, for she could put him on his backside. But Cyril was his favorite target for his antics. When he received a note from him early in the morning, it only solidified that Dalton was going to disappear today. He wished that he had the power to go invisible, rather than freeze the life out of things.

That would *actually* be useful.

Dalton looked at the note again. Cyril's delicate handwriting lay across the scroll neatly. Cyril never rushed when he disciplined Dalton. It was even written in the tone Cyril always used with Dalton when he was serious. If it was possible that handwriting contained a tone, Cyril made it so.

Dalton,
Absolutely do not pull your usual with me on this, but I have been called to an urgent meeting with your father, his Majesty. I will resume our usual session this afternoon, for he

has let me know that this meeting will be rather lengthy.

I cannot spare you details, but I encourage you to be on your best behavior today, especially since those around the castle now know who you are.

As soon as the meeting is over, I will come and get you.

Be in the correct place, or Gods help you and me both.

Yours truly, and sternly,

Cyril

Dalton loved Cyril dearly, with all his heart in fact. He owed so much of his life to him, especially that of his ability not to freeze over hell twice from the corners of his bedroom. He also owed him as a father would a son, speaking that he was the closest thing to a father he had.

But Dalton had spent five years alone, and he relished the feeling of being disobedient. It was disrespectful, cheeky, and immature to blatantly disregard what Cyril wanted. Dalton knew that Cyril always had his best interests at heart, but he also could not fight the itch to rebel in ways that kept him afloat with his father. Especially after being released so suddenly.

He was engaged in a game of power with his father, but was playing just enough to shift the balance. *How far could I push without repercussions?*

When he was alone all those years, he made do by pulling pranks on servants and reading to his heart's content. But he was also flawed, causing Cyril irrefutable pain when he ran, made a break for it, and came back broken by his father's hand. It did not matter that the King did not raise his physical hand, but he commanded his beatings with his voice.

And that was enough to condemn him in Dalton's eyes.

Dalton shook his head with one last look at Cyril's note, and headed for the door.

✦

The courtyard was as busy as it had been the day Charmaine sauntered through with Lawton. Except this time, it was Randolph on her arm.

It looked so different than it had two days ago, stained with the memory of her friend's murder. It was cleaned up to look exactly as it had when she arrived. If Charmaine had not been there, she would not have known the King had savagely murdered a girl. Her heart shattered the moment he drove the sword through her neck. Gwendolyn had shown nothing but kindness to Charmaine, even weeping herself when James had been gravely injured.

Gwendolyn did not deserve a death like that.

Randolph came to her door this morning, asking if they could go for a walk. He said he had wanted to check in on her and Charmaine happily accepted, eager to move on from the horrors she had seen as of late.

Randolph and Charmaine spoke softly to one another, him avoiding bringing up anything dark that had happened in the past few days, and her avoiding the Royal family at all costs. The women of the courtyard gawked at them non-discreetly with open mouths. The sight of a man of such high stature and good looks on her arm inspired jealousy. She even noticed men looking at her.

For all the improper behavior that he frequently expressed—occasional cursing and consistent wine drinking, Randolph was also very skilled in proper behavior. His demeanor on their walk was the epitome of everything she imagined a member of the Knights to be. He walked beside her as an equal, not trailing behind submissively, but not in front of her in a display of masculinity.

She rounded the corner of the courtyard again, agreeing on their fondness for James when Charmaine noticed a fluttering sensation in the pit of her stomach. She darted her eyes from left to right, trying not to draw attention to what she was experiencing. Taking a deep breath in through her nose and out through her mouth, she tried to discreetly push away her discomfort. Charmaine scanned the courtyard for a door, or a potential distraction if she turned right there and right now.

She heard the group of women who they had passed numerous times—who gawked at Randolph as if he were a God among men—gasp. Charmaine quickly turned her head, breaking all illusion that she was listening to Randolph talk about James's obsession with swords, and she saw *him*.

Strolling through the courtyard, with no look in particular of a care in the world, was the Prince.

Dalton.

In the sun, he came to life, rather ironic as he was the future King of the First. His hair was illuminated, the white gold of his hair complimentary to his pale flesh. Even from there, the freckles across his face seemed to be brighter, as if they too were born in the sunlight and reflective of its joy. His eyes seemed darker, the blue deep and all encompassing.

He was smirking too.

He looked nothing of the man she met on the first night when they attended the ball. His gaze was that of the man she saw when he walked into the throne room for the first time. This was the mask. This was him as he was born to be, the ruler. Charmaine had seen him dragged out of the castle to this very courtyard by the lapels of his tunic by his father. His face had been red and his eyes flamed with rage as if he had been fighting.

But she had to swallow the bitter reality that they all stood there and watched Gwendolyn die. It was something they could not take back.

He was dressed rather simply—his tunic a white silk—rather see-through in the sunlight. He was so skinny, Charmaine realized, hollowed out. His pants were leather with matching boots similar to the garb Randolph wore. The clothing of a knight. His shirt was wildly tucked in at the front, his shoelaces unlaced as if he had been in a hurry.

Upon seeing him, Randolph froze.

⸙

Dalton strolled into the courtyard casually. It need not look like he was on the run.

Even though he was.

This was his favorite game to play. He almost set a bet with himself as to who would find him first: the Royal Guardsmen whom he had evaded at his door with a little frost magic display, or Cyril.

Dalton did not plan on being busted by Randolph. The son of the—

Dalton silently cursed himself for following the itch that continued to consume him without realizing it. Destiny? He thought not.

As he strolled into the courtyard, the usual women dropped their jaws at his holiness. He heard whispers of his white hair. The physical attributes of his political standing were the center point of gossip, not shockingly. But it was *her* face that rattled Dalton the most, the look of awe and pain.

Could she feel it too? Was she as broken by the loss of a simple girl as I was?

Dalton nearly spat at the look on Randolph's face as he walked toward them. In Dalton's defense, there was nowhere else to go. But it was truly his tone that put Dalton off the most, a dog of his father through and through.

"My Prince, what are you doing here?" he said through gritted teeth.

Dalton paused, bowing to them in the rudest way imaginable.

So dramatic.

His white hair shifted forward and then backward as he shot up. His hands interlaced behind his back in a disgraceful gesture.

It took everything in Dalton not to laugh this entire courtyard into a winter wonderland. Instead, he looked at her and the frozen tundra knocked the wind out of him. Her violet eyes filled with a horror that almost made Dalton apologize for his indecency, his fake bow to one of the slaves of his father. Yes, he had held his ground and shown his disapproval when Ronan had dragged Gwendolyn into that council meeting, but *he hadn't done anything.* He had not even raised a finger. Dalton was not one to go toe-to-toe with his father any day, but he had tried.

Her facial features betrayed nothing, telling Dalton she was used to masking her emotions, but her eyes… they told another story.

"Sir Randolph. Miss Grimes of Brinn," Dalton said, pulling his mask back up after being temporarily disarmed. "I simply wanted to enjoy the beauty of the day like the rest of us fine people. I only wanted to… explore whatever it was that drew me outside today." He looked at her as he said it, the violet in her eyes flashing dark with recognition.

Ah ha! She did know what I was talking about.

✦

Randolph's tone had rattled Charmaine beyond her wildest imagination. The sheer ice that came from it sent a feeling down her spine. *This was the other side to the man.* This was the Knight. Doing his duty to his King. And Dalton reveled in exposing him.

Charmaine knew what he was talking about. He felt it too, and without asking, he received his confirmation.

"DALTON, PRINCE OF THE FIRST KINGDOM?!"

As Randolph opened his mouth to unveil more Knighthood duties on his Prince, a short man entered the courtyard. He could not have been taller than a child. His skin was rather wrinkly, covered in old spots. His eyes, however, were a bright blue and alive with a wintery rage. His voice, although meek and mild, carried a volume to it that commanded the entire courtyard.

This must be Cyril, the man Dalton had spoken of before, who had been standing with him at Gwendolyn's execution.

"DALTON, PRINCE OF THE FIRST KINGDOM," he repeated upon seeing them, stomping with his short arms flailing wildly as he came toward them.

Dalton spun toward him and then spun to them again, a smirk crossing his face. "Ah, sorry to leave you both so soon. I had so much to chat about." He winked at her, leaving her mouth agape at his impropriety.

He extended his arms as if to embrace the old man, saying, "Ah, Cyril. I wondered when you would catch up to me! Short game of hide-and-seek today."

The man looked as if he were about to explode. His cheeks were a fiery red. His arms pounded against his sides as he stomped and his mouth was in a straight line, pursed by anger.

But his eyes were still bright, even loving, as he

approached the Prince. It was evident that this Cyril loved him. His tone indicated differently. "Boy, your father has been looking for you left and right. I left you strict instructions to *stay put*." He rubbed his wrinkled hand over his eyes, as if he was tired from running after Dalton on more than one occasion.

"Does he need an escort, Cyril? So, he does not evade you again?" Randolph chimed in, a darkness in his voice Charmaine had never heard before. Not from him.

Cyril seemed to notice that they stood behind him. Until then, all his energy was directed at Dalton. Charmaine did not think it unusual, for Dalton was impossible to ignore.

"Sir Randolph, what a pleasant surprise. The King is calling a meeting of all those at your little… celebration, my Prince. Best we be there before the bells chime."

Dalton strode forward, all confident as he put his arm around Cyril as if he were a boy. "Ah, Cyril, my good fellow, let's be off then to see Daddy dearest. Let's see what horror he has in store for us today." He turned around, his eyes dark as he looked at Randolph. "Sir Randolph, feel free to walk behind me."

THIRTY-THREE

fter multiples glasses of wine the other night, Elena and James had agreed to meet in the rose garden.

Honestly, Elena had been avoiding James all of yesterday, the same as she had been avoiding everyone. But she had particularly avoided James. There were multiple instances over the course of the prior day when she could have crossed his path. She swore he had tried to get her attention with a not-so-subtle wave of the hand, but she had diverted down another hallway.

Everything with James had moved so fast. Whatever that *everything* seemed to be. She did not love him by any means. Her wits somehow remained relatively intact, while she tried to navigate life at this disheveled court. What scared the Ten Kingdoms out of her was that she thought she *could* love him. Her palms were sweaty and her heart threatened to burst from her chest when she pondered it too long. She could not keep up with this court's insanities.

James was undeniably gorgeous. He was the male version of his sister. Their coloring and features were nearly identical. Elena still did not know what his sister was like—

if she was anything like him—but if she was, then she thought she would enjoy her company the same. His eyes were her favorite thing about him, the violet color so full of vibrancy and life. He did not seem to be afraid of much, another quality she most admired. And he was kind. He did not treat Elena like a Princess; rather, he treated her like a person. She did not realize how much that meant until she met him.

The memory of the servant girl's death hovered over her, a constant. The moment was a marking point, pivotal in her journey at the castle. She knew for certain that things did not just happen to happen. Elena could not wrap her mind around the horror she had experienced, or the nirvana that had crept into her life in the aftermath.

So, she had agreed to meet James, because if anything was proven the other day, it was that life was uncertain. And she had to face this, or she would go mad.

James gallivanted across the walkway to come down to the garden. She figured this was a rather safe place for them to be today. Let the onlookers see this young man near her, for it did not matter to her. Her mother never said who she had to marry, rather that she wanted it done and an alliance to be secured.

He flashed a grin worthy of the Gods themselves and approached her without hesitation. He grabbed her right hand from her side and kissed the top of it lightly, his lips upon her hand leaving her breathless. A chill shivered down her spine, the small display of affection rattling her to her core. He made her feel like a young girl again. There was real power to be had when one lived like they were young, instead of on the verge of adulthood and gaining a Kingdom.

Her mother's expectations be damned, James Grimes was beautiful.

"Good afternoon, Princess," he whispered as he held her hand between his. They were rough and calloused, the hands of a man who had spent his life working and training.

She wished the people saw that side of Dalton, the side that James presented himself with, for he was covered in more scars than the eye could see.

Scars were not diminishing; they were becoming.

"Good afternoon, Mr. Grimes."

"Formalities? You ruin me."

Elena looked from side to side before hitting him with her free hand. He tipped his back, laughing loudly.

"You will ruin me if you keep up these displays of affection."

His eyes turned darker. His gaze filled with intensity. "Have I gone too far?"

"No, not at all," she stammered, realizing her joke might have been a bit too forward. Not everyone was as accustomed to her humor as Dalton.

"I do not want to jeopardize anything you might have going on... I did notice that you and the Prince..." His eyes flashed with hurt.

Elena stopped him, for she was the one now who was howling. "DALTON?!" she shouted, laughing between gasps of air. "Dalton is like my brother. He is my favorite human in this world, and I would lay my life out for him to live not but another second, but never would I consider him *romantically*."

He looked rather stunned, eyes drifting up and down Elena's body as if taking her in for the first time. He whispered, "But you are both royalty and beautiful."

Elena blushed. "Do not tell him that. His ego is bad enough."

He smiled, a dimple appearing on the right side of his cheek. Ten Kingdoms help her.

"He seems rather humble, for a Prince."

He tried to play it off casually, but Elena knew that they both had seen Dalton and his sister dancing at the ball. Charmaine had looked at Dalton in wonder, as most girls did, but the difference was that he had met her gaze.

Dalton could never hide from Elena, no matter how much he tried. And he had without a doubt looked at Charmaine with a softness he only reserved for his most cherished. Elena would know; for that was how he looked at her sometimes when he did not realize she was paying attention.

"He has been through more than the average Royal," she said, allowing her admiration to come through.

"I can see that you care about him deeply."

"But I do not love him," she said, lifting her pointer finger at his face.

"But you do not love him."

His smile was damning.

"And you? Did you have any beautiful ladies back in your home?" Her question hung thickly in the air.

"My sister is the only beautiful lady I dote on." He smiled as he said it, but it did not reach his eyes.

"I have seen how you two are together. You are close."

"She is the only family I have."

She could not hide her shock. Her own family was complicated as it was for royals, but she never dwelled. It was only her and her mother, and she intended to keep it that way. "What happened to them? If you don't mind me asking."

He paused, taking a breath before he said, "My mother had... abilities. Abilities that got her killed. Looking back, we hardly knew our father. He perished from illness when we were children."

"How old were you?"

"I was twelve. Charmaine was ten."

"And how old are you? I never thought to ask." She suddenly felt childish for asking so many questions.

"Twenty."

"Nineteen," she answered without the question being asked.

"You are a baby."

"A powerful baby."

He plucked a red rose from the bush nearby, impervious to the thorns on the flowers. "For you, powerful baby of the Fourth Kingdom."

"You know, the Roses here are quite mystical. They have a history to them. Planted by Queen Ciara on her coronation night, for she wanted a garden that was beautiful and yet dangerous." Her finger trailed the inside of the flower, hoping the scent of roses would imprint on her hands for the afternoon.

"The more I learn about her, the more I believe Queen Ciara and I would have been quite the duo." He kept his gaze on the roses around them.

Elena huffed a laugh, thinking of all the tales she had been told in her life about the dark Queen. There was no way she would deny that James probably would have brought out the best in her as King Cian had. "I wish Dalton had someone like Ciara did. The crown can be lonely."

His eyes connected with her own, burning with a fierce intensity. "But its weight does not have to be worn alone. It is so heavy that nobody should have to bear it without help."

She almost snorted, but held in the impropriety. "Help is rare to come by."

"Help is offered to those who deserve it," he offered on the offensive.

"And I am deserving?" She touched the tip of the thorn on the rose softly, careful not to prick herself.

"Nobody is more deserving than the woman who saved my life."

Elena paused. "Is that what this is? You are simply grateful to me?"

"No!" he half-shouted, terror spiking across his eyes.

Elena could tell that he was not just spending time with her out of admiration of one of her abilities, but she could not help lashing out at him.

"You are not indebted to me? Feeling like you owe me something because I did you a favor? Honestly, James, I figured you would be better than that, not unabashed about hanging out with a powerful woman. A future Queen." Elena kept pushing, despite feeling like she was the villain. But this was what she did. She pushed when she did not need to. She became the evil of her own narrative. She did not quite know how to be anything else. Her mother had ensured that this was who she was at her core. It might be insensitive, or unbecoming of a Princess, but it was her truth. As a royal, you had to have a thick skin against the world in order to survive.

"That is not what I meant at all," he whispered, pain flickering across his eyes.

"Then tell me what you meant!" she shouted, her feral rage coming through in her tone as he cut her off.

He leaped toward her as his mouth connected with

hers in a passionate embrace. It was slow at first, as she was stiffening and taken off guard. His rough hands cupped her face with a gentleness that she had never known before. But she was not made to be handled gently.

Elena Leclair was not breakable.

And she kissed him back.

She was hungry for the feeling of his lips against her own. He moaned softly as she parted her lips again, her tongue sliding gently into his mouth in a desire for pleasure. He tasted of smoke and ice, a jarring juxtaposition that left Elena craving more. She ran her hand through his hair slowly in an attempt to tame its wildness. She was breathless, overwhelmed by the sensation that she had finally come *home*. Elena could not explain the heat of James as he ran his hands down the bodice of her gown. She did not care that they were in the rose garden and that this could become a Royal spectacle.

All she cared about was him and this moment.

As she breathed into him, she began to have flashes. Different moments in time that she had not seen when she used her powers on him to heal his wound.

She saw a child running through the castle walls, laughing uncontrollably. She saw James holding her hand in a carriage, his eyes full of worry and temptation. She saw Charmaine, and heard a voice she could only assume belonged to her say, "Tell me that James would be proud of that child." Her heart broke into two—the most intense sadness she had ever felt in her life, looking upon a black casket covered in white and red roses.

Without warning, Elena shoved him away. She was breathing heavily. The fire that had been built in the moment became suffocating.

It was too much. This was all too much…

"Elena..." he said, breathless as well.

His cheeks were pink, but was it from the flush of the moment or the memory?

"Why?" she crooned, feeling tears drip down her cheeks uncontrollably. She never cried, and she was mad that she was doing so now.

"Why, what?"

"Why does this keep happening? Why do I keep seeing—" she trailed off, unable to say it aloud.

"Elena..." he tried again, but was rather speechless. That cool swagger that normally dripped off of him now stifled with realization. With fear. With longing.

Elena grabbed him, hugging him fiercely. "It is as if every memory, every moment, makes less sense, but is clearer."

"I could *feel* the emotions this time. I could feel the longing and the sadness and the love—"

"Did you see him?" she asked, the tears continuing to pour down her face. She could not admit who he was, for she did not know for certain, and she could not admit what they both knew out loud. The moment they said it, it would become real.

"Who?"

"I have never... I have never experienced such..."

"Joy? Pride? Elena, what did you see?" He grabbed her hands, his own shaking. "Elena, what did you see?"

"What did you see?" she asked, suddenly so afraid of everything else she saw, but not that. Never that.

"A field of burning roses. Petals falling from the throne room. A heavy winter storm..." His eyes were rimmed with silver now, the epitome of pure happiness. But they were so sad, so broken.

Did they not see the same thing?

250

Elena put her hands on either side of his cheeks, stroking his jawline with her thumbs. "I do not want what I saw."

I do not want it if it means losing you. I do not want any of this power if it has any truth in it. Losing what we could have is not an option.

"We do not know what capacity these... moments are coming in. Maybe they are not reality. Maybe they are not memories or visions at all, but rather just moments, signs from the Gods."

"The Gods have not cared about us in a long time."

"There is always time to start, and change."

He took her hands off her face with an understanding of what she was feeling that was beyond any level of discernment she ever had with Dalton.

"To accept this at face value—" she said, but her throat began to close up.

Would it be stupid to accept these visions without any context? Would it be correct? Why did we continue to have flashes of moments in time? Was there any truth to them?

"All that I know is that you are kind and you are strong. When I am with you, I feel as though I am ignited from within."

"I have not known you long at all, but I can agree." Her mind circled back to that boy again.

Was it her son? Who was the child? Why had James not seen any of that?

"Then that is all that matters."

"Then that is all that matters," she agreed.

They pulled apart from one another and walked slowly out of the rose garden toward the castle entrance, when Cyril bounded toward them. He looked flustered, per usual. There was a level of apprehension when he saw

Elena, like he wanted to say something, but knew the mastery of the conversation was not for the moment.

"What is it, Cyril?" Elena asked, not sure if she was referencing the look between them, or whatever he had come to say.

"The King has demanded somewhat of an audience. Best be on our way, Princess." He dipped his head slowly to James, smirking and his eyes alight as he whispered, "And you too, Prince Consort of the Fourth."

THIRTY-FOUR

harmaine's teeth chattered incessantly. It was peculiar that King Ronan had wanted an audience with the crowd, and it rattled her to her core.

He could not have found magic again so soon?

A steady sense of caution had been at the forefront of Charmaine's mind since Gwendolyn's execution. After speaking with James, she realized that life at court was no different than life in the villages. There were threats everywhere, specifically for people like her. People who possessed magical abilities.

Gwendolyn's execution was wrongfully fulfilled, but she could not help but wonder why the girl had taken her dagger to begin with. It was obviously beautiful, an ornamental weapon.

Did she know it had magic within it? Did I subconsciously know? Is that why I picked it up?

They continued walking toward the throne room at a breakneck pace. Charmaine slowed down, falling behind Randolph, who had met up with Lawton along the way. They were both stiff and rigid as they walked together, whispering among themselves. No doubt they were both concerned about the spontaneity of this call by the King.

How could you not be, when it was obvious the man was mad?

A hand grabbed Charmaine's lower arm and she turned her head slightly in response. Her breath caught when she realized it was Dalton's cool hand. He silently put a finger to his lips, hushing her impending question with a gesture. She nodded as he dragged her into the open door on the right, closing it behind them noiselessly. The look on his face was all mischief, and Charmaine suddenly became hyperaware of her surroundings.

She looked around and realized that they had entered a library. There were stacks of books beyond those that were sitting on the shelves that lined from the marble floor to the ceiling. The books looked like they had been rummaged through, uncharacteristically disorganized for a library. Dalton sauntered toward the middle of the room, and sat on the edge of a table that was not as filled as the others.

"We need to talk," he said matter-of-factly.

"About what exactly?" She looked around in wonder at the thousands of books that lay before her. She had the overwhelming urge to open them and read the first lines. That was her favorite part of reading, being exposed to the first moment of someone else's story.

"You. Me. This *feeling* I get when I am not near you. Gwendolyn. My father. Mercenaries. Anything and everything." He threw his hands up, annoyed.

Charmaine clenched her jaw. The directness of him took her off guard. "I do not know what to say. To any of that."

"But you do feel it. I am not crazy." He stared at her

with one eyebrow raised, impatient.

"You ask it like it is a question." She did not know why she always felt bold around him.

"Madness is not without question. I am my father's son." The bitterness in his voice caused her shoulders to tense up.

"You are not your father's son." She did not know why she said it. It was not as if she truly knew him. But it felt like the truth.

"How would you know?" he spoke, reading her mind. "You have barely spoken to me since your brother tried to sacrifice himself for my father. I figured after we had talked... after we had danced, that we could at least be *friends*." The word hung in the air like a bad joke.

She smoothed her skirts and replied, "I have not tried to avoid you. I am sorry if it came off that way."

"You would think I would be rather used to being avoided, given my precarious living situation." A smirk brewed on his face; one dark eyebrow still raised.

"Your living situation? You are a Prince!"

"A Prince who has spent more of his life in the bedroom of his castle than actually frolicking around the castle!" He shot back, getting off of the table as he stood abruptly.

She whispered, feeling like a fool again for being bold, "When you said you would not be locked away again..."

"I meant it. *Literally,*" he snarled.

"I do not know why I am drawn to you," Charmaine mumbled, so low she doubted he heard it.

His eyes softened, and flashed from rage to regret as he looked her up and down. "You perplex me."

"And you perplex me."

He smiled, that quizzical look reignited that had been

there during the party. "Explain it. What you feel, maybe it is the same as what I am... *feeling*," he spoke with desperation.

Charmaine closed her eyes, imagining what she had been feeling these last few days. "It is like a pit in my stomach. As if there is an invisible thread... I know if I followed it, the feeling would evaporate as I did so. As if giving in was the only cure."

He blinked slowly, taking in every word. "When I came to your chambers after the explosion..."

"You followed it, didn't you?" She was not sure if she was breathing.

"Yes, but I also wanted to see you."

"You said you were checking up on me." She definitely was not breathing.

"I was. I needed to make sure you were safe."

She grabbed the edge of the table she was standing next to for support, since she did not have James to lean on. "You are not like the Prince I imagined you to be."

He sat up straighter, his lean arms crossed in front of his chest in both irritation and as a shield. "I am not the ruler the world depicts."

"Your father is," Charmaine said with disgust, realizing her tone after the fact.

"He is predictable, if not consistent." She could not believe he was making jokes about his own father.

"He is a murderer. Gwendolyn—"

He stepped closer to Charmaine, cutting her off. His lips parted slightly as if he had filtered through his thoughts before deciding which one to voice. "When my father told us in the council room... I feared for my life that it was you he had planned to execute."

"Me?"

"I... I can feel it. I was not sure at first, but I have been rummaging about the library," he said, gesturing to the mess around them. "And I started to read anything I could about *attractions*..."

"It?" she asked, her eyes going glassy. *Don't say it don't say it don't say it.*

"I can feel it because I have it too. I was not sure at first, but now that we are alone... It is different than the draw, though. It is not an invisible rope, but rather a thumping. One that I feel radiating off of you. One that I understand too well."

"We cannot discuss this, not here."

He laughed; he actually laughed. "Then where are we to discuss it? For neither you nor I can escape this stone prison."

"Nobody... nobody can know." Fear blasted through her blood, turning her number by the second.

"Why did I see you?" he asked, his eyes full of dark mischief. "Why did you ask me that, Char? That was the question you asked me after I found you. You were upset about your brother, rightfully so. You asked me if I could see you."

"I do not know." She wished this answer was the truth, but she was tongue-tied.

"There has to be a reason. An explanation." He paced back and forth. Long fingers ran through his unkempt white hair.

"Would Cyril..." She did not know why she brought up the old man. Maybe some small part of her thought he would know the reasoning behind their *attraction*, but another part of her was terrified that he would sense her magic.

And then he would tell Dalton.

And then Dalton would know, and Dalton would have to tell his father.

She did not think he would, but she could not take that chance.

Dalton laughed at the mention of his elder comrade, his ethereal nature overtaken by the hilarity of the comment Charmaine supposed. "Cyril does not tell me anything until it serves the *greater good*. I am not sure where you are going with that, but I have noted that you are evading the question all together."

Charmaine leaned against the table she had grabbed. "You say greater good as if it were a curse."

"Is it not? A prophecy is another fancy word for a curse, if you ask me." He spun around, his hands on his hips as he twirled through his thoughts outwardly.

"Do you not want to be who you are?" Charmaine could not possibly understand this boy.

He paused, turning his head around. His blue eyes connected with hers as a chill came over her. "I have never asked for anything, lest to be me. To be free."

"And you are not you?" She was stupid for asking, but she genuinely did not know. She had to keep him talking about anything while he was alone with her. Anything but why she had asked him such a bone-headed question.

Why was she so thick sometimes?

"Shackled to a prophecy and my father's disposition is hardly being free, darling."

Suddenly, there was a clamor at the library door. Charmaine heard the hands of someone rattling the door with indistinguishable yelling. She jumped. The noise frightened her. Dalton, on the other hand, just rolled his eyes.

He stepped toward her, silent as if the voice outside

could potentially hear them.

"Meet me at the Hall of Portraits tomorrow night. We are not done here."

Without another word, he strode toward the door, and opened it with caution. Charmaine noted that his shoulders visibly picked up. His tone changed to a Princely demeanor as he said, "Ah! Cyril! Elena! Oh, and James, your sister is here with me. We were just chatting. Small detour before Daddy dearest's meeting. Are we off now?"

"Boy," Cyril growled, a warning.

"Char?" James said. His head peeked around the corner of the door.

Dalton opened the door fully and ushered her with him as they walked into the hallway.

Princess Elena looked Charmaine up and down, her soft brown eyes a warm embrace. She stood next to James, power reincarnate. A golden crown was seated atop her head, only enhancing her glamour. Her auburn hair was violent among the white walls of the castle, the color so vibrant it reminded Charmaine of autumn leaves just before they fell. Elena smiled softly, her painted red lips only enhancing everything that was already beautiful about her.

Charmaine gazed at her dress longingly. The white lace clung to every corner of her lean body. The shoulders of the gown were capped at the sleeves, the lace acting as a delicate embrace to her shoulders. The tops of her breasts were exposed, but not in a scandalous way. She looked regal, *strong*. The jewels that graced her neckline were a beautiful light blue, shining brightly like sea glass at sunrise. She almost looked like a painting. She was that stunning and bright in person.

Beside her, James Grimes looked like a King. His dark hair was wild. His tunic and pants were a stark white, contrasting his dark hair. His eyes looked radiant against the coloring, his white dressing causing them to come alive with a fire Charmaine did not know could exist in the color purple. She raised her eyebrow at her brother, who attempted to wave her off with a soft smile. Dalton seemed to notice Elena's disposition as well, looking at her with the same expression that Charmaine was giving James.

"Later," Elena whispered to Dalton, her voice final.

THIRTY-FIVE

"Who is that?"

"That is the King Protector. He saved the Prince during the battle," a man answered, his voice filled with an anxiousness Charmaine did not expect people of Ronan's court to express.

What did the people of court have to fear?

Dalton charged up the stairs of the throne. Charmaine's heartbeat quickened at the sight of him, even though she had never left him. His outfit was still in disarray from his escape earlier. A chill ran down her spine, remembering him a few nights ago, splattered with blood in this very spot.

"What is the meaning of this meeting, Father?" he said, irritation lacing every word.

Charmaine's cheeks flushed, as she noticed Lawton smirk.

"How is your brother shagging a Princess already? How long has she been here... ten minutes?" Lawton whispered. A light chuckle escaped him.

Charmaine wanted to elbow him, but she refrained. Hurt overwhelmed her, realizing this was the first time she had really seen James with *her*. He had told Charmaine that Elena healed him, but Charmaine did not know they had been seeing one another outside of that isolated incident.

Princess Elena extended her lace gloved hand forward for the King to kiss in greeting. His lips grazed the lace delicately as he rose to meet her gaze. A smile parted on his lips, as if relaying a message only she could understand.

Queen Aine stood beside her husband, her anguish over his gesture to Elena obviously bothersome. Charmaine looked toward James, whose fists were clenched so tightly that she was surprised his hands were not broken. His jaw was set, but she held her tongue. Lawton held him next to her, his eyes alight with humor at the physical anguish of both of them.

James let Elena go to the King, but his eyes betrayed him. Squinting, there was a fever there that she had never seen before. A protective nature that she did not quite grasp, even with her jealousy.

In what nature did my brother continue to meet the Princess?

King Ronan stepped forward, his arms extended in an embrace as he bellowed to the crowd, "Good evening, all, and welcome, Princess Elena. The First Kingdom is thankful to have you for this momentous occasion."

Dalton's brow furrowed as a chilly breeze flowed through the room. Charmaine's hands tingled, the sensation of the draw reaching out. Singling her out. Elena's bloodred lips shifted into a line, unimpressed by the King's presence and nonetheless irritated.

"Father…" Dalton whispered as an icy breeze picked up in the throne room, his words carrying a hidden message.

Ronan was not deterred. "Over the centuries, our two kingdoms have exemplified a powerful rule and hold on the eastern side of our world. We have always been close, given our elemental heritage. Forged by the Gods, our descendants lived up to that of the Kingdom of the Fourth's legacy to divulge our new kingdom of frozen power. We are forever grateful for the lineage between our two dynasties," the King said proudly.

Charmaine saw her breath form in front of her, puffs of hot smoke. Lawton paled.

"What is it?" she asked, unsure of the trajectory of the king's sermon.

"Ten Kingdoms save us all," Lawton said as his teeth began to chatter.

"King Ronan," Princess Elena said softly, her eyes a typhoon of power, as if to stall this moment with her gaze.

The King took a deep breath. He would dare not acknowledge the power his son wielded. The hypocrisy of the act was disgusting.

The frozen air caused him to cough, stepping forward as he continued, "I have been in contact with Princess Elena's mother many times over the past years. We have always had a dream for everlasting peace." He looked around the crowd, pausing for dramatic effect. "It has always been a goal of my legacy to unite our reigns once again. A ruler for both kingdoms, to consolidate our power with that of our elemental brethren."

Dalton looked as if he was going to be sick.

"He *cannot* be serious," Lawton whispered.

"I am here today, in front of you, my loyal subjects, to formally announce the agreed upon engagement of Princess Elena to my true heir, Prince Dalton."

The temperature of the room plummeted. Icicles

formed instantaneously on the ceiling as Dalton turned on his heels and stormed out. Princess Elena stood among the crowd of castle dwellers, stunned as everyone else to find she had been promised to the one true heir. Cian's heir apparent. The King remained atop the stairs by the throne. His blue eyes glared at the spots of ice on the marble floor that his son had left as he stomped out of the room.

THIRTY-SIX

"ian save me," Cyril whispered to nobody in particular as he walked out of the throne room. Ronan had really put them in it now.

Cyril knew he should not have revealed the prophecies to him, not *all* of them. He kept so many of them from him since seeing how he had responded to Eben's years ago. Cyril had gained an understanding many years ago that one could not intervene with fate and the Gods if they were not willing to pay the price.

Over the past one hundred and seventeen years of his life, Cyril had become a secret keeper. They did not teach the history of the Gods anymore, not since the times of Cian and Ciara. The Ten Kingdom's history was lost to the will of time, purposefully disbanded when they stopped giving powers to royals of the mortal world. Cyril wondered if he would be permitted to start teaching again, to bring back the history that was lost.

There were three Gods of stature, masters of elements and magic beyond the wildest imagination of the Kings and Queens of today. The Kings and Queens of Old had known, but knowledge was power. And the Gods wanted to prevent anyone from acquiring enough power to reignite the fire that lived in King Finn's tyrant heart.

Rightfully so.

An arranged marriage with Elena and Dalton? Cyril laughed, hysterical. Not only was it a disaster, despite their fierce friendship, but Ronan *hated* the Fourth Kingdom. He never wanted an alliance between the two Kingdoms. It was a miracle that Elena Leclair had come there to secure some type of alliance between the two Kingdoms.

Unless Ronan had been planning it all along?

Cyril reached into the depths of his mind, vast and filled with prophecies of the world he could touch with his presence. He could not decipher one against the many. None came to mind to explain the clairvoyance; nothing at all.

An engagement between the First and Fourth? Did the Gods not foresee this?

No matter how hard he tried to find some semblance of an explanation, anything that he could give the boy to latch onto, he was short of an answer for the prophecy: Dalton's rise to power and the violet Queen.

Was Elena the violet Queen? Her arrangement with the Grimes boy seemed prevalent. I don't know how anyone could ignore their display of affection in the Rose Garden earlier. And Dalton? What in the actual Ten Kingdoms had he been doing in the library with the Grimes girl? Had he absolutely no common sense? Was he trying to be executed like the serving girl?

Cyril groaned, and put his hands to his eyes, exasperated. He was a terrible Thinker. He used to be good and prolific. Now this whole castle had become a storm, one which he was not sure how much longer he could weather. Cyril could only imagine what his friends would have said to him all those years ago.

He was thankful that all Ciara had come forth to say was that the King of Snow was coming. She would have had the right to beat him senseless and tell him that he was the worst of his kind.

Maybe old age has made me futile and weak.

As he rounded the grand marble corner, he saw the Grimes girl in front of him, staring at the intricate detailing of the walls with wonder. Cyril could not help but walk over to her, unsure the next time he would catch her alone.

"The walls of this castle are hundreds of years old," he said, slithering up beside her.

Her youthfulness made Cyril almost envious, the bright light in her eyes so full of curiosity and wonder.

She only smiled at him in return, although it did not meet her eyes. She looked sad, even defeated. "It seems there is a history to everything here."

"History is our past. We cannot escape it, even if we try."

"A curse or a blessing," she said, not pondering it as a question, but as a statement.

"I think it depends on whose eyes history is reflected in." Cyril linked his fingers behind his back.

She turned to him. Her eyes filled with fear. "I heard... I heard you have been here a long time."

"Quite," he murmured.

"Do you miss the way it was?"

Surprised by her question, he paused. "Very much, sometimes."

"How did the world get here?" She ran a hand through her black mane, curls falling forward over her shoulders.

Cyril pondered again, landing on, "In order to be remade, it must be broken again."

"Dalton told me you only say things when they are *allowed* to be said."

Cyril laughed and it bounded through the halls. "Dalton spews a lot of nonsense, but with this, he is not full of it."

She smiled at that. Her purple eyes lit up. "Do you know the destinies of many?"

Cyril nodded, unsure for the first time in his one hundred years what he could reveal and what he could not.

"What is mine?" There was no hesitation in her voice.

"I am only revealed things as they come forth. The Gods decide when I am allowed to know, and how much I can give away."

"What happens if you were to give away something you were not allowed to have?"

"My heart would stop beating," he said rather bluntly.

Her voice became very low, afraid of the marble walls themselves hearing what she was about to ask. "Is he really who the world thinks he is?"

"The second coming, Miss Grimes." He nodded. He believed wholeheartedly that he was able to share this with her. He would take on the odds of death to make sure the world knew.

"What is my destiny?"

"I have not foreseen you, my dear, not in the ways that are reliable and true."

"It was worthy of a shot," she said, smiling sadly to herself. Disappointment radiated off of her aura.

"Are you not without purpose?" Cyril did not know why he was still asking questions. This girl was not his responsibility. Only Dalton. Only ever Dalton.

"I have not had sight of who I am in a long time."

"What makes you, *you?*"

She paused. "I have some... peculiarities. I have been told I am kind—"

"No, not what others say about you. What do you like about you?"

She held a finger to her bottom lip, scratching it slightly with the top of her pointer finger. "My empathy. My wanting to understand."

"That, my dear, is your drive. To unveil your destiny. I always tell Dalton he needs to embrace who he is."

"And who is that?"

"Our King." He had no qualms about spewing that truth.

She slightly snorted to herself; the gesture refreshingly genuine. "He knows that."

Cyril nearly doubled over. "Does he? Mind you, when has he ever stepped forth? Commanded the room?"

Her mouth was agape for a moment before she said, "I have not known him very long."

"And neither has the world. It is not the amount of time you know someone. It is what they have done with that time."

"You do not think he is ready?"

He unlaced his fingers. "I do not think he knows what ready is."

"Aren't you the one to help him?"

Cyril smiled; his teeth showed in a wide grin. "There is only so much a Thinker can do against the odds of destiny."

Cyril parted from the girl moments later, after reflecting on what it meant to be a ruler.

A leader.

A commander.

He missed Ciara. The world was terrified of Ciara at some points of her too-short life. They had nicknamed her the Queen of Fury for a reason. But she ruled with fairness, justness, despite all the terror that she could create with her power.

He missed Cian too. Cian was the man who fought with all that he had to save Ciara from herself. He was the man who built their kingdom from the ashes when the world had nearly bowed at the feet of King Finn.

But that was a story for another time.

They would not have let this get so wildly out of hand.

Cyril opened the door of his chambers and sat down on the yellow day-bed that was on the left side of his room. The fabric was soft and comfortable, a piece that he had taken with him throughout the years as a constant. As he moved to lay down, he heard a knock at the door.

He scoffed angrily, sitting up and concocting an insult to hurl at whoever was at the door. He imagined it was Dalton, finally coming to his senses regarding his engagement.

Maybe we could talk strategy, find a way to use this to our advantage to get more freedom at the castle.

Cyril opened the door hastily, bristling with anticipation. He could not hide the look of shock on his face when James Grimes stood before him. His face was flushed as if he had been running. His eyes were sad, but full of a triumph he had not seen in the throne room earlier.

"What can I do for you, Mr. Grimes?"

"I need to talk to you."

Cyril gestured for him to enter.

And so, they talked. For almost an entire hour, James gave him the rundown since Princess Elena healed him. The visions, the emotion, and the kiss that had happened between them moments before he found them. Cyril smiled to himself at some of the visions, his eyes closing as he imagined what James had been telling.

"Most peculiar," Cyril said when James finished.

"What does this all mean?" he asked, desperation crawling back into his voice.

"It is hard to tell. I have never seen someone have such intense visions brought on by physical contact."

"Is there any truth to them?"

Cyril paused, unsure what to unveil to the young man. Elena had more variance power than any other royal he had met. Was it possible that she had the properties of a seer as well? He breathed in and out rhythmically, begging for an answer from the Gods. The words tumbled out of him. Permission to share them had been granted.

"A healer and a destroyer. A Princess will find love with the one who can see in darkness and accept it. A new age will be forged. A King born out of the unseen and winter—"

Cyril opened his mouth to continue, but his throat began to close, a signal that it was all the Gods allowed him to say. "I cannot continue with the prophecy."

"So, there is a child?"

"Some sort of child, yes." Cyril nodded, aware of the danger of the conversation. If he revealed even a drop of information more than the Gods deemed appropriate, his heart would stop.

Cyril had unfinished business, and was not about to die revealing a prophecy that was not James Grimes's destiny.

James gasped, overcome with emotion.

Power of the visions radiated through his hands as he took James into an embrace, steadying him with his own power. "You must not tell anyone what you know. I posed a great risk to the both of us by revealing what I did."

"Between you and me." He stood up, taking his leave through his chamber doors.

Cyril stood to follow, in his old age and curiosity unbidden in his ability not to ask what was on his mind. "You told me what you saw, James. But I have to ask... this child, whoever he may belong to... He may not be the child of you and the Princess. I can see where your mind is and how you look at the Princess. Did you ever see yourself with him? Have you tried to look beyond the images at the true meaning? There could be a warning there, something ominous the Gods want Elena to know that you happen to be privy to."

James turned to Cyril before he left, his eyes grave, but his expression serious. "No."

"Does that make you apprehensive?"

"I trust the Gods to lead us back to the world we deserve. If I am not a part of it, then so be it."

Cyril snorted at his ferociousness. He was definitely a brave young man. "You trust the Gods who do not trust people? You do know why King Cian's power has not returned for over one hundred years... There has been nobody *worthy*. Nobody *capable*. The Gods do not take prophecy and power lightly. We have forgotten their names for a reason."

"Then let us serve the only man they have deemed worthy of Cian's legacy."

James Grimes was many things and adamant was one of them.

"And you will accept their dictation, at face value, even if you see a destiny that you do not yet understand?"

James looked back to him, unable to make direct eye contact as he slipped from the room without another word.

THIRTY-SEVEN

harmaine tore down the hallway of the castle as if the mercenaries were on their doorstep once more. Her lungs battled for air against the constraints of her corset. Her intricate gown that had made her feel so beautiful now was like shackles against her skin. Her breath was irregular. Her heels clicked unconventionally against the marble floors of the castle as she ran as fast as she could.

Her power was flickering, threatening to return—an unstoppable force against whatever resistance she had built up since arriving. She was so tired, so exhausted.

She yanked open the doors to her chambers with all her might, not daring to look to see if any eyes had followed her since she burst through the hallways. Upon slamming the doors shut, she took to the teal chair in the corner of the room, and thrust it against the door to ensure nobody could enter from the other side. She paused and looked down at herself as she breathed in the power that consumed her. When she was escaping Brinn, the change was effortless, same as it as had been when she was in the throne room.

But *this*—this was the way it usually happened, and it terrified her so.

Inch by inch slipped away, the colors of the world lighter and the intensity of them dulled with each breath she drew. Her heart sank with that familiar feeling of distaste for who she was, and she wondered why this part of her lay dormant. She leaned up against the wall. Relief that she had made it to her chambers before she was lost to sight washed over her like a tidal wave. The cold white marble of the wall she leaned against was smooth; soothing to all that remained of her senses. She did not know if that was because she had seen Dalton and Elena—those who clearly had magic—take hold of their lives that left her calm.

They didn't live in fear.

She walked over to the mirror and saw nothing in the reflection. It was as if she did not exist at all. When the power took hold, that was all there was. She had nothing left to her in the eyes of mortals.

Maybe that was the scariest part, losing yourself when you were still there.

THIRTY-EIGHT

or the first time in her life, the power that overtook Charmaine did not disarm her.

Instead, it calmed her.

Rooted her.

She achieved peace.

When she awoke the next morning to the sun kissing all that lay in her chambers, she no longer felt the fatigue of her gift.

That's what it was, truly. A gift. Maybe it was time I started to think of it as a blessing, rather than a curse.

This was the first time she did not fight it when it came on. Granted, she was alone, and she was terrified, but she let it take her. Pride filled her, for she had embraced it. Let it consume her. It did not define her.

And she was okay.

She stood up quickly to look in the mirror, to be sure that she had returned to her normal state. She saw her black curls first. Her violet eyes popped against the color palette of her features. A smile overtook her face. She admired herself for the first time in a while. She was present and she was there. She had completely forgotten her training and the strategies that her mother had tried to teach her to prevent the surge.

Instead, she did the exact opposite of what her mother had told her, and for those brief moments, it felt *good*.

She heard a knock at the door and rushed to remove the chair before the person on the other side tried to shove past the barrier she had created. As soon as she did, James came in a second later, his cheeks alight with color and his stride wistful.

"Good evening, sister," he said cheerfully.

"What has you in a mood?"

"Can't I be in a good mood?"

"Sure, but knowing you, there is a reason." She tried to sit inconspicuously on her bed, even though she was clearly wearing her same garb from yesterday.

"Just glad to be alive, that is all." He spun, pretending to dance, before he popped onto the edge of her desk.

"That we all are, I suppose."

"Wait, did you say evening?" she half-shouted.

"Yes. Why?"

"James, I slept through the day. I..." She laid a hand to her forehead.

"Are you alright?" His voice was latent with concern.

"I slept through the day!" she half-shouted again, as she strode toward the dresses in her closet. She had promised to meet Dalton, and she would not miss an opportunity to figure out what was going on.

"Are you alright?" James asked again, moving toward her.

She grabbed a simple teal gown with sheer sleeves. The dress had an ornate bodice with pink roses detailed across it. She snatched a pair of black shoes, throwing them on underneath the dress with haste.

"The change... It must have knocked me out for the entire night and day," she whispered.

"You changed?!" His voice cracked with agony, as if he blamed himself for her admission.

"No, it was not like it normally was. I was alone... I was okay."

He did not look like he believed her. "You are okay? No pain? No problems?"

"None," she said, as she began to undress. She motioned for James to turn around, and he did.

"Where are you off to?" he asked as he spun. Curiosity entered his voice as he changed the subject. He did not want to dwell on her changing without assistance in the castle, especially so soon after Gwendolyn's execution.

"To meet Dalton," she said, not thinking before she spoke. Like usual.

James stilled; his voice weary. "And why would you be meeting the Prince? Charmaine, we caught you yesterday with him in the library. Are you sneaking around with him? Do you think that to be wise? There are genuine opportunities for you to find happiness here. Randolph, for one, is a good man—"

As she pulled up her dress, she turned to face him. Her irritation unjust, she knew, but she could not stop. "Just as you were caught multiple times embracing Princess Elena, publicly? Mind you, that is Dalton's *fiancée*. They are to wed, James. And you were seen holding her as if she belonged to you at the execution."

James's eyes flashed with hurt. Charmaine knew she had struck a chord, but she could not help the pain that stirred within her. Charmaine and her brother were so close. She told him everything and vice versa. This divide that had come between them since coming to the castle

277

had affected her more than she wanted to admit. She missed her brother, and seeing him with Elena had shocked her.

How had I not known? How had he not told me?

He opened his mouth to reply, but then closed it. His eyes darkened with an emotion she did not understand, and for the first time since he entered the room, she noticed the dark circles under his eyes.

Had he not been sleeping?

"I will see you when I see you then," he said quietly, before leaving her chambers.

She made a move to stop him, to apologize and explain what she was feeling, but she did not follow through. She had made a mess of things, for sure. It was best to let him go, and they could figure it out later. He needed time as much as she did.

She prayed to the Gods that Dalton was still there.

Charmaine rushed down the halls of the castle toward the Hall of Portraits. The door was closed when she arrived and her heart sank in response.

Was I too late?

She opened it with a grunt and closed it behind her quickly. She did not want to be followed, least of all by James, who she was sure did not retire to his chambers after their interaction.

She turned around as she caught amusement spread across Dalton's face like wildfire. "Did you not think I would be in here?"

"I am sorry. I figured you left before I even got here." She smoothed her skirts, her fingers shaking ever so slightly.

"I keep my promises when they are made. I do not take them lightly." He smiled softly, and took a few strides toward her. "Have you been to this place before?"

"Yes, I came here with Lawton when we first arrived at the castle. It seems like ages ago." She was not sure she should admit that she had visited this room twice with Lawton, but she sensed that Dalton did not care. There was no accusation in his gaze.

"Time moves differently here. A few days can feel like a few years, in my experience."

Her heart shot up with pain as he said it. The weight of his words took hold. "Is there a reason you wanted to meet *here*?"

"Nobody really comes here. Nobody wants to admire our Kings and Queens. I figured we'd be... alone."

She strode over to his portrait, smiling sadly as she looked at how young and different he was, immortalized in the painting. "You were so... different."

He smiled, and touched the portrait with his long fingers. They swept over the golden frame as if it were a tangible memory. "The world was a little different, I suppose."

"Do you miss her?" Charmaine blurted, covering her hand with her mouth afterward with a few fingers.

He looked at Carinthya's picture next to him, his eyes glassy in the dim light. "Sometimes. Does that make me a horrible person? That I do not miss her every waking moment?"

"I think grief can be as imperfect as we are. It is all about the passing of time, the manner in which it happened... I do not believe grief is linear."

"I am sorry again that you lost both your parents so young."

"I am sorry that your sister was lost to us all."

He snorted. The Prince of Snow *snorted*. "She was a

firecracker. I do not remember much. I have blocked out rather a lot from memory, but I remember her ability to get her way. She was cunning and smart. No doubt, if she were here today, this whole mess would have been cleaned up by now."

"Would she have ruled?" Charmaine felt lesser for asking about the politics of her own kingdom, but it had been so long since she had any formal education.

"No, the firstborn son takes over if a daughter or daughters are first. So, she was dethroned upon my birth." There was no hint of shame in his response.

"If the world was not as it was, would she have ruled?" She was genuinely curious.

"I think she would have. I think she would have been good at it too. People would have probably called her the Queen of Snow, the second-coming of Ciara." He laughed to himself, as if his own title seemed to bother him.

"Was she like you?"

Was she like me?

"The only thing icy about her was her heart."

Charmaine smiled at that. They walked in tandem down the hallway, gazing upon more royals. The faces of history that determined the fate of their world today.

She paused in front of a portrait she did not recognize. The man had an intensity in his gaze that the portrait captured perfectly. His green eyes squinted and his brow was furrowed. He had red hair tied in a knot behind his head. There was no name underneath his portrait, like many of the others. The difference, however, was that below the portrait there had been a nameplate, but where it had been was now a burn mark on the wall. It was as if someone had attacked the nameplate, trying to erase it from memory.

"Who is that?" she asked Dalton.

"King Finn."

"That is King Finn?" she replied in surprise. "I would have thought that Ciara's murderous father would have looked more like—"

"A monster?" he finished; his eyes sad.

"He does not look out of the ordinary."

"But he was quite the spectacle. So much so that his own daughter killed him for the crown." Ice lay latent in every word he spoke. "She did it out of fear, out of the fear of what the world would be like if he were to live another day in it. And because of that, she became the monster. She became the one thing she feared above all else."

"Why was his nameplate destroyed?" Charmaine asked.

He touched it softly, his long fingers trembling so slightly she figured it was a trick of the light. "I do not know."

She turned to look at Dalton closer, the curvature of his mouth parted slightly as he looked at King Finn. "You are nothing like him, you know."

He smiled at her as she said it. A dimple appeared on the right side of his face. His blue eyes seemed darker tonight, more haunted by whatever he contemplated.

"I am sorry I was so direct with you in the library. I am afraid, due to the condition of my life, that I have become unaccustomed to the way I should speak to people. Particularly people who have shown me nothing but kindness and understanding."

She blinked twice, rather shocked by the apology. She smiled. "I am sure Cyril would love to hear that."

At that, he laughed loudly, his head tipping back.

"It must have been horrible, being locked up like a caged animal," she whispered.

His smile was vicious. "Do not worry, darling. I am still caged."

She moved closer to him. The gravity of his words settled in as he took a step closer to her. That tugging sensation returned, but for the first time, it was when she was near him. She could pinpoint it.

"A King should not be on a leash," Charmaine said, moving the white hair out of his face. She wanted to ask him about its coloring, why it was black in his portrait and so different now, but she could not draw a full breath. He was so close to her and he was so *beautiful*. She had not forgotten what it was like to see him for the first time, that ethereal nature blooming for all to see. There was something about him up close, though. His angelic features were less bright. He looked more human than God.

It suited him.

"A King is always on a leash. The difference is that I know how long mine is."

He put a long finger to her lips, tracing them mindlessly. The intimacy of the gesture stopped her from breathing entirely. His touch was grace itself, a power that she had never known before. She wanted to tell him this was stupid, and there was no future for a girl who spent their time chasing Kings. She thought back to James, encouraging her to see a man like Randolph differently.

But this was the only man she saw differently.

He leaned closer, his breath smelling of mint and ice. "May I?" he whispered.

She nodded her head slowly, knowing what she would allow. He leaned closer to her, his eyes never leaving her lips. He moved slowly, as if he were afraid she would tell him to stop.

She realized, in that moment, she would never tell him to stop.

His lips grazed hers gently, and then they were kissing.

He tasted of blueberries and snow. She gasped, unable to stop the frozen fever that had taken over her. His hand was pressed into the small of her back, gently coaxing her to him. She could tell—despite being locked away for five years—he had experience, for he was not rushed, nor was he anything but deliberate. She imagined before Ronan had taken his freedom away that he had been quite the catch for the ladies of court. She had noted all this time how women gawked at him, not just at his power, but at his charm.

Who are you? Not who you think you are supposed to be, but who are you, really?

She knew the answer, though. He was kindness and sympathy. He was pleasure and sarcasm. He was wonderful and wondrous.

The positioning of his lips was methodical, for pleasure rather than to satisfy the heat that ran between them. He groaned slightly into her mouth, reciprocating how she was feeling. This was not Charmaine's first kiss, but it was the first kiss where she felt like herself. The boys in Brinn were inexperienced and unsure. Dalton, for all that he was, was confident. He took what she gave and gave it right back. She ran her hands through his hair as they moved backward toward the wall. Without warning, her head hit a portrait, connecting with the corner of the frame. Charmaine whimpered with pain, jarred momentarily from what they were doing.

"Is your head okay?" Concern flashed in his eyes. He pulled back from her, his eyes wild with an emotion

Charmaine could not place. His cheeks were flushed pink, despite his pale coloring.

Heat rose in her own cheeks.

"You should return to your chambers," he whispered as he moved a curl from her face.

"Do you want me to return?" she asked, not sure what she was pushing for. It was not as if anything more could happen between them.

"No. But I want you to be safe above all else." His gaze never left her. His long fingers stroked the side of her head that collided with the frame. "I am sorry. I should not have put you in a position like this." He looked scorned, as if he had ruined her.

What he did not realize was that he could not ruin someone who had nothing to lose.

"I do not regret it," she said, her voice breaking. "Do not push me away in the name of social status."

He smiled at that, as if the whole world were a joke to him. But his eyes were sad. "Never in the name of social status. Come, let me drop you off. It is late and I am afraid if we linger—"

"If we linger, what?"

He smirked, not answering her, but instead wiggling his eyebrows. His blue eyes were now shining, his expression clearly fighting a laugh. Her face turned to flame as he reached out his hand to hold hers, and they exited the portrait gallery.

THIRTY-NINE

andolph, naturally, found himself in the tavern. Again.

Lawton did not join him—not yet, anyway. Where Lawton was concerned, Randolph found that he never requested or admitted that he even slightly enjoyed his company. Some part of him, deep, *deep* down, definitely enjoyed the friendship of a boy his age. It had been many years since he had had someone in his life that he considered a friend. He locked that part of himself away when he retreated from his destiny three years ago. The part that craved friendship and love openly. He had murdered it just as he had destroyed everything else that once mattered to him.

Deep within his bones, destiny hummed. It was becoming harder to hide, especially with Charmaine and his own budding friendship. He had been avoiding Cyril too, fearful that the old man would coerce him to listen to another prophecy.

So, Randolph did what he always did, he pushed down his fears and his lust for oblivion because that was who Randolph was at his core.

A coward.

When he cared about people, they always got hurt. But with Charmaine and Lawton, he knew they had been hurt before. A lot.

Maybe that's why they were drawn to one another. Maybe hurt people are forced to navigate life together because in some sick manifested way of destiny, we need one another to stay whole.

Randolph looked around the tavern, which sat at the bottom of the hill in Thallgan. The walls were bare; wooden. Villagers were crammed from wall to wall, men and women alike looking for release —a moment away from their home lives or whatever they too had been running away from.

There was something unwaveringly comforting about the small village and the realities that Randolph observed time and time again. Over the past few years, he had become alarmingly comfortable with the elderly couple who sold bread, the children who ran amok in the streets, and the drunkards who sang the King's praises in this very tavern.

In another life, that type of behavior would have disgusted him. His wicked father would have thought that behavior to be shameful. Anything that was not an exhibition of brutality was considered weakness.

Sure, he could laugh about it now, smile in remembrance of some of the memories that he was able to make with those he loved. However, they were few and far between at this point.

The bad always overtook the good for Randolph, no matter how hard he tried to ignore it.

"I will take a pint, please," Randolph said to the bartender.

As he lifted a tattooed hand, which Lawton had pointed out a few visits ago—*it made him famous in towns all over the First Kingdom*—the bartender froze. His gaze was locked on the ink.

Ten Kingdoms save me.

He was on the verge of causing a scene, but reined himself in for the betterment of his own reputation. He did not know what rumors the knights had spread of him, but he figured if anyone was responsible for his reputation, it was Lawton. His big mouth did not serve him any which way, except to run Randolph's name in places where it should not have been uttered.

No, you are overthinking again. Lawton was the one who told you that the townspeople had fears about you, since you work for the madman yourself.

But that was exactly the type of person Lawton was. He pushed and pushed and could make a person believe something until it became fact. He never meant malice, at least not to Randolph. It was a gift, that ability to make anyone believe in anything, rather than a scheming curse, but Randolph would never admit that to him.

He would not admit a whole lot of anything to anyone. He did not inspire shit.

"Sir?" Randolph replied as he strategically moved his hands out of vision for the poor bartender who still looked petrified.

"I am sorry, good sir. We have heard so much about you."

"I hope you only believed the good things," he said, smiling and flashing his white teeth. He kept his arms out of sight, and rolled down the sleeves of his white tunic, so all but the roses on his hands were covered.

Despite his sultry disposition, Randolph knew how to

charm. It was one of the traits he had not lost to the flames of his prior life.

The bartender's green eyes flashed with emotion, and Randolph decided he did not care enough to understand it deeper. "One pint coming up, Sir Randolph."

"Atta lad," Randolph whispered under his breath, so low that nobody heard him. Appeasing people was exhausting.

Within seconds, the pint was delivered and Randolph moved to sit in a booth by himself. He sipped the ale and let the warmth of the alcohol seep into his veins. The sense of autumn spread through him. The familiar sun he ached to see from his childhood suddenly made him nauseatingly homesick. It was the only sensation which he could equate it to—the end of summer and the rebirth of the seasons. That moment when the skies opened and the sun peeked through the trees. It left nothing in its wake but utter joy. Randolph still felt the Seventh Kingdom's sun awakening after the dark months. The moment the sun touched him, he erupted into flames.

Randolph laughed out loud, a tattooed hand quickly flying to his mouth in response. *Home,* he almost vomited at the nostalgia. *What was becoming of me?*

He put down the pint with haste, and it spilled over the sides in response to the abruptness of the gesture. He could not remember the last time he had referred to that miserable place as home.

Or when he had thought of the wretched place.

While he lived there, it had been anything but home. A cell. Confines. Chains. Any synonym used to describe being shackled would suffice.

His head hit the wall as he threw it back in exasperation. A slur of curse words ensued, for that surely would leave a bump. Randolph decided that this solo adventure to leave the castle this evening was rather benign. He moved to stand, his leather pants cracking slightly due to the length of time he had been sitting. He always tried to wear his newer leathers to more inconspicuous places: taverns, parties, and council meetings. If he was able to break them in prior to the cry of battle, he felt like a part of him would be more prepared.

And Randolph was nothing if not prepared.

He left the ale at the table, unsure if he ever wanted it to begin with, or if he simply wanted an excuse to leave the castle.

An engagement between two royals was no small feat.

He pushed through the crowd of people, his flower-covered hands making waves as he separated those who crowded the passage to the door. After a plethora of excuse me's and pardon me's, Randolph emerged from the tavern heavier than when he had walked in.

Immediately upon hitting the cool air, he took off for the castle. His boots smashed against the pavement, the only sound and sensation which could keep his mind from wandering back to the Seventh.

That's the last time I go to the Beloved King without an escort.

He rolled his shoulders forward and backward as he continued to jog up the long hill to the castle gates. He had walked down earlier, sure of himself in his decision to break away from the castle, but he wanted to run now.

Running was the one thing that relaxed him. He did not get to do it enough, due to his own precarious schedule and servitude. With every step, his lungs opened up, his knees drove higher, and his arms pumped with ease. His breathing never turned ragged, though he could feel his tunic beginning to weigh with sweat.

Randolph welcomed the pain of running, relished it. It freed him from the confines of his inner fire, and the plague which was his overthinking mind.

He despised these types of weeks where he had nothing. No tasks, no journeys, and no quests. Those types of things were the reason he had shown up on Ronan's doorstep three years ago. He needed purpose. And unfortunately, he had reached the point in his service where he could climb no higher. He was the head of the legion of the First Kingdom at nineteen years old. Even his elders bowed to him and respected him.

But nothing was ever good enough for Randolph.

Without even realizing, he rounded the last corner as he shot for the golden gates of the castle. He immediately thought of Charmaine and when he had first taken her there. Another one of his mistakes: bringing that poor girl to the castle. She had experienced pain there in the short time he had known her. The attack on the castle. The brutality of the serving girl's decapitation. The interactions with the Prince which had obviously stressed her further.

Randolph could add Charmaine to his ever-growing list of guilts.

He took a deep breath as he unlatched the key necklace he had decided to wear tonight. Ronan had given it to him a few years ago, in case he did not have a sword on him. Only the knights with swords could open the castle gate without some type of magical influence. It left questions and rumors among the Knights and King. How did the mercenaries get in, unless someone had let them in? It was a puzzle to him, yet another task on his plate to figure out.

As a child, he heard rumors that the King of Snow

would be able to open the gate with nothing more than a blast of winter wind, but he did not know if there was any truth to that.

A lot of his childhood had been a lie, after all.

He looked at the key before he put it into the slot. It was no ordinary key. It was the tip of an old knight's sword—to whom it belonged, Randolph had never been informed. The Kings of the First Kingdom did not give out swords to anyone.

He inserted the tip and the gate thrummed as it had that day Charmaine, James, and his group of knights had entered the castle. He almost hit himself in response to the feelings he was swarmed with when he thought about his comrades who were sent on a mission, leaving Randolph behind. It was almost as if the King did not trust him fully to leave.

And despite everything, that hurt Randolph.

"I should see her tomorrow, apologize formally," Randolph whispered to himself as he shut the gate behind him.

Yes. I will see Charmaine in the morning.

FORTY

alton awoke in a daze.

He tossed and turned all night, restless. He could not wrap his head around it all, and by, *it all*, he meant Charmaine.

He did not understand her kindness, her willingness to understand, and her ability to want to learn about everything. For someone who had endured so much pain, she was so full of life. She wanted to understand him, as she did this place. She saw who he truly was, and he felt it when she kissed him.

Rather, when he kissed her.

She did not look at him as if he was the future King. She looked at him like he always dreamed of being looked at, like he was a person before any of the titles and romanticization. Dalton was normal around her. It was easy to spill out information.

Ten Kingdoms, he even talked about Carinthya in front of her. Something he never did.

Ever.

He got dressed quickly, coming out of his morning stupor with each dramatized motion. He knew the expectation from his father was to have a dinner with him tonight, per the reminder Cyril had given him so graciously this morning, yelling in his ear before the sun came up. Dalton did not know who would be in attendance, but he could only guess it would be his fiancé, the Grimes siblings, and esteemed members of the Royal Guard.

So, Randolph would be in attendance. Lovely.

It was not that he had developed recent animosity toward the man, but he did not like how he prowled around Charmaine as if he owned the girl just because he rescued her from Brinn. He pretended as though he were just, and his world was on the cusp of reaching the ideals the First held so dear that everyone now called them laws. However, the laws he believed in were the laws that came out of his father's mouth. They were not laws, not anymore. They were treason.

Dalton knew Randolph was not a savior, for he wore his sins like a tapestry on his skin. He was familiar with the concepts of those from the Seventh, and what he had said when he showed up on his father's doorstep—

Suddenly, there was a knock at the door. It opened with a blast of irritation. Elena walked in as he finished pulling his purple silk tunic over his head. She looked quite beautiful today, a red dress and red lips to complement the fire of her hair. Her skin looked like silk at midnight, dark hue radiant against the coloring of her clothing. It was a shame he was not in love with her, for he was certainly attracted to her.

"Where in the Ten Kingdoms have you been?" she asked, slamming the door behind her.

Ah, the familiar sting of her loving personality.

"Me? I have been nowhere and everywhere."

293

"You are my *fiancé*, and this is how you are going to treat me?" She was smirking, but her eyes were troubled.

"What's wrong?" He could read her like a book.

She ran a hand through her curls. "What's wrong is this entire situation! How dare you leave me to rot in the throne room, James on my arm looking as if he were to be sick—"

"What's with you and the Grimes boy?" Dalton lifted an eyebrow.

"What's with you and the Grimes girl?" she shot back.

"Touché." He grabbed his boots and laced them with care. "You have to be careful."

"Me? You are the one with the chains off! You have to be smart, Dalton. He will lock you up again, I know it—" Elena was rambling. It did not happen often, but it was her major indicator that she was off balance, scared.

"He would not dare lock me up again." Dalton's voice was heavy, but he meant every word. He would take a blade through the heart before he let himself rot there again. Now that he had tasted freedom, there was no going back.

"How do you know?" Her voice was quiet.

"Because he needs me. Something is off, Elena. I can feel it. The attacks at the castle, the way he has been demonstrating his powers at the castle, the execution of Gwendolyn... Something has him scared and running."

She paused, and her eyes searched his face. "And you think our wedding is another flex of power?"

"Of course. It gets me out of here and your mother off his backside. Double win for Daddy."

"You do need to be careful, though. The three times I have nearly caught you both, it has been so *obvious*." Her full lips were pursed. Concern flooded her deep brown eyes.

"I cannot deny my feelings," he settled on.

"I am not asking you to. I am asking you to be smart. I am sure James does not want to end up on the executioner's block." Her face turned a sickly color for a moment. He heard her heart beginning to pound in her chest. "And what of you?"

"What of it?"

"Do you not want her?"

Charmaine.

"I barely know her." It was the truth.

"Do you not want to get to know her?" Her question was poised, but he could hear the alarm in her voice.

What did she know?

"I would like nothing but."

"You need to talk to her."

"Tried that last night."

"And?"

"Ended... unexpectedly." Dalton smirked, letting Elena think whatever.

She rolled her eyes, but they glittered. "We need to buy ourselves time."

"Time can allow us to fix this." He gestured between the two of them.

She extended her hand. "Then let's go for a stroll before dinner."

The moment Elena left Dalton's chambers, she regretted it. They entered the courtyard with a robust sense of laughter, themselves again despite the precarious situation. They did not know what Ronan was planning. Cyril seemed to be spitting out destinies as if they were playing cards, and a girl had lost her head. They had just been falling back into their old ways when they saw them.

Randolph stood in the middle of the courtyard, kissing Charmaine's hand and whispering quietly to her. Elena could not overhear it because of the thundering whip, as Dalton's power cracked the moment he saw them.

Elena almost ran at them, to shout at her and demand to know why she was entertaining Randolph, but she understood. To be a woman in this world was to make choices and to entertain the likes of men.

Wasn't that what she was doing right now? Playing the game?

Charmaine had as much of a future with Dalton as Elena did with Charmaine's brother. The admittance left her heart in two. The difference between them, though, was that she was not the one to accept her fate at first value. She wanted more. She wanted a life of her choosing.

Charmaine probably did not think much of choice.

"Sir Randolph!" Dalton shouted, his eyes feral, but his voice calm.

A winter storm erupted around them as those in the courtyard scattered to ignore the pelting of hail. Charmaine looked at them, her eyes wide in alarm.

"My Prince?" Randolph asked, squinting through the ice to see.

"I demand an audience with the lady. Alone." Dalton's voice was that of a King.

"Is it an audience if you are alone?" he shot back.

Ten Kingdoms, those from the Seventh were so—

"Now." Dalton's voice was lethal.

Randolph bowed to her, before turning to Dalton to do the same. He walked by Elena and took her arm, steering the two of them away.

"Are you trying to be executed, Randolph?" Elena

asked as they turned back into the castle, her cheeks stinging with the transition of temperature.

"He did not claim the girl," he said, smirking at her. "He has you. Remember?"

⚜

Dalton knew his rage was ridiculous, but he could not pull the plug on his power. When he saw Randolph holding her hand as if they were lovers beginning a courtship, Dalton could not manage.

"Let's get out of the snow," he said curtly.

They made their way to her chambers. He could see her hesitation, but Dalton did not care about the formalities. He was not sure he ever did. There was nothing good that ever came of them anyway. Dalton and Elena's forced engagement was a prime example.

They entered her chambers with haste and shut the door quickly. He whirled around and ran his hands through his hair in exasperation.

What was I doing?

"What is it? What was *that*?" she asked. Her eyes filled with alarm as she nervously twirled a curl at the end of her hair.

"I saw you with him, and I—"

"You what?" she challenged.

"I lost control, okay? Is that what you want to hear?! That little tether I feel when I am not with you felt as though it had been yanked. I could not do anything but unleash whatever my power had been building—"

She looked as if she had been struck. "Dalton…" She took a step toward him and paused, as if she were not fully aware of what she was doing when she moved, and was now taking it back.

"There is no rhyme or reason for me acting like this," he said, more to himself than to her.

"Then *why* are you acting like this?"

"Do you not feel what I feel? When we are not together… Even if we are together now, it is starting to come up."

"What is coming up?" She sounded tired.

"That tugging… the draw between us!" he half-shouted, trying to keep it together. The winter storm continued to rage outside. He saw it through the stained-glass windows.

"Dalton, we cannot talk about this."

"Why not?"

"Because we do not know what it means and you are still on a *leash*," she said the word with a venom Dalton did not know she was capable of.

"I told you the leash does not bother me. It is better than a total lack of freedom."

"It might as well be *chains*, Dalton!" Now she was the one shouting.

"Shackles are bearable when you see the sunlight." Dalton did not know why he was egging this conversation on, or why he had even brought her back there in the first place.

"They are not if you bear them alone."

He looked at her, stunned by her resilience. "Why was he kissing your hand?" He was a fool. Let her see that. Let her hate him for his feral jealousy.

"He has been kind to me since the start. James does not want me to shy away from—" She stopped.

"A potential match with him?" He hated the words as he said them.

"A match with him would be advantageous. I have no future with—"

"With a Prince. And you need to protect yourself, in any way possible," he said, barely a whisper. He was boiling. Threads of power threatened to snap unless he unleashed himself somehow. He had to do it fast before this room became desolate, and he covered the entire world in ice.

His solution was that he started to laugh.

You cannot be with a prince, but you can be with Randolph.

His laughter was quiet at first and then became louder. His breath shot out little snowflakes with each exhale. The dramatics of the whole thing were the perfect release from the never-ending depths of his power.

"Do you think this is funny?" The question was clearly more for herself than for him. Regardless, he held his tongue as he collected himself. "Why do I feel… like *this*?"

He straightened the collar of his tunic, repositioning the crown atop his head. "I have been reading… Trying to understand and find anything… I have seemed to run out of luck. And books. I am sorry I brought you here. We should not have spoken and I should not be… quite the way I am."

"You have been alone for so many years—" she started, clearly unsure where to go with that. Dalton quirked an eyebrow, encouraging the discourse. "Do you think you do not know the difference between infatuation and desire?"

Dalton laughed again, despite his heart hurting at the involuntary jab. "Do you think I do not know what it means to love and to be loved?"

"You cannot say that you love me."

"I do not," he answered a little too quickly. "I do not love you, but you intrigue me. You are kind and fierce. You do not back away from me like I am some Godly Prince who could murder you with a dash of power. He is not good, Charmaine. He does not deserve you." He meant every word.

"Are you jealous? Do you know how it feels to be jealous? To feel as though your heart has been betrayed, and to want something so badly from another person that you would do anything to get that feeling back?" Her violet eyes flamed with anger.

Dalton could not say that he did, but he could not let her win. Instead, he put his mask of cruelty back up before he unleashed on her. "Just because I live with shackles, does not mean I live without a heart."

And with that, he stormed out.

FORTY-ONE

t was as if the very memory of Dalton sitting there, which was probably hours ago, would not allow Charmaine to get up.

If she got up, it was as if their interaction did not exist at all. If she got up, she would have to accept these *feelings* for him. Whatever that meant. He had called it an attraction, a draw. If she got up, she was going to revel in their budding friendship. If that was what it was. If she got up, she would have to go through it all again to realize that she was no longer allowed those joys. Whatever joy meant in this ludicrous court. If she got up, she would have to escape this draw she felt for him, for it was too dangerous. And putting herself in more danger was not an option she could embrace.

Her eyes were no longer wet with tears, but her head hurt. Water. She needed water. She stood and made her way over to the tray the ladies-in-waiting had brought with them earlier. The golden chalice was filled to the brim with cold water. She took it in her hand, admiring the structured glass, the snowflakes feeling real as she ran her fingers over the design. She poured herself a glass full. The sensation hit her lips and took her mind off of Dalton for as long as she drank. She put down the glass, her head no longer as heavy as her heart.

The doors to her chambers burst open with no warning, and she yelped in surprise, only to find Randolph staring back at her.

"Do you have a moment?"

She nodded in reply.

What in the Ten Kingdoms was going on today?

"I did not mean to get you in trouble with the Prince. I know he is fond of you. And I know you admire him." His brown eyes were lethal, but calm.

"It was not your fault. I have been a bit of a mess lately." It was the truth, rather the only truth she had known.

"You have come into so much pain. And this place... well, even on a good day, she is not the easiest to navigate." His smile was filled with kindness, something she needed to see after Dalton's outburst. "I did not mean to make things harder for you. That is all."

"I appreciate it." She meant that truth too.

"I will not keep you, but I wanted you to know that you have a friend in me, no matter what the Prince said." He ushered himself out of the room before waiting for her response, his strong jaw set. "See you at dinner."

FORTY-TWO

he garb Cyril brought to Dalton's chambers was no more than a petty costume.

"You absolutely cannot be serious," Dalton said to him, repulsed at the white regality of the whole thing.

"You cannot seriously still be fighting with me on everything, Dalton. Are you tired? I am," Cyril spat, as he gestured once again to the white dressings lying against his green silk sheets.

The servants who made his bed had defiled the thing. His poor bed, saturated by King bullshit. The horror of the jewels against the white fabric.

Who in the Ten Kingdoms did they think I was?

"This is the outfit of your engagement dinner, Dalton. To the very powerful and future Queen." Cyril was pacing now.

Dalton stifled a laugh at the sight of his fingers twitching against the side of his brow. A gesture he had long come to understand as Cyril's deepest frustration.

Dalton thought of being smart in his response, but all he came up with was, "I can think of prettier women, with fewer knives."

His mind went to memories of Elena from their childhood, one of the only children he was able to see within the castle walls before he unleashed on his father. Royals were always under some level of lock and key. Elena was strong, verbally intelligent, and she was exquisite with her knife throwing abilities. They always got into such trouble with one another. She was an incredible woman, and would make an incredible Queen, and wife, one day. But that was a choice they should make for themselves. Even Queen Ciara had been able to choose to marry a commoner.

Knowing Elena as long as he had, Dalton was shocked she did not murder his father on the spot. And by the way she held the arm of Charmaine's brother, it was clear she was taken with him, even in the short time she had known him.

Charmaine. The draw of her drummed under his skin if he focused on it. She was somewhere in the castle, within this wing. He was called to her, like a piece of his inner puzzle was still shifted out of place. It was not missing while she was there.

He sighed and Cyril looked at him with squinted eyes, his lips curving into a smirk. "Who is prettier with fewer knives?"

Ten Kingdoms.

He made an exasperated noise. He threw his head back as he ran a hand through his white hair. Cyril smiled. He knew. He always knew somehow.

Dalton made a mental note to ditch him somewhere later.

"Put this on my dear, Princeling," he said with as much sarcasm as he could. "Dinner is in ten minutes." He strode out of Dalton's room, turning around once before he closed it and said, "She may not have knives, but she definitely has a draw."

✠

James waited for Elena outside of her chambers. He was dressed in all white, signifying an allegiance to the Kingdom. To Ronan. Elena knew it was purely ceremonial, but it did not mean she liked seeing him like that. Dressed like the enemy, while Ronan still ruled. She wanted to skin the King alive for surprising her like that, working with his mother on a secret engagement that neither of them knew the truth about. They would pay for this, taking her freedom.

Her heart softened at the thought of Dalton. He had not known freedom in the last five years. Ten Kingdoms, maybe he never knew it at all. He was kind when he needed to be, and had a life to himself that she had never seen before in a royal. He could be cruel, but that was not his nature. He cared about people deeply. He deserved to be King one day, and he would be a good one.

But Elena would not be his Queen.

Sure, we would be happy. We would be happy and powerful, but that wasn't enough.

That was not love.

She took a deep breath and gazed at James. He was unlike any man she had ever met. His ferocity did not come from his birthright or his life for his Kingdom, but that of his sister.

Charmaine. She was beautiful, a woman version of her brother. But as weird as it sounded, there was no other way to dictate it. Her curls were long and thick, hitting the middle of her back. Her skin was porcelain, her eyes a sharp violet. It was unbelievable that they were not royals, for

305

they were beautiful, dignified, and diplomatic.

She thought of James when she first met him as they walked, his body bleeding as he defended Dalton and his father. Giving his life for what he saw in others.

I had to help him.

I thought of it again, the surge of power that went through me as I wet my hands. They glowered fiercely as the water encapsulated them, as if I were wearing gloves of water. They glowed as I touched him. The intimacy of the gesture connected us.

I saw flashbacks of his life in pieces, the love for his mother and sister, the raids on their home, his love for swords...

When I took my hands away, I could not let him leave me. I was trapped, his strength and beauty encompassing all I knew.

I thought of what it was like to have his beautiful hands run along my skirts, his wound closing as I shared with him some of the greatest beauties of my life. Tears ran down my face as I saw glimpses of my life ahead and his as well. When healing, I could see beyond, only for seconds, as if the water could show me visuals. I saw James again as I replayed the memory, Dalton kneeling before him. I saw a boy with brown eyes with a crown against his head.

Elena had shown him memories again last night, his eyes bright with wonder as they spent the whole evening in her chambers together. They seemed to be making up for lost time. Her heart pained for him, but if anyone would get them out of this disaster, it was Dalton.

She smirked as she had watched Dalton squirm when his gaze fell upon Charmaine in the courtyard with Randolph. The Prince was infatuated with her presence, so much so, that he could not stand still. His power radiated off of him like he was a newborn, unable to control it for a second. That thread of control he had snapped and there was no reeling him in.

Elena had gotten good. No longer did she fear an outburst or accident among her own court. She had mastered control before the gifts themselves had reignited. *Except with James. That was the first time that she had flashes of memory outside of her powers of healing being used.*

But she pushed that out of her memory now.

None but Cyril, Dalton, and her mother knew that she, too, had received gifts from the Kings of Old. No doubt that was why she was paired with Dalton and forced into this marriage. If the other Kingdoms also had heirs with insurmountable power, they would need an alliance, and a good one at that. She had been wondering about the Seventh...

"We are here," James whispered in her ear, breaking up her thoughts.

They strode into the ballroom. For the first time, she realized how well she matched the castle walls. Her gown was white, irritating to her as it was that James wore the same color. The design was strapless and fitted at the bodice. The bottom half was a full train, similar to a dress she would wear if she were attending a ceremony.

In a way, she was.

Her informal funeral.

Elena vowed silently to herself that she would get them out of this. Dalton did not want her, and he sure was not someone who did what he was told. They would escape this, and she would see her destiny fulfilled.

She heard Dalton before she saw him. His white garb was regality at its best. She stifled a snort thinking of how much he must have resisted wearing it. Dalton never wanted to wear the crown, but he failed to remember that he *was* the crown. Upon seeing her, his face darkened, but his blue eyes maintained their cool. He did not resent her; he resented this. This engagement.

Upon seeing James attached at her arm, he smiled, scheming. "Welcome, my love. And James."

Before she could answer, Lawton walked in with Charmaine. Dalton tried to mask his emotions, but resistance was futile. His eyes brightened and his lips quivered. His hands went to his sides and began to shake.

Cian save us.

Elena instinctually strode over to him, beckoning James to stay there for a moment. She may not want to marry him, but the last thing they needed was another ice storm inside the castle because Charmaine looked beautiful in her white gown.

Her eyes were sad as they landed on Dalton. Elena cursed herself for playing the role for a second, hurting both of the Grimes siblings. She would have to find a way to talk to her later, sort things right. But not now.

Charmaine strode to the seat labeled with her name. Randolph strode in next, his garb a regality without the title. He was breathtaking, but he followed Ronan too blindly. He was taken with his role, rather than the man he *really* was. Elena saw those tattoos too. The mark of the Seventh…

She smirked at Dalton's icy gaze as Randolph kissed Charmaine's hand and helped her sit at the table, sitting next to her after she took a seat.

"Come, fiancé," Elena said, her tone clipped.

Elena and Dalton sat directly across from them, her hand fighting frostbite as she clenched his. The cold was blistering, but she would not let go of her friend.

Elena whispered into Dalton's ear, "Keep it together."

He nodded and took a deep breath. James sat next to Lawton at the end of the table, and the King and Queen strode in to sit on either end.

Ten Kingdoms save us all.

"Thank you all for joining us this evening for such a wonderful celebration, for dear Elena and Dalton."

Dalton let go of her hand, cool instead of frozen, as he chuckled softly. She held her breath, praying he would keep it together.

"Oh, dear father, yes. What a wonderful way to celebrate a marriage that neither party is interested in, nor cares to be a part of." He threw back the champagne that had been on the table before they arrived, smirking at his own undignified behavior.

Ronan did not fall for the bait. He took a deep breath, steadying his smile as he read the horror across other's faces at the table. Only Randolph seemed poised, his fingers tracing Charmaine's atop the table. A public display of affection.

Elena wanted to leave so badly.

Dalton noticed. "Randolph, good sir." He threw back Elena's glass of champagne, the bubbly alcohol spilling down the front of his mouth like a savage.

Queen Aine looked at him in horror. Randolph met his gaze, unfazed by this behavior.

"Randolph, will you take Miss Grimes here like you take my father?"

James stiffened and Elena held her breath. *Was Dalton trying to die tonight?*

She flashed him a warning look as if to say "*Leave it alone.*"

He ignored her.

"What do you mean, Dalton?" It was Charmaine who spoke.

Horror flashed across his eyes. *Surprise.* He did not expect her to comment.

He leaned closer, willing himself to be cruel. To push his real persona away. "Will Randolph beg for redemption from you, like he did my father?"

James stood up, and Elena along with him.

"Dalton," Queen Aine spat.

Elena knew as well as anyone in court that the Queen had no love left for her second child, and the fact that she had even uttered his name had the room silent.

Dalton smashed a fist onto the table, leaving a sheet of ice in his wake. "How dare you speak to me like you love me, Aine."

Charmaine stood up, putting down the glass of champagne which she had just sipped. Horror spread across her face, blatantly irritated at Dalton. Her violet eyes brimmed with rage, but Elena guessed that Charmaine had no idea what Dalton truly referenced. Not many were privy to the torture that Dalton had suffered over his life.

Charmaine lifted her pointer finger to the door, all command in her voice as she gritted out one word that had Dalton scurrying like a child. "Now."

As they left, neither of them turned to look at those who remained at the table. Elena was shocked at the forwardness of the moment. Not many women had the courage to stand up to Dalton's nonsense.

Elena pieced together that their conversation earlier had gone well.

Guards followed them as Dalton exploded past them, waving them to stay away. The doors locked down the hall as dinner was brought to the table.

"Dig in," King Ronan said.

⬧

FORTY-THREE

Dalton caught her arm, following her as she tried to divert him.

"Charmaine," he yelped as she turned suddenly, entering the throne room. If they were going to have another conversation, she did not need the spectacle of it happening in her chambers. Again.

"Dalton," she said, exasperated, closing the doors behind her. "This is not you. That was not you. It is not your heart."

"You cannot possibly deny whatever is going on here, between us. This… *feeling*," Dalton spat. A familiar coldness returned to the throne room now that they were out of the bustle of the dining room. He pointed his finger at the door, and launched his frozen power at the lock, sealing it shut. "Or is it that your doting Knight has filled your head with the lies of my father, that you have come to resent me just for existing?"

"Resent you?" she said accusingly. Fire began to burn within her.

Gods, he was frustrating.

"I understand that my position makes things

complicated," Dalton started, pacing back and forth with his hands interlaced behind his back. His lean arms shifted beneath his formal dress wear uncomfortably. His breathing was uneven. Strenuous.

"Complicated?" she shouted. "You cannot be serious. This—"

"And I never formally declared any sort of intention or indication of my feelings for you. I cannot explain to you what I feel when I am around you. It is beyond any personal connection… this draw..." he continued, still not looking at her.

"Dalton," she said, pinching between her eyebrows as if to obliterate herself out of this conversation.

He continued to ignore her. "I have been thinking for some time. I understand that our moment in your chambers was inappropriate—"

That was enough. She interrupted him, shouting, "Dalton! Ten Kingdoms, Dalton, why can't you just be normal—"

He interrupted her, his voice like living death. "I do not know how to be normal."

Her soul prickled with blind irritation, despite how frightening his tone had become. She understood what he said, and she knew she was being unfair, but she was not sure how to help him. Pain bristled off of him and she desperately wanted to relieve him of it. He had been through so much, but she had been through a lot as well. Hurt flowed out of her freely too, whether he realized it or not.

She had lost everything, and all she wanted was for someone to be there for her. She was distanced from her brother. Randolph was trying to get closer to her, but she could tell he withheld a plethora of secrets. The only forthcoming individual in her life stood before her, and yet he could not express to her what was going on in that charming head of his.

And it was maddening.

She took a deep breath, washing the chaos that stirred within her away. "Then why do you not at least try?"

He laughed. He actually laughed. His white hair spilled wildly in front of his eyes, unveiling him as broken and disheveled. "Do you think I ever wanted this?" He gestured around the room.

Charmaine could not bring herself to reply. Her mind wandered to the first night she had seen him. He seemed so together and appeared to embrace all that had ruined her. She had been shocked by him, his cadence in conversation and easygoing nature. He had been ambitious in his moments alone with her, speaking of a better world and talking to what she most deeply desired: peace. But this boy in front of her now had none of what she had found so charming. This boy before her was brazen, irrational, and so pent-up with unrelenting chaos that Charmaine could sense the chill radiating off of him.

She had never wanted to understand him more.

"Wherever I go, chaos follows me. I never asked for any of it, Char. I do not bloody want it. I do not want this crown. I do not want this *life*." He fisted his hair, the curls snow white against his pale hand. "I have only wanted to be loved, Charmaine. My father has always looked at me like an object. I was his heir, a son who could carry on his legacy. But when my power awoke, I was a threat. I was better than him. He has done more to harm me than to better me."

She gasped. "He hurt you?"

"He never laid a hand on me. He has been very

explicit at that, but I don't see a difference. Neither does Elena." His eyes glistened with tears, but he was strong. He did not break eye contact as he spoke. "My own mother has not looked at me with love since my sister was taken. She does not care for me. She hates the reminder that her second born is everything that her daughter could not be. I am alive. I am powerful. And my sister is dead."

"Dalton, I am so sorry."

He waved her off, not accepting her apology, even though she meant every word. "You insinuate that I am abnormal, and you would be correct to do so. I may be a Prince, but this life was not given to me. I forgive and forget because I have people who kept me alive. Cyril kept me alive—mind, body, and soul."

The throne room was suddenly icy, bitter. It was hard to breathe. Focusing, she took three deep breaths. *In and out. In and out. In and out.*

"Charmaine, I do not want the power that runs through my veins, especially when it brings me this much pain." The cold air came out of his nostrils in puffs as he forced breath.

"This happens frequently?" Her lips began to tingle slightly, and she touched them with her pointer finger, figuring it was the numbness of the air taking hold.

He blinked twice. Upon entering this room, his eyes were wild, troubled with something deeper. Now they spoke of the horrors of his past. She had no idea, and she was guilty of being a terrible friend. "More frequently as of late."

"Has anyone noticed?"

A small smirk returned to his face. However, it did not lessen the freeze around them. His smile was tame, reeled in by the fear that still lingered in his eyes.

Running his hand through his hair, he said, "Did you

know I was born with raven hair like my father? 'A spitting image of him' the nobles used to say. My mother in particular was always commenting on how I looked just like him."

Charmaine nodded, not in agreement, but to show him she was listening.

Dalton paced, the winter surge around them not bothering him. "When I was ten years old, I awoke one morning to a rather large gray streak in my hair. Upon seeing me at breakfast, my parents were stricken with fear that I had been cursed." He chuckled at the distant memory, physically waving it off as he placed his hands on his hips in defiance of it. "They must have brought in every healer in the Kingdom. From border to border. Nobody could figure out why day after day, week after week, my features began to shift from the darkness of my father to... well, how I am today." He gestured to himself, shamed by the thought of his difference.

You are beautiful.

"After many months of agony and my parents watching over me like I was dying," he started. A sudden bitterness overtook his voice. "I was sent by my mother's grand thinking to the Tenth Kingdom."

"To the Thinkers."

"To the Thinkers," he chided back, a thin frost appearing at the ends of his hair. He did not seem to notice. "When I arrived-begrudgingly, I might add-I was taken to Thinker Eben. My personal favorite. After much meditation, medication, and what felt like hours of staring into his crystal ball, he revealed to me my destiny."

Spitting the word destiny, she noticed his fingers were beginning to have ice on the tips. "Dalton..." she started, not wanting to bring attention to it if he had not yet noticed.

How often did this happen to him? I felt it before, saw storms and ice, but never like this.

"Do you remember what I told you... that day... that we..." he stammered, his eyes pleading for confirmation of not what she had heard, but what they had done.

When they had kissed.

"Yes," she managed to get out, trying to avoid looking at his freezing appendages.

"A King of the Ages. The true king. My sovereignty is undeniable," he said, making a mockery of what she imagined to be Thinker Eben's voice.

"Are you saying you do not believe it?" she asked in a whisper. She would have laughed if it were not so cold. And if she were not thinking back to her mother's own foretelling. Before she could recall it, she pushed it away and focused on the broken boy before her.

"It does not explain why I am the way I am." Rage flowed through his voice.

"Dalton," she gasped out. Her vocal cords strained against the frozen tundra that had become the throne room. "Dalton. It is so... cold."

His head snapped up, looking her over, noticing for the first time what he had created. What he had done. "Ten Kingdoms..."

"H-how do you stop it?" she asked, fighting her teeth chattering. She would not leave him in there to his thoughts. He needed a friend. He needed her.

"I do not know," he said, sadness covering his eyes. He gazed down at himself in wonder and disgust. "It has never gotten this bad before... Well, actually, it did once..."

"Look at me," she said, motioning for him to come closer.

"Charmaine," he said, unsure of her motives.

"Come look at me, Dalton."

He walked toward her, the frost on his hair now droplets of ice, his strides filled with an uncertainty that was not his persona.

"Charmaine, I am—" he started.

In response, she lifted her arms slowly, and touched his jawline. He closed his eyes. The visible breath came out of his nose slowly now. She knew what she had to do, but she knew it was wrong.

She had no future with the King of Snow.

But she kissed him anyway.

Their mouths collided in a soft embrace, his frozen power falling away from him with every touch. She was undoing him, and he was her undoing. Where their last kiss was a blizzard, destroying everything in its path, this was the first snow of the season. New, beautiful, and a promise of something new. Her heart ached with the sensation; this was wrong. But she could not stop.

He knew it too. His hands no longer felt frozen against her waist. His breath was no longer visible in the air before him. His hair now clung to him, defrosted and soaking wet.

He smiled, continuing to kiss her jawline and moving down her neck to her collarbones. The purple bodice of her dress suddenly tight and hot against his torso. Just standing there sent chills all over her body, even though his power had been deescalated. She did not want him to stop. She never wanted him to stop.

He groaned her name, and in response, she found her hands running through his wet hair, desperate for him to touch her more.

Without warning, he pulled back.

She leaned closer to him again, her arms still

interlaced around his neck. "Dalton, I will not break."

"It is not you I am worried about breaking," he told her. He used his pointer finger to lift her jaw so that he looked directly at her. "Charmaine." He breathed out, his eyes glassy at the words left unsaid between them.

"We cannot do this again," she said in one breath, her mind fuzzy.

"Talk to me, Char. Please," he said into her ear as she stood up, putting physical distance between them.

"You are the future King of the First Kingdom," she stated, lifting her gaze begrudgingly to meet his. She did not have to look in a mirror to know her violet eyes were filled with pain.

He nodded in reply, acknowledging his title.

"You are engaged, Dalton. A match fit for the century. A way to fight off the mercenaries." A justification for that dinner, spewing the nonsense of the King.

"Do you even know him?" he asked her. There was no bitterness in his voice, no vengeance, and she knew who he was asking about.

"I hope he will let me in one day," Charmaine whispered. It was the truth.

"Do you feel a draw to him?" he asked more pointedly as it began to flurry in the throne room again.

Looking up in wonder, she answered honestly, "No, I do not."

His features softened with relief. The snow that began to fall around them was beautiful, crisp, and a promise of a new season. Of a new life.

"I cannot break off friendship, and you cannot defy your father. I do not want to arouse suspicion, and Randolph is a good man... I care about him."

"And I cannot break off mine. Not while I do not

318

understand *why* my father is doing this," he said, that near-perfect playful smile appearing on his face.

She thought of Princess Elena, her desire for something more, her acceptance of her duty to her kingdom. She did not love him, not in the way she needed to. She thought if she were there right now, she would cheer Dalton on, begging to have herself released from the clutches of their parents.

"I plan to defy my father, Charmaine." The flurries of the room stuck to his eyelashes. "I will defy kingdoms, as is my birthright. I am better when I am around you. In the short time that I have been around you, I have been in more control than I ever was with Cyril… and more out of control. Gods bless him."

Admiration filled within her. The future King of the First thought of her as an equal. A counterpart to his power, a fuse detonator.

"Charmaine Grimes, this is not a proposal, but a promise," he said, a chuckle escaping his beautiful mouth. He plucked one of the Godly rings off of his finger, a simple band with a blue sapphire atop it, and held it between his thumb and index finger.

"I promise to stop being so Gods-damned moody. I promise to do everything I can to understand our connection. I promise to be not just your King, but your friend, in any capacity that might be. I cannot go another day in this castle or in this Kingdom without telling you that you are all I think about when we are apart. I can feel you. I can feel where you are. I can feel my power being quelled by you. I need you to train with me, and Cyril, of course. I need you to be mine." He kissed the top of the ring. The stone glittered against the light snowfall around them.

He gazed up at her. "That is, if you will accept me for all that I am."

⁕

Dalton and Charmaine awoke tangled in the silk sheets of her chambers. Dalton had no idea how long they had spent together, telling one another stories in wonder and talking about whatever this was. They had just fallen asleep, so pure in the nature of friendship.

Dalton was suddenly ill, as if the wine from last night had an agenda for vengeance. But he had not been drunk, for he only drank two glasses at dinner. He was not much of a drinker to begin with, afraid of what it would do to him, since he spent so much of his time within the confines of solitude.

But why did it feel as if I did drink too much?

He sat up carefully, afraid of waking her up. He smiled, for every emotion that he had been feeling since she had arrived had come to fruition. There was no reckoning and no going back for him.

He made a move to stand, and his head throbbed instantaneously. He walked over to her desk. The wine glasses they had ordered their servants bring them were still full of the liquid they poured.

How was I such a mess if I hadn't continued drinking?

As if in answer, the door creaked open slightly, revealing a livid Cyril standing at its keep. His eyes were flaming, but his facial features remained soft.

Ten Kingdoms, this is great.

"What?" Dalton whispered as he made his way over to him.

"What do *you* mean, 'what'? Come here, boy."

Dalton stepped outside to see him holding two wine

glasses, the chalices that they had been using last night at dinner. "Are you trying to partake in round two?" Dalton said, laughing.

His face was grave. "No, not with this wine." He gestured to the inside of the glass, where there was a root of a plant sitting at the bottom of the glass.

"Root of the lily," Dalton whispered, his hand going directly to his face.

"Do you remember what it does?"

"Who drank from those glasses last night?"

"Dalton..." His tone was warning, as if Cyril did not want to admit to Dalton what he knew. What they both knew.

"Ten Kingdoms!" Dalton yelled before covering his mouth with his hand.

Why was he so obnoxious sometimes?

"Cyril..."

Root of the lily was an extremely powerful potion. It worked quickly, for it dulled the senses and made the user indulge in inebriated decision-making. The way they had both acted at dinner... Dalton knew that could not all have been a side effect of the root.

That kiss had been done of their own free will—he knew it.

Hadn't it?

"By the looks of things, it seems as if whoever planted the lily root knew what they were doing."

"Who could have done this?" Dalton said, sinking down the wall behind him.

Cyril sat next to him. "You think all is lost this morning because of this hidden reality. Whatever happened between you two, you know I cannot condone right now. You think the world is less beautiful now, don't you? Given the hideousness of a potion. But boy, beauty is not the standard of our world. Don't you understand? It is the treasure; that perfection defines us because we think that is what defines success. We think it defines the traits that lead us to becoming a better part of ourselves. But that is not the truth at all. It is the moments when we rise above our flaws that define us, and trust me, boy, you have many."

Cyril shook his head as the door parted slightly, as if there were more he wanted to say. Dalton saw the black hair and curls before he heard her voice. He had to tell her the truth, of course, for this was a disaster even he had not foreseen.

"Charmaine..." Dalton said, standing up hastily and his head pounding as a result.

"I will leave you to it," Cyril said, choosing now as the time to back out of his life.

Dalton gave him a vulgar gesture before they reentered her chambers.

"Charmaine, I need you to know that—"

"I heard you both. You are not very quiet."

"And?"

"And I suppose the lily root took hold of both of us last night." She barely looked at him as she said it.

Was she disappointed, or rather, embarrassed?

"There's nothing I—"

She cut him off, lifting her hand in warning. "You have shown me incredible kindness and surprised me beyond my wildest imagination. You brought me *hope* for this Kingdom once you assume the throne. You are a good man, Dalton, and I... I would never want to stop you from fulfilling your duties."

"Nothing I said—" he stopped and quirked up a smile, proud of the way she was taking control of the situation. Proud of the way she was taking control of her life. He took her hands. "Nothing I said was a lie."

"But how could I know that? You have been locked away all these years. How do I know you are genuine with me? I am laying myself out for you, Dalton. It was improper enough that we did what we... did."

The kiss. The falling asleep in her chambers. Talking for hours.

"Do you have regrets?"

"I have apprehensions." She took off the ring, which he had gifted her last night, and held it out for him to take back.

He took a deep breath, for this was going much better than he expected. "Then let me break them," he said, taking the ring and sliding it back onto her finger. "Keep it. I like the way it looks on you."

IV

THE KING OF SNOW

FORTY-FOUR

Queen Aine had not made eye contact with her husband in five years.

Even now, his hand was braced against her own, but there was no *looking* at one another. They lost the luxury of love and lust many years ago, when they had made the gravest mistake of their lives. It cost them their Kingdom, and more importantly, their children.

"This is bad, Aine," King Ronan grumbled as his hand ran anxiously through his raven hair.

Normally, Aine would not describe anything related to Ronan as nervous, but things had changed so much as of late. The arrival of those two from Brinn... Their son being unleashed...

Despite Ronan hating her and Aine hating herself, she tried to calm him. "Worse than the mercenaries attacking our people? Making you look like—"

"Damn what I look like! He is *here*. He has come for what is rightfully his. He will stand at nothing, let no moment go by, while he takes the world by the throat and throttles it over the edge." He released her, pacing back and forth holding his crown in his hands.

"Do we have time?" Her voice was barely a whisper.

He shook his head, still not looking at her. "I thought we had more time, with the girl and boy from Brinn. I thought we could convince the commoners to stand against the threat. To put a name to the discourse which has overtaken our narratives."

"We never tried to right it," she whispered. It was admittance to all the worst things she ever did. The commitment her husband had made that she had not tried to dissuade him from. It had cost her everything, and she deserved to lie in ruin.

"What is the point when you are not worth redemption?" he spat, throwing his crown on the ground with a crash.

"Do we have time?" she asked again, even though she did not care to know the answer.

She hoped her death would be painful. It would be what she deserved. Her poor Carinthya… Her poor Dalton. She deserved all that was coming to her, and she was ready to embrace it with open arms.

"I need to speak to the King," Ronan whispered before stalking out of the room, leaving Aine once again alone, without even a look.

FORTY-FIVE

lena's servants braided her flaming hair into one long rope that ran parallel to her spine. The braids started at the scalp of her head, near her hairline, and grew methodically until they met at the apex of her neck. It was heavy, pulling on her hairline with an effort that already gave her a headache.

She laughed, hysterical almost, for today would be the ultimate headache.

Her servant from the Fourth, Meredith, painted her eyelids with a silver mixture that left her dark skin sparkling. She looked like starlight. She wondered if her new husband would love the homage to the First Kingdom, or if he would be disgusted that she flaunted her new status. She braced for the latter.

Her eyes watered, but she pushed it down, down, and down.

Her husband.

Her mind thundered with the prophecy that rang on repeat in her ears. She knew in her soul that she was not the Violet Queen. She was not the woman who would save everyone in the Ten Kingdoms.

However, as true as she knew it to be, she could not seem to find the words to tell anyone otherwise.

King Ronan was madness reincarnate. He was all that she had heard of King Finn from the reigning days of Queen Ciara. It was no wonder to Elena that Ciara had killed her father, who forced her hand one too many times in the name of self-entitlement. She promised herself that if Dalton ever gave the word, she would murder him herself.

Her heart skipped a beat when she thought of her husband-to-be. The pounding in her chest was not for lust or romantic gain; rather, it was out of pain. She could feel Dalton's pain always, whether they were throwing herbs at the castle walls and running amok, or sobbing in the arms of one another. That was a part of her healer powers, and she was always keen to heal Dalton.

There was always pain for him.

Wiping her eyes clean from the water that began to build and breathing in a silent sob, Elena vowed never to be the cause of Dalton's pain. Out of all the vows she was expected to make today, that was the one she would never break.

Her hands shook violently as she reached for her glass of water. The usual poise that she carried vanished with the confidence that normally beset her shoulders.

She was completely and utterly broken at this point, submissive to the whims of others.

"You look beautiful, Princess," Meredith murmured, her blonde hair shining in the light.

Elena could not disagree. The makeup highlighted every curve of her face and the dress left little to the imagination. The white fabric of her wedding gown hugged every muscle and curve that she had worked for over the years. The simplistic nature of the gown held her accountable to the way she aspired to carry herself. The ensemble was not a distraction; rather, it was a mirror to the inner workings of her soul.

She was the girl who would kill for her friend's happiness. She saw her destiny and that of the child she did not understand. She was laid bare for the whole world to see, all Ten Kingdoms to pass judgement on her for marrying the Prince of the First in an advantageous match.

She hated herself for it.

Before she could reply to Meredith, thanking her for her hard work, the doors to her chambers opened slightly. She saw wild black hair and thin fingers closing the door behind her. Her breath hitched and she ushered her servant out of her chambers with a maddening dash.

"Leave us," she commanded. The voice of a Queen.

James Grimes stood before her, his cheeks flushed and his eyes alight with fire.

"Elena," he said, his eyes trailing up and down every inch of her body. She suddenly felt hot and exposed, the fear of what she would go through laid bare before her in an agonizing display of wants and needs.

She was brazen and cold and fearful. She could not play the games of politics when under the spotlight. All she could do was hold her head upright and try not to burn with the rest of the world. She wanted to serve her country well. She wanted to change her world for the better. She needed to do the bidding of her mother. She needed to serve the wishes of the First Kingdom. But what she really wanted and what she really needed? He stood before her now with hungry eyes and a wild heart.

"Why did you come?"

He flinched at her tone.

"I came to check on you..." His voiced sounded different. Defeated.

"I need you to step out of the way," she whispered, afraid of her internal fire melting the longer she stood before him.

He did not move.

She took a step closer, her hands shaking and her mind wary. She did not know how much strength she had left. *How much willpower do you need against the one you want the most?*

"Move," she hissed.

He did not move.

She took another step closer. Her back was sweating now, her breathing unsteady. She reached for her water glass she had set down on the table and gripped it with all her might.

She needed to hold something to stop her hands from shaking.

He did not take his eyes off her face, that violet sadness and understanding full-fledged.

He still did not move.

She closed her eyes as she walked toward the door, faster now. He let her pass as she reached an arm toward the door. She made contact with the golden handle as she simultaneously felt his familiar touch grace her elbow.

She screamed as she whipped around, realizing before him what he had done.

Her power reached out, flinging itself in full force at him. *She did not want to be touched. She had not been in control this whole time...*

In the blink of an eye, she was sobbing and yelling,

dropping to the floor with a thud as she reached for his arms. There was nothing she could do to comfort him, to make this *fine*…

She looked at him as he turned his head to meet her— a long, jagged slash along his cheek the only reminder that she was a true monster.

Her hands trembled violently, throwing the glass that contained water to the ground with a clang. He touched his cheek, the new cut that lived there as a reminder of what she could do.

Of what she could manipulate if she lost control.

"I am sorry," she huffed. Her hands ran through her braid, causing it to come loose at the ends. Her control was slipping, all sense of what she was supposed to be lost forever to the power of her innate abilities.

She was all power and had no control.

He stood up. His eyes flashed, not with betrayal or anger, but a sadness so deep that it froze her blood.

"James," she croaked. Tears poured down her face.

He did not look back as he walked out of her chambers.

Dalton was losing his shit.

He paced around his chambers. The anguish of what was to come raced throughout his mind. His rage was thunderous, uncontrollable. He stepped on the cobblestones beneath his feet and heard the *crunch* of the ice he was creating. Normally, this would pose concern for him, but now, it was almost therapeutic. These little bursts of his power seemed to take the edge off of his overall demeanor. He pressed a finger to his lips, biting on his fingernails in a maddening display of irritation.

Not only was today his wedding day, but he could not get Charmaine out of his mind.

And he wanted to murder whoever gave him that dose of lily.

His mind did somersaults, twisting and turning with the memory of her touching him. His cheeks blushed even now, his lips hot and raw as he recalled the way that she had looked at him. The way she had said his name made his power crackle throughout the castle. Even the memory of them sleeping in bed together, tangled in the silk sheets that graced her chambers, had him writhing hours later.

She had smelled of honey and lavender, a fresh gust of wind, and the fires that had destroyed her town. He wanted to hold her and get all the details of her life out of her. He wanted to punish everyone who had harmed her. He wanted to know every minute detail of how she had come to this castle and how their fates unassumingly seemed to be intertwined in a whole scheme. It was maddening to him. He did not understand before, but he understood now. She had something about her that was special. Something that set her apart. She was a part of a scheme that he had no part in planning, and it drove him *insane.*

And none of it had been bloody real.

He wanted to scream and unleash his power all over this castle. He wanted to go to her and find her and tell her that he wished the whole thing were real.

It had felt real to him.

But today was his wedding day, and he was losing his shit.

He looked out the window as he continued to walk in circles. The sun began to set in a hue of purples and pinks. Normally, he admired it, but he had nothing to applaud today.

He would be married—to his best friend.

He knew he could have been dealt a worse fate. He could have someone like his old nursemaid, Velanceia, old and fat with hands like a man. Elena was stunning and intelligent. He never had to explain the inner workings of his mind to Elena. She anticipated every move of his like they were playing chess on the continent's stage.

But he did not think about her. She did not invade his dreams or have any sort of draw.

She was not Charmaine.

"You are pacing so much, boy, you are going to leave tracks in the cobblestones," Cyril muttered impatiently.

Dalton snorted, but continued nonetheless. "I will pay for the damages. You can tell father dearest not to fear."

Now Cyril snorted. The familiar banter that Dalton held so dear to himself caused him to slow down in his routine movements.

"Come, boy. Get your wedding garb on."

"I cannot believe you are going to make me do this," he muttered, pausing in his tracks. The ice turned to slush beneath his feet. His boots crunched on the cobblestones with the sensation of half-melted snow.

"I am not making you do anything, boy. Your father is."

"As if I need reminding," he muttered as he ran his hands through his hair. "He has gone completely mad, hasn't he?"

The question lingered in the air for a moment too long. Dalton smiled at the hesitation that befell him. Cyril opened his mouth to reply, but Dalton beat him to it.

His pointer finger raised with a salient point as he whispered, "Now if it is madness that has befallen him—"

Cyril cut him off, grabbing him by the neck of his

black tunic. Fear shone in his deep blue eyes and his lips were pushed together so hard they seemed to turn blue. "Regicide, my boy, is *not* your answer."

"Isn't it the answer to everything, though? Think about this, Cyril. If I accidentally fell into him with my dagger this evening—"

"I am serious, *boy*. You do not wish to walk the same path as Queen Ciara, or others we may know. I forbid it, and I promised King Cian that none of his ancestors would take the road of the Queen of Fury ever again."

Dalton pondered this for a moment, his eyes quizzical, but understanding. He knew there were lines that he could not cross with Cyril. The memory of Cian and Ciara was one of them.

He would never disrespect the memory of Cyril's greatest friend. As he would never disrespect the origin of his power.

"But she became Queen. She saved the world. She united it." Dalton let that passion creep into his voice, one which he reserved for matters of state. He believed in Ciara's cause and would never allow her memory to be disrespected. She brought the world to its knees and helped it back up again.

"And she paid the ultimate price. The Gods do not favor regicide, my boy. They never will." Cyril's voice was stone-cold.

"And why is that? The Gods should take a hard look in the mirror and—"

Cyril put a finger to his mouth before he got carried away.

"And they never will. It's *unforgivable,* Dalton." The way he said the word was terrifying to Dalton, instilling that primal fear he had felt only a handful of times in his life.

That same fear that flowed through his bones the first time his power erupted, when the cruel hands of the Gods touched him and awoke his gift.

"What would they do to me?" His voice was very far away, but he asked anyway. He had to know. He had to know his options.

Cyril released his shirt, realizing now that he had been clutching it so intensely it was now crinkled. "They would kill you, just like they did her."

And that was that.

Charmaine stood in the throne room holding her brother's hand. Her mind flashed with the memories of the night before, the passion and the friendship that she had felt had been *so real.*

The way he said her name last night was unlike how anyone had said it before. His hands touched her in ways she did not know a woman would want to be touched. She had never been so desired and felt so beautiful. Her cheeks even heated now, thinking of the boy who was not supposed to be seen, caressing her as if she were the only woman in the world. She almost giggled, hot with embarrassment, thinking of the way that she had touched him. Something primal had overtaken her as she took more of him than she had ever taken of a man before. She was been scared at all. If anything, she welcomed it. Relished it.

But she knew it was a lie.

She stayed passive when she awoke in the morning to find him sitting in the real throne in her room, facing the window. She knew by his posture alone that something was horribly wrong.

"Dalton?" she asked.

He spun around quickly, his smile dashing, but not quite meeting his eyes. For a future King, he did not hide his emotions well. Rather, he wore his emotions on his sleeve.

But she would not tell him that. Not now, and not ever.

And he told her. He showed her the glasses and sworn to her that he did not mean to take advantage of her. That it was completely inappropriate for a Prince to do such provocative things with a common girl. He would soon be married, and he did not want any harm to come to her.

Her power slipped out and she knew without looking that her toes had gone invisible. She held steadfast, not breathing, and not even flinching as she tried to regain any semblance of control.

She refused to falter.

Not in front of him.

She opened up her mouth once he had finished apologizing. She knew he was waiting for her to say something. Anything.

The words escaped her then as if she were in an empty room, "I wish it was real."

She tuned back in to the present. James's hand was soft and cold, waking her up from her feverish memory as he stroked her hand. He seemed different tonight. The casual fire that always burned within him had gone out. She noticed when he strode into her chambers earlier that a slash had appeared on his face. There was no blood, but the cut was clean and delicate. It was as if the wound had not wanted to be deep and had not meant to cause harm.

She would ask him about it later.

As her thoughts continued to run wild, trumpets blared throughout the halls. She braced herself, taking a deep breath, and leaned her head against the shoulder of her brother.

She had to be there for him as much as he had to be there for her.

✦

Randolph swung his sword in the courtyard. His muscles ached for relief. The power he wanted to relinquish so badly had built up to the point of no return. He slipped out of the ceremony once the trumpets started, beaming for the outside world and a relief from the madness which seemed to be overtaking his King every day.

He had to fight. He had to train. He had to do *something* to keep history from repeating itself.

Memories of his past flooded in and out of his mind without any semblance of rhyme or reason. His power reaching a tipping point was too much for him. He had been standing in the throne room to watch a royal wedding, and was nearly knocked on his ass by a memory of his life before. Thankfully, this was not the first time it had happened to him, so he knew what to do. He breathed in and out, releasing enough smoke to take the edge off.

The second the focus was on the happy couple, he fled.

It was like his history would not give him the peace he deserved. *Did the Gods think I needed to suffer more?*

He slashed his sword against the invisible enemy once again, the wind whipping as he breathed through the motions. The blade glistened in the moonlight and vibrated with the familiar hum of training.

He had been so stupid earlier. He had actually gone to talk to Cyril. To see if there was anything in the future, or if he had anything to report on. Randolph hated the

Thinkers by proxy, but he did not hate Cyril. He merely avoided him. For Cyril knew the truth about everything, so why would he subject himself to talking about it?

When he arrived outside of Cyril's chambers, Cyril was gone. Randolph knocked twice and gave up.

Just showing up at Cyril's door was progress, so that would have to do for now.

As he retreated back to whatever he was doing, he heard Cyril and Dalton speaking in the chambers nearby. *The Prince's chambers.* The words rang through his mind. He heard them so clearly. Cyril was discussing Queen Ciara, and how King Ronan's fate was not Dalton's problem. Randolph did not know the trajectory of the conversation, but it was enough to deter him from visiting Cyril anytime soon.

If Cyril could not provide guidance to Dalton with his father, he would be no use for Randolph's journey to redemption.

Randolph lashed out at the air again, his body strategic and brutal. He breathed through his power, heating up as he pushed it down further and further. He had picked these strategies up as a child, back when he was afraid of hurting those he loved. He noticed the Prince had started doing the same thing, and Randolph was silently grateful that he had picked them up too.

Randolph would have told Dalton of them years ago if he had known the Prince struggled as such. The Ten Kingdoms did not need two rulers to bottom out and meet the same fate as the Queen of Fury.

FORTY-SIX

andolph could not hide his surprise when Thinker Eben came to his chambers to retrieve him to meet with Ronan. The King had not wished to speak to him since he went on his mission that brought Charmaine and James to the castle. He seemed different in the past few years. The madness and cruelty from within had taken over with each waking moment. He was losing it, most said, and that was for certain.

Randolph thought he had already lost it, but it was his handling of Gwendolyn which solidified it. Randolph had been in denial for a long time, refusing to see the animal behind the King's persona. Despite everything, Ronan saved Randolph's life by allowing him to serve there. But there was a line, and Ronan was desperately approaching it. Ronan had zero drive to rid this world of the mercenaries, it seemed. Rather, he tried to pawn off the issue onto others. There was no accountability, no leadership. Only instilling fear and hatred among the aristocracy for something that could not be controlled. *Magic.* That was all he had done with his rule.

Randolph set his jaw as he entered the throne room to

find King Ronan pacing. He wore all black, a jeweled crown atop his head, even though there was nobody there to see it but Randolph. This was no ornamental display of power for Ronan. He was the King every given moment of every day. He was murmuring to himself as well. Randolph caught no part of it except "He is here."

Why was I so nervous? It is not as if this is the first time I have been alone with Ronan.

The King looked up as he heard Randolph's boots clicking on the marble floors. His eyes had dark circles under them. Clearly, he had not been sleeping. The closer Randolph looked, the worse the King looked.

"My boy," he said. Even his voice seemed off. He looked haunted.

"Your Majesty," Randolph said, bowing his head slightly. He tried to push away the encroaching memories of the first time he had seen Ronan. It was only three years ago, but they had both been so much younger then.

"I needed to speak with you urgently, for I am leaving tonight." The King looked around as if he were being watched, despite them being the only two in the room.

"Leaving?" Randolph asked, unable to hide the shock in his voice. The King of the First could not just *leave*.

"I need to go to the bordering villages and see the mercenaries' desolation. I need to rally the people, and we need to *stop* this."

Randolph's jaw dropped before he could stop it. *He wanted to stop this? After all this time? There had been so many killings and attacks over the past few years from the enemy that could never be given a face.*

"Why now?" Randolph asked, his voice curt.

He was surprised at himself for being so forward, but something about the King's disheveled appearance made him feel he could speak out right now without repercussions. Ronan was off and Randolph would take advantage of it.

"After the meeting I am about to call, I am going because we are at an impasse. There have been too many years of attacks, brutality... my poor little girl..." Ronan ran a jeweled hand through his raven hair, demonstrating erratic behavior which Randolph had pointedly ignored until this very meeting.

Never did the King speak of Carinthya. Ever. *What in the Ten Kingdoms was going on?*

Ronan continued. His blue eyes pleaded as he put his hands on Randolph's shoulders. "You need to watch over my son. Make sure he does what he is assigned to do this evening until I return."

"Assigned to do? Your Majesty, I do not..." Randolph was speechless.

This behavior was unheard of from Ronan. Delegating his power while he went on an exploration? It was completely out of character.

And Randolph could not imagine Dalton listening to a word he said.

"Be a King-maker, Sir Randolph. I am sure you remember how."

Randolph stepped back. Ronan's forwardness shoved him backward.

"How dare you bring up my circumstances," Randolph whispered. His hands were red hot at the fury which consumed his bloodlust.

Ronan released his shoulders, recognition igniting on his features. "Kings do not let other Kings fall, Randolph Eniar. You will do well to remember that."

Randolph's hands cooled slightly, anger subsiding

with every breath he took. *In and out, in and out, in and out.*

He took a pointed step toward the maddened King, his hand on the hilt of his sword. He lifted the weapon slowly. The sound of the blade against its holster upon removal was the only sound that could be heard in the room. He held it to the King's temple, careful not to even cut a hair off of his head.

"Kings do not let Kings lay waste to Kingdoms they no longer deserve," Randolph spat before sheathing the sword into his belt once more.

Ronan laughed, bristled and unhinged. Randolph turned and started to stalk toward the doors, done with whatever madness this was when he paused.

Ronan breathed deeply and said, "I told you this years ago, boy, and I will tell you again. You did the world a favor."

And with that, Randolph was gone.

FORTY-SEVEN

uckily for House Saphirrus and House Leclair, the wedding ceremony had been swift.

Dalton and Elena now sat at the foot of Dalton's bed in awkward silence. Elena's wedding dress lay across the navy and gold chairs in the corner of his chambers. It had been disregarded because neither of them cared about the ornamental symbols and relics which made up their false marriage. Ronan sent them to Dalton's chambers to consummate their marriage, to which they both nodded to the lunatic who wore the crown.

Luckily, Ronan did not care to send a party to watch. That was the custom in the First Kingdom, as it was for all the other Kingdoms, but the current ruler could ban it if they felt it appropriate.

His father was a deviant, a menace to society, but at least he had an ounce of a soul regarding this. Dalton was not one for customs. He let a small part of himself be grateful.

Dalton was surprised, shocked even, by Elena's control that she had demonstrated at the altar. It was not in Elena's nature to hold back, to bow before the incorrigible. Her face had stayed stoic, repeating the vows as if they meant something to her beyond her sworn duty. She was the eternal flame of his life, an unstoppable force, which raged from the Fourth Kingdom as a beacon of all that he wanted to be, yet could not. To Dalton, Elena was the strongest woman on the continent.

And now, he was her husband.

"This is ridiculous," she said, crossing her hands over her nightgown. Her red hair spilled down her back in a wave of fire, beautiful against the flames of the candles which sat around the room.

Dalton fell backward, lying on his bed parallel to her as he chuckled. "Glad we are on the same page, *wife*."

A hand smacked his thigh. "Do not call me that."

"Okay, my *Queen*," he said, intentionally lacing venom on the word.

There was no shame in this beautiful, best friend of his being his Queen. Dalton had no doubt that she would make a damn good one. But neither of them wanted this. The word was cursed, as were the both of them for their shit luck.

She growled, deep and low in her throat. "I will kill Ronan for this."

Dalton sat up, and concern furrowed his dark eyebrows. "Elena, I do not want you to lose your head."

"What does it matter? I am lost anyway."

Dalton brought a hand to the side of his head and rubbed his eyes, exhausted. "You know, we could work this in our favor."

She quirked up an eyebrow, her brown eyes dark. "How could we possibly make this work to our advantage? Marriage is not reversible, Dalton. We do not have that luxury as royals."

"Well, for one, it could be *worse*, Elena. You could hate me. I could be a brute. I could want a child, an heir. We need to look at the positives." He spoke truths she already knew, but he also understood her well enough to know that she needed to hear them.

"We are royals, Dalton. You might have been locked up too long to understand such a thing, but trust me when I say that we only get one shot at this. And we cannot take another."

He pressed his tongue to the back of his teeth and he made a clicking noise as he took a breath. "But, Elena, years in the box taught me to think on my feet and always be one step ahead, if not two."

"Do tell. Enlighten me, my *husband.*" She leaned against the back post of the bed, scooting to get comfortable.

"Think about the First Kingdom and all it has to offer you. I am a Prince, a believed possessed member of the royal household who has inherited King Cian's power. Father will not hurt me while that rumor circulates, especially now that I am out. I can offer you *protection,* because I will be damned if you face my fate or Gwendolyn's because of your abilities."

Elena bit the bottom of her lip nervously, but gestured for him to continue. "Go on."

He smirked, leaning closer as he went on. "You are forgetting to read the playbook, Elena. Look at the whole portrait before you judge it accurate or not. A marriage between royals *can* be terminated."

She shot forward. Her long nails ran through her hair in exasperation. "I am not willing to lose my head."

"And neither am I. I quite like it where it is. It is pretty too. I quite like my nose—"

She cut him off with a smirk brewing on her full lips. "How, in the name of the Ten Kingdoms, do we get this annulled?"

"So you can be with the Grimes boy?" Dalton had to ask.

"So we do not lose our heads because your father is *nuts*," she said curtly.

"Noted. We hold onto this marriage. We play the game. And when my father dies, for he surely will, we can claim that he was mad. Madness and declaration are things the Thinkers cannot overlook, Elena. They will have to grant our wishes. And you can go on and be with your Grimes boy, and you will be safe."

"Dalton, it could be years," she whispered, calculating in her mind every hour that she would be unwillingly shackled to her best friend.

"And we could have fun. You know, I would never force anything between us. I quite like just being your friend."

She smiled softly, her harsh exterior breaking down. "I know your heart, you weirdo."

"So, what do you think? We pass out in this bed tonight, as friends, and claim madness upon my father's death?"

She laughed softly, the hatching of her plan reminding her of all that Dalton was. He was playful and mischievous, but he was her greatest love in this world. No, it was not romantic, and it never would be. The best love was that of true being and belonging. He could offer that. And her head.

"I will be your Queen," she agreed as she wrapped her arms around her best friend in the entire world. The hate in her heart was duller than it was moments before.

"And I will be your King."

❦

FORTY-EIGHT

hen the castle fell silent, Randolph made his way back to the throne room to pay his respects to the Gods. It was not something he did often, not since he had come to the First Kingdom. But it was something which for the first time since he had arrived there that he *needed* to do. He had no urge to speak to them since he was a child, for his father had beaten the Gods out of his comforts a long time ago. He had always been taught to rely on himself, and not those who had abandoned him.

Randolph never believed that the Gods abandoned him. Looking back, they might have been there the whole time.

With a groan, Randolph shoved open the familiar doors of the throne room to unveil the white masterpiece which was the First Kingdom's center stage. Randolph crept forward, suddenly unsure of himself, to stand at the threshold of the throne room, and looked at the First Kingdom's seat of power as he fluctuated between seething anger and unbridled pride.

He touched his fingers to the bridge of his nose and squeezed gently. His tattooed fingers pulsed with a raging sensation that he had not felt in three years. Not this intensely. Randolph closed his eyes and welcomed the fire in his veins. His hands were hot to the touch, but infuriatingly refused to burn him.

He scoffed, irritation flooding his vision, as he conceded another moment when the chaos must be kept at bay.

Randolph moved toward the empty throne. The room dazzling among the moonlight and the stars. The throne, in all its marble white glory, was a beacon of all that King Cian represented in stories. He was everything a King should have been. He was loyal, fierce, and a comrade to all. His wife sacrificed her own life in order to give him a chance at a better world, no matter how long it took to build one. Randolph knew that Ciara was called the Queen of Fury for her temperament, but it was a testament to Cian that she became better for it. For him. For them. For the First Kingdom.

Randolph whispered his name; his full and true name as he bowed before the throne which started the world that he swore to protect the moment he stepped through those very doors. "I am Randolph Cian Eniar, and I pledge myself once again to serve in your memory, my beloved King," he whispered underneath the stars.

He closed his eyes as he bowed his head. His short brown hair fell forward, grazing his forehead as lightly as a feather. He lifted his brown gaze and smiled at the beauty of power and legacy. A weight lifted off of his back after speaking his full name to the wind.

He rose slowly, his knighthood armor glistening against the white reflection of the evening sky. The sword that hung from his belt clamored against the floor, shoving him violently into a vision.

✦

I stood at the threshold of the Seventh Kingdom's throne room as it began to shake. A violent fire cracked around me without warning. The flames danced at the edge of my fingertips, threatening to incinerate all that got too close. They whipped as easily as if they were the wind, devouring the oxygen in an unbearable blast of heat. The flames struck like lightning, though it did not burn the hands from which the flames escaped.

They were my hands. Hot tears poured down my face as I struggled to take a breath. Primal instinct had taken ahold of me. I was not a child in this instant, not anymore. I was possessed by the Gods. I knew it.

And the Gods did not deem themselves victims.

My hands trembled as I continued to stretch them outward. Instinct roared at me not to let go. My hands were the weapon of the world, were the words I could not say. In that moment, the sight was beautiful and raw, but sprouted such hatred in the fires I forged.

'Stay back,' I wanted to scream at my sister. She was the one I was trying to protect. She was the only reason I was willing to stand up to the King.

Stay back. Stay back. Stay back.

I breathed in the smoke as the guards in front of me choked on the black clouds. The familiar tinge of the flames bristled against my cheek, but I no longer felt the urge to cough. I no longer struggled for breath like my human counterparts did.

If anything, I was alive. I breathed in once... twice... three times. The black cloud traveled down my throat and electrified my blood. The flames grew hotter and higher, the blaze of the fires alive with a thirst for vengeance.

I screamed and relished in it, thrashing as I struggled to contain my power aimed at the guards who now backed away, afraid of being scorched. They cursed me, telling my sister that I was the child of the Evil God who had just slayed his father. A smirk appeared on my face as I tried to maintain any semblance of control. Let them think what they wanted.

Damn them all.

A child of the Evil Gods. A disgrace to my birthright. An embarrassment to the throne of the Seventh Kingdom, for which I had been destined to one day hold.

The Evil God did not kill his father.

I had.

I had committed regicide—the crime which even the Gods themselves could not forgive.

I deserved to be cursed. I might as well be one of the Evil Gods themselves.

But my sister would live. My sister would know freedom. And that was worth the cost that I was doomed to now pay.

I knew as I screamed that the flames that erupted from me were flames of my own pain. They were born of flesh and fire, a curse which had erupted upon seeing my father's hands wrap around the hilt of the accursed knife. I had been momentarily stunned at the elegance of the weapon, the jewels hanging off of it in a dazzling array of starlight against the candelabras of the Seventh's throne room.

I was dazzled before I was terrified, and now I relished all the madness that had awoken within me.

The heat cracked around me like thunder as I crushed the blade of the knife against my fingers. The blood of my hands mixed with the blood of my father. The flames did not come from fear or regret. They were flames born of sadness. Flames born out of the grief of a child who had just lost their father—their King—to a blade no longer than a finger.

I lost my father—no matter how the story would be

told—that remained at its core.

I had to do it. I had to do it. I had to do it.

I was no longer the beautiful child who had graced the halls of his father's stead.

I was no longer the Prince with the brown hair and the auburn eyes, beloved by his people.

I was no longer the child of the prophecy to rule the lands with an iron fist and a heart of glass.

I was banished. I was the spawn of the Evil Gods. I was to be forgotten. I was a murderer.

And yet, I smiled as the flames ignited my whole body, feeling peace, yet losing it all.

He touched his head to the floor, wishing to ground himself permanently in these emotions. "I am so sorry, Reine," he whispered, unable to bear the weight of the phantom crown he wore.

Randolph found himself on his knees moments later, his breath unsteady, and sweat furrowing his brow. He wiped it with the back of his hand. Not for the first time, the roses took the brunt of a distant memory. He breathed in through his nose and out through his mouth, the sensation of the cool air of reality a harsh contrast to his nightmare. He coughed slightly as he rose. His armor suddenly seemed heavier than when he had entered the room.

FORTY-NINE

harmaine stepped through the threshold of the throne room the following afternoon, no less nervous than she had been on the first day she arrived.

She walked among the noblemen and noblewomen who supported Ronan's reign, afraid that her own scent would trigger her magic and expose her for all to see. Hope blossomed within her, despite her own paranoia. Due to the draw, she knew Dalton would be there. His father had called a meeting and celebration among the castle dwellers a few hours prior, and Charmaine only dreamed that the meeting was nothing like the last they attended.

She laced her fingers, draping them behind her back as she looked down to admire her attire. She would never tire of that. A new servant came to her chambers today—Athelred, he had called himself. He seemed rather nervous, and peeked around corners within her room as if he were missing something. Charmaine did not ask what had befallen the serving boy to make him jittery, but if she had to guess, then maybe he was previously assigned to Dalton. She knew as well as anyone that he could be quite difficult.

Athelred brought her the most beautiful blue gown she had ever seen. The entirety of it was velvet, smooth, and flowed behind her like a river. The neckline was rather low, but her long hair somehow made it more modest, due to how much it covered her shoulders and back.

She turned her head from side to side, not seeing Randolph or James. She had not seen James since their spat the other day, and something did not feel right about it. She never went this long without speaking to him.

A gust of wind blew throughout the throne room as Charmaine made her way off to the side to stand among the common folk.

With a jump, a voice whispered in her ear, "No reason to draw attention to ourselves today, especially *you.*"

"Hello, Lawton," she said, trying to hide the amusement brewing in her tone.

"Who gave you that beautiful dress, darling?" he asked, looking her up and down.

"Athelred. My new serving boy brought it in for me."

Lawton looked as if he were about to burst out laughing. Instead, he said, "Dear Gods, I thought they sacked Athelred."

Before she had the chance to ask what that meant, thunder cracked among the walls of the throne room as the King made his entrance. His powerful stance was heightened by the velvet navy cloak that draped around the floor. His crown perfectly fitted above his brow, a white gold, shimmering in the sunlight. His hair was a stark contrast to his son beside him, black and cut close to his skull. The cut of a soldier, rather than The King of the First. He was a handsome man, only corrupted by his own government's inability to be successful. Like all men in power, power changed him. Not for the first time,

Charmaine saw the crippling effect it had on Dalton. The outbursts and the tundras that came out from his regular emotions…

She thought of all the whispers of her childhood about the royals. Cruel, menacing, haters of magic. Haters of people like her. Her heart skipped a beat. It was so far from the truth.

Dalton was royal, and he did not hate her.

"Welcome all. Today we plan our strike back within the next two days, which the council and I have deemed necessary. We must fight the mercenaries on all fronts. For too long, we have avoided, as a court, the horrors that lie beneath our mountain," Ronan's voice rang true throughout the halls.

Lawton snorted. Charmaine dared not to breathe.

"I have brought with me today two very important guests. Children of Brinn, the only survivors of the great attack." He gestured to her, his blue eyes blazing.

Charmaine paled, feeling Dalton's eyes glaze over her in fury as if they were saying, '*You aren't a prize to be paraded around as if you've won the war yourself.*' She dipped her head to him, as if acknowledging it was going to be okay.

"If you may." He gestured, signaling to them to tell the truth. Their story.

James stepped forward, purple eyes hot with fury. Charmaine tried to hide the resentment that flooded through her. She had not even noticed he was so close to her among the crowd.

James told most of it, embellishing where he needed to embellish, adding where he thought it advantageous, and eliminating any remnants of the story that they did not yet understand. Blood roared in her ears when she thought back to the mercenaries in Brinn, their words just as haunting now as they were then. Their insinuations that they knew her and were looking for her.

Acting on instinct, Charmaine came forward and held James's hand, her anchor in this life. This was how it always was for them—her the quiet centerpiece, all eyes on her when she was with him—but him doing all that mattered. He explained the truth with such prose that the King himself was rendered speechless.

Charmaine could not yet forgive him for not having been open with her, for changing, but she wanted him to know that she was there.

Despite being so close to her brother, finally, after what felt like years apart, Charmaine could not stop focusing on Princess Elena. Her eyes were large and full of emotion, watching her brother with such a generous care that Charmaine wished for the first time in her life to be anything other than what her power presented to her. She wanted to take away her pain. Or to destroy the engagement between Dalton and her, so she could have what her eyes said she really wanted. Charmaine guessed that it was James.

James finished speaking, releasing her hand as they took a unified step backward.

The King looked pleased, a terrifying grin spreading across his face. "Thank you, James. May I remind you all, he saved my life and my son's during the invasion. He selflessly came between us and one of those monsters, sacrificing himself for his Kingdom, although he has already lost so much."

James faintly blushed, as did Charmaine. She did not think the King would acknowledge the ultimate sacrifice that her brother almost made. She was still terrified of him, but being praised by a King was nonetheless something to be proud of.

"James, come forward, son. There is another reason I wanted you here today, boy."

Randolph stepped forward, revealing himself, his gear glistening in the reflection of the windows through the stained glass. His tattoos attracted the light, as if the flowers missed being in the sun.

"Did you know about this?" she asked Lawton pointedly.

"No," he said, clearly not pleased at the reality that, for once, he had been left out of the loop.

Randolph walked toward the King, turning around to face James. James's hands were interlaced behind his back, as the King commanded him to bow before them.

James obliged.

It was Randolph who spoke, King Ronan's hand on the shoulder of his favorite soldier. "James Grimes of Brinn, for your utmost demonstration of bravery and commitment to your Kingdom, I hereby pronounce you a member of the King's Knighthood. A brother of mine, now and forevermore."

James looked up at Randolph. From behind, she saw his shoulders relax, and understood what this meant.

Hot tears ran down Charmaine's face before she could even determine why. *Was it the fact that my brother was to be pledged in service forever to a King who only took action when it best suited him? Or because, for once in his life, James had a purpose other than me?*

James rose with the sword Randolph had been holding in his hands. Without warning, they embraced and the crowd in the room erupted into claps and praise.

Her brother was a hero.

She looked at Lawton. His eyes were squinted as if trying to understand this moment—to discredit it or find the motive.

"And now, we celebrate this new era we are about to embark on. No more fear will live among our men. Today, we start to take back the First Kingdom, and drive the mercenaries out." Ronan smiled, looking years younger than he had before. He lifted his arms and the crowd suddenly dispersed, exiting the throne room and walking toward the gardens.

Before she could say anything, James strode toward the main opening of the rose garden. As she made a move to follow him, a cold hand lightly touched Charmaine's forearm. She turned quickly, not shocked to find Dalton's deep blue gaze staring back at her. When she opened her mouth to speak, he put his pointer finger to her lips, urging her to be silent. He beckoned with his other hand to a different opening to the gardens, which they had taken the night of the first ball.

They walked together in haste, making sure to stay incognito among the crowd. As they descended the grand staircase, hardly containing their laughter, Charmaine was hit with the familiar scent of roses. She would never get over the high vines and plethora of white and red roses that adorned the walls. She decided that she much preferred pretty things to have thorns.

When they reached the bottom, Dalton paused and lifted his arms as he spun wildly.

Charmaine could not contain her laughter. "What in the name of the Ten Kingdoms are you doing?! You look like a child."

"I wish child me could see this day," he said as he continued to spin. "My father *finally* deciding to do something against this enemy who we know nothing about, and who has terrorized our people for too long."

"It was rather amazing," she whispered, suddenly feeling funny about complimenting the King.

He stopped spinning, putting his hands to his waist as he breathed in and out with a bit of a strain. "I haven't done much in the past five years," he said with wistful energy.

"You have a life which you should be proud of, Dalton. You are a survivor. You are here, standing at the forefront of your future Kingdom. You are out. You are free. I know you think you wear shackles, but you have the keys to them. You can make your own choices. I know you are going to be the best ruler one day."

He looked extremely taken aback by her words, his dark blue gaze heavy. She saw sadness, admiration, friendship, and peace all at once. She knew she was being forward, but that was who she was. And she was tired of Dalton thinking he was less than because of what his father had made him out to be.

"You are power, Dalton. And you need to show the people that. I can see it. Ten Kingdoms, I have felt it!" She laughed. "You are my friend, and I admire you more than you know."

He blinked away a tear so quickly that Charmaine was sure she missed it. "Are you sure you aren't a princess yourself, Charmaine Grimes? You give a hell of a better speech than I ever could."

"Nobody gives hell like you," she deadpanned.

A wide grin exploded across his face. "I know you came here under shit circumstances. And I know that is not very princely of me to say."

"Dalton…"

"No, let me finish. You had your little speech." He raised an eyebrow playfully. "You have had shit. Complete and utter shit."

"Dalton!" She was a second away from hitting him.

He held up his hands defensively. "I promise I am going somewhere with this. Despite all that, I have never been more impressed with someone than you and your brother. When you came here and I met you for the first time, you opened up to me in ways that nobody had in years. For you, I was not a prize to be won or a chess piece to control. I was someone you could talk to without judgement. I knew nothing of anyone here at court, other than those who I met prior to awakening with my power. But fate brought me to you for some blasted reason, and it is the greatest gift the Gods could have given me. No matter what you think of my father and that regime he claims are knights, I have to say I can think of nobody more deserving of the ornamental title than your own brother."

Charmaine blinked away tears. "And you say you cannot give a speech? You are full of it."

She wrapped her arms around his neck and breathed in the scent of snow and blueberries, which was becoming familiar to her. She never imagined a world where she would be privy to hugging a Prince, being comforted by his familiar smell, but there she was. "I never thought he would want such a thing—James, I mean—to become a knight."

"We never know what we want until it is right in front of us, or thrown into our laps," he said as he pulled back, his blue eyes shining.

"You sound like you know from experience." She blushed.

"You know you are not the first woman to tell me—"

He started as smoke wafted to their side of the garden. "What in the name of Ciara is that?!" Dalton said as he began to cough.

Charmaine's entire body seized up, the memory of Brinn all too fresh in her mind. She did not think she would be so affected by fire, but clearly, her body remembered every moment. Her jaw was clenched. Her hands flew to her mouth and nose in an attempt to breathe clean air. Dalton's hands were on her in a second, moving her away from the crowding smoke and the cries which were raising in volume.

"Dalton," she choked out, her coughing more aggressive as the cloud became thicker.

"Whatever you do, do not stop moving," he said, coughing just as much in return.

Screams battled throughout the sky as they tried to run, racing against the clock to get as far away from whatever this was. Whoever this was. They bounded up the stairs of the castle as they reentered the throne room. As they blinked the thick smoke from the rose garden from their gaze, they wished they had stayed down below.

Bodies collided in a passion of blood and determination, the knights versus large men who looked all too familiar. They were dressed in gold, their armor painted with blood and their swords glittering against the reflection of the marble castle. *Clang.* The knight before her attacked the mercenary with a vengeance for justice. As she stood, her chest heaved against the corset which confined her ribs. She could see that those who believed in Ronan had been moved by his words earlier.

"FOR THE KING!" one shouted.

"FOR THE PRINCE OF SNOW!" someone shouted.

"FOR THE PEOPLE OF BRINN!" another shouted.

Swords collided again in what had become an eternal struggle for power. Dalton's hands suddenly gripped her shoulders, trying to sideline her. She tried to push off of him, feeling empowered by the King whom she had spent years hiding in fear of. Maybe, there was some good to be found in evil.

"CATAPULTS! THERE ARE CATAPULTS IN THALLGAN!" a voice shrieked.

"WE HAVE TO MOVE, CHAR!" Dalton yelled, a cough wracking his chest as he tried to shove his weight into hers.

She screamed as she saw what Dalton was tugging her away from. The corner of the throne room had been decimated by pelting boulders, clearly coming from down below in the citadel of Thallgan. She was so overwhelmed before by the chaos of the battle that she had not seen the greatest threat which lay before it.

The next boulder to rise looked as if it were in slow motion at first, gliding toward her with grace and patience. Dalton was screaming at her as he tried to move her body, but she had no control.

She was frozen.

She was horrified.

She saw the massive rock fly before she heard the *crack* of white marble, and then, everything went black.

FIFTY

lood roared in Dalton's ears as he ran from the infirmary to the throne room in a mad dash for Cyril. He received word after taking Charmaine to safety that his father had fled the castle and was out on business. Apparently, entrusting the entirety of the castle to him.

Dalton had not found one piece of his new bestowed responsibility to be out of kindness and his father's belief in his princely capabilities. He knew it was because everyone was thinking the same thing; Dalton was the Prince of Snow. He was just being used in another one of his father's games. Leaving Dalton in charge was a chess piece on the board of politics.

Dalton breathed heavily as he moved around the castle dwellers, careful not to touch anyone or make contact with any bare skin. The last thing he needed, that they all needed, was for him to hurt someone with his power. He was on edge more than he cared to admit, and if he had to play this role, he could not be anything but the epitome of calm.

Easier said than done.

As he dashed through the castle, he spotted Randolph among the knights.

"Sir Randolph!" he yelled, no bitterness in his voice as he announced Randolph's title.

Despite the chaos they had just endured, Randolph did not look rattled. He bowed his head to Dalton and listened attentively for his orders. "Yes, my Prince?"

"I need you to go down to Thallgan for services. I want you to make sure the people are not harmed, and to bring supplies with you, in case they were. Those catapults were put up in that town and who knows the damage they caused before they started firing boulders at the castle."

The corner of Randolph's mouth rose. Dalton assumed that was his attempt to smile. Randolph turned his head and beckoned to his remaining men to follow him. "I will bring a few of these men with me, and I will return when all is settled."

Dalton thanked him and his men for their service. He meant it.

At last, he spotted Cyril, running amok among the people to make sure they were okay from the attack. Moments after the catapults started, the mercenaries seemed to disperse. Their motive was clearly to inflict suffering and fear, and not to end them all. They were probably looking for his father, and when they discovered he was gone, they cut their losses.

"My boy!" Cyril shouted as he walked over to him.

"Cyril," Dalton breathed as he threw his arms around the old man.

"What is the occasion?" Cyril sneered, but emotion cut through his voice.

"It is Charmaine," Dalton answered, pulling away.

The image of it came again, her fear paralyzing her at

the recognition that the mercenaries and the fire were once again in front of her. Dalton had tried to move her, but to little avail. He could still hear the sickening crunch of her head against the marble, as the boulder collided with the pillar behind them. It had chipped apart like shattered glass, and a sizable piece had flown right into her left temple. The moment the life momentarily left her eyes was when Dalton decided he could no longer bear to be parted from her. She was alive, but she did not stir when he used what strength he had from all the years in solitude to drag her to the infirmary.

And he had never felt such fear. Not in his entire life.

When he got her there with the assistance of noblemen, the knights who had been around him checked for wounds on his body. They demanded that he sit still, in the name of the crown. Dalton begrudgingly let them inspect him as he stood next to Charmaine's body, which had been moved to one of the infirmary beds.

With a startle, he was informed that his power had created a shield of ice around him in that moment, freezing his blue tunic in the name of frozen defense. He looked down at the tunic for the first time, and noticed that the shirt itself was a cool damp. He sat up dizzily, the effects of that much power being exerted so mindlessly starting to take effect.

But it was her that he was concerned about.

The blood had pooled around the back of her head, and Elena was nowhere to be found with her power. Dalton knew he was acting rash and had no place in his position of power to care for a commoner, but he did not care.

He cared about nothing but keeping the girl that held his soul in the palm of her hands from harm.

✤

Charmaine was floating through time.

She was detached from her body. The grogginess of sleep that had overtaken her was completely debilitating. She lifted her head to look down at herself, thinking it funny that she had not changed out of her clothes from earlier. Her vision was spotty and her hand flew to the side of her temple in response to the sharp pain that erupted there. She hissed under her breath, and suddenly felt a hand touching her free one, comforting and steady.

As she came to, she visualized Randolph kneeling before her bedside. His brown eyes were heavy and shadowed with dark circles. Blood crusted his tattooed fingers and hands. The flowers that appeared to be nothing more than the sins he had claimed all those nights ago now looked as such. He looked up, his eyes steady with relief, but his face pained.

"We once expressed nothing but apologies to one another, Char." His ivy-inked hand grabbed the collar of his white tunic as if that were all he had to hold onto. "But do not patronize me by sending me there again. Friendship is so hard to come by in this castle, and I hoped I would have you as one of mine."

"What happened?" she asked, leaning back onto the pillow of her bed slowly.

"I fear destiny has claimed that you have no place with princes, Charmaine." His eyes darkened to a deep amber that reflected the golden stars of the sky outside.

"Randolph, I did not mean to bring this on us," she whispered, her eyes closing slowly as exhaustion took over her once again.

He leaned forward, his tattooed hands stroking hers. The gesture was not romantic, but that of longing, a desire for friendship and understanding.

"Charmaine, I heard them. Why were they looking for you?"

She rolled over, her head pounding uncontrollably. "I have not been able to discern that for myself, Sir Randolph."

He huffed a breath. "Charmaine, I am going to tell you one of my secrets. I have been trained my whole life to sense magic." His voice was as soft as the pillow beneath her head.

"Then why don't you turn me in?" she replied, groggy.

Alarm would have spilled through her, but this was clearly a dream. Randolph would never know anything about magic. He worked for the King. And the King hated magic.

Sleep was taking her again. She knew it, but she held on for another second as he whispered, "Because then I would have to tell you *everything*."

✥

Lawton's change overtook him as it always did. It was explosive, heart-pounding, and a head rush that never ceased to amaze him. He had no idea how he acquired such power, why he was blessed. He was not royalty.

Lawton appeared behind Randolph with the intent of starling him, but his momentary practical joke was silenced when Randolph held a short sword to his neck before he even had the chance to open his mouth. "Ten Kingdoms, Randolph, nothing gets past you anymore."

Randolph snorted in reply, almost a growl. "Do not sneak up on people who know you are coming. What do you have to report to me?"

"Ah, there is my favorite knight."

367

"I am serious, Lawton. No time for games. I was just in Thallgan for the past six hours assessing the situation. By some divine intervention of the Gods, they kept the town intact and did not cause the villagers any harm." He sighed in relief. "I notified Dalton already. What do you have to report? Speak clearly and quickly, or I will not be as gentle next time."

"Cian save you, you are in a mood tonight." Lawton smirked, even though he had no doubt that Randolph would hit him without a second thought. He could see the tattoos. Some sick twisted part of him wanted Randolph to throttle him. Those muscular arms trained for hours a day, yet he never lifted a finger. Lawton wondered what it would be like to touch them, run his own thin fingers on Randolph's inked skin.

He really had to go to the tavern more, so he did not do anything stupid.

"Prepare to go to Brinn. Ronan came back moments ago and told the council members that his move was to parade throughout the lands, rallying support and fighting battles that we could win throughout the First."

Randolph stabbed his knife into the table beside him in response, the wood splintering erratically.

"It is a terrible plan, I am well aware, but at least we will not be stuck here like sitting ducks anymore. Maybe we could even call for aide—"

"You are right," Randolph said. "Even though the First Kingdom has never been one to make the call."

"Maybe we can make it for them." Lawton smirked.

Randolph picked up the knife, the blade twisting between his fingers as if he were playing an instrument. "Or maybe we need to go to war to finish what has been started."

When Charmaine awoke the next morning, James told her that the Prince of Snow had not visited her yet, for he had gone on an exceptionally long walk with Cyril.

"All night?" she asked James.

"It seems so."

She managed to speak a few words to him, learning what had happened to her and how the Prince of Snow had tried to drag her limp body toward the infirmary. Her entire body ached; her head half bandaged from the wound she had acquired. The castle dwellers and the King never anticipated such an attack. The ferocity of the mercenaries was unstoppable. James also informed her of Ronan's speech earlier that day when she was sleeping.

Ronan had said, "*Knights will accompany our brigade, but will hang back on our expedition. These are the people of our Kingdom and they need to see us with open arms. Dalton will ride with Elena, a show of the unity of their arrangement. I will ride in front with Queen Aine. Together, we will all show the world that the Kingdom of the First is fighting back with a bitter vengeance. For Carinthya, and those who never received justice.*"

Charmaine complimented James on his incredible memory, to which he said that he memorized the speech, repeating it over and over, in the hope that she would awaken and he could recall it. She threw her arms around him then, drinking in the smell of her remaining family.

When the sun set, Dalton decided to check in on Charmaine. He had avoided her successfully, but it was starting to become ridiculous. He did not want to see her because the terror that wracked him earlier left him bottomed out. He had tried to stay busy, avoiding confronting anyone who left the infirmary about her well-being. He even attended the council meeting his father had promptly set up when he returned. Cyril promised him that if he heard even a word of her decline during the day, then he would get him.

Cyril never lied to Dalton. So, Dalton and Cyril wandered the castle grounds together, pondering the cruel ways of destiny and trying to understand why in the name of the Ten Kingdoms Ronan had left Dalton in charge.

The attacks, the catapults, the plan of his father to march right into the enemies' hands—none of it seemed to fit right together. Randolph had told him too that the mercenaries did no harm to the people who lived there. Sure, they had threatened them if they were to intervene in their destruction, but the villagers seemed to believe the mercenaries were under instruction to proceed that way. It all had to mean something in the eyes of destiny. But Dalton was not sure what it meant.

He entered the infirmary and found Charmaine stirring.

"Dalton?" she asked, her voice full of slumber. Her violet eyes fluttered slowly open and closed, unsure if this was a dream or reality.

"'Tis me," he said, smirking as he kneeled before her bed. She sat up slowly, groaning with the effort. "I am guessing you are still feeling the effects of the catapult?" he asked, trying to be lighthearted when her injury had caused him to go ballistic. He was so scared that his own power was silenced. And the shield that he had thrown up with his power? It had been like wearing a second skin.

Wielding that much power should never be that natural. Not in his circumstances.

"I never want to hear the word catapult again," she whispered as she leaned against the backboard of the bed.

"Catapult," he said before he could stop himself.

"Why haven't you come to visit me?" Her violet eyes dulled.

"I went on a walk," he replied frankly.

And he had. Despite being a fool at all times, Dalton could not deny that when things were difficult, it could be hard for him to open up. But Charmaine did not push, for she read him like a book.

"I think James told me that, or was it Randolph?" she asked herself. "I think Randolph came to visit me."

"No matter," he said. "We need not discuss that tattooed bastard. I wanted to ask you something."

"What is it?" she asked, clearly trying to contain a budding laugh.

"Ride with me and Elena tomorrow," he pleaded.

"You saved me." It was an admittance. A thank you.

"And I would very much like the opportunity to do so again, or maybe next time I will be the one who needs saving. You do owe me one," he said, readjusting his crooked crown.

Cyril had nearly verbally assaulted him for wearing a Princess crown today, so thin and ethereal. It was decorated with leaves and pearls, something his sister had worn before she was lost. It was subtle, and it brought him comfort to be close to his sister's memory, while he had been dignified this temporary position. His white curls flowed overtop of it and hid the power that the decoration was to his head. He liked it that way.

Hidden power was his style. Or at least it was until he was almost hit by a boulder in the throne room.

"The draw the past few days has been... agonizing

since our time in the throne room. I used it to find you among the chaos of the room… I am sorry if I hurt you."

She blushed, even though he knew she probably had not intended to. "You never hurt me."

"Damn catapults," he said, his white teeth flashing.

"I told you not to say that word again," she groaned, her head falling back as her hand flew to it.

"Catapult," he whispered again, loving the feeling of being with her. This freedom. This lack of judgement. It was the most beautiful thing in the world.

Gods, he loved friendship.

"I only hoped I could be next to you, not only for your company, but for my own fears and contempt. It is all rather selfish lately."

"You are scared?" she asked quietly and he knew what she was thinking. *How was Dalton scared of anything?*

"Terrified, actually." He smirked.

"Of what, might I be so forward to ask?"

"When have you not been forward my lady?" He got up to pace, controlling his own power, keeping the cap on the untapped potential of his frozen world.

He had replenished himself naturally over the course of the day. His mind was at ease, and so was his body. It came back to him as energy did when one slept. Charmaine watched him, waiting for him to make the first move. "Earlier, when my father was speaking of the plans, parading me around… I thought of Cyril, arguing for my autonomy as if I were a boy, not just some chess piece to be maneuvered. The way that he also knew my sister… He always wanted better for both of us."

"Cyril did that for you? For both of you?" she asked, her heart warming at the sound of Cyril's companionship for Dalton. And lurching at the reminder of Carinthya.

"Cyril has always done everything for me. The only man in the room willing to go toe to toe with my father on anything regarding me. But not this."

"This?" she asked, confused.

"Yes. This parade of *equality*." He spat the word with such hatred she was not sure if it was really Dalton standing before her.

She had hit her head damn hard. His usual lust for life, his energy, his kindness had vanished.

"You know as well as I that there is no equality in this Kingdom. Look at you... You might be one of the most beautiful women I have seen in my entirety of life, and I cannot be near you without receiving vindication from all those who work to control me." He ran a hand through his white hair, his skin turning light blue from containing his frozen rage to himself. Forbidding it to project onto her.

"You think I am beautiful?"

He paused, his lips trembling. "The most." He took a deep breath. "I do not want this crown that sits atop my head, but if I must, I want to wear it well."

"Why do you want me to sit with you and your fiancée?"

He paused, his cheeks now flushed with the same blue tint, his lips purple. His eyelashes were coated in snowflakes. If he looked at himself in a mirror, he was sure he would be in horror at his lack of control after being so worried about it all day.

"I want you to sit with me and my wife because you make me a better man. You challenge me to think differently about the world. You make me better. I feel grounded when I am with you. And I am terrified of being presented in front of my kingdom for the first time and losing control when I have been locked away for the past five years. I need all of this not to be for nothing."

With a newfound strength and certainty in her voice, she said, "You are the true King of the Snow Kingdom, and I will sit next to you and your *wife* tomorrow. I will help you show the people what you have shown me."

She wiped a tear from his eye as his power left him.

"And what is that?" he asked, kissing her lightly on the forehead. His wet lips crowned her with the remains of his frozen fury. He knew he should not associate with another woman, especially since he was married, but Charmaine was his anchor to sanity. And he had almost lost her.

It would not happen again.

She threw her arms around him. He was momentarily stunned against her before he relaxed. The forgiveness for the injury, for acting out against the draw's wishes... She did not blame him for one part of it. "That the Prince of Snow wears his crown well."

FIFTY-ONE

n the early hours of the morning, when the grass was full of dew and the sun was still asleep, they set off for the remains of Brinn.

Dalton's hands gripped his kneecaps the entire ride, on edge about leaving the castle in such a gallivanting way. He felt the brigade was dishonest, for they were sitting ducks out in the open together. Although, having Elena and Charmaine with him seemed to calm his nerves a bit. At least he was surrounded by friends.

The ride was longer than he had anticipated. The grassy forests and hillsides of the First Kingdom were vaster than he anticipated. Not that he had given it much thought before.

Ten Kingdoms, how far had James and Charmaine walked?

He looked out the window again like a petulant child, taking in every blade of grass and every gust of wind. The world was beautiful, lest he forget.

Dalton had sworn a vow to Elena before they left that he would not unleash himself during this carriage ride, like he had at dinner and in the courtyard.

"The carriage is inescapable if you freeze us in, your Majesty," she had spat.

It had been so childish, all of it, to lose himself time and time again in the name of insecurity and fear. However, he could not help but laugh at their faces, particularly his mother, who he did not give one damn about. Everyone had been so terrified, realizing that by locking him away they did not subdue him. They only caged him until they released him. He could always become a monster and he would never forget that.

But flaunting it every once in a while was a lot of fun. He was sure the Gods would agree. Given time.

Charmaine was silent most of the ride, but she did not sleep. Dalton noted her simple garb today, her plain black gown rather unruly for a ward of the castle. He caught onto her symbolism, however: black for mourning.

For the sake of the Ten Kingdoms, she had a right to be upset. She lost so much. Her father in some way. Her mother in a fire. And then her home in a blitz of mercenary violence.

She looked much better today. With Elena's unhinged healing magic, she was almost completely back to normal, except for the dark circles under her eyes. Elena could not cure sleep deprivation and night terrors.

Dalton leaned closer to Charmaine as a village outline appeared on the horizon. He smiled at the present, which he held for her in his pocket, proud of his thievery skills while his father had been off playing God and he had been dedicated to being King for a moment. Dalton silently decided to refer to the dagger Charmaine had procured all those nights ago, and the weapon which had lost Gwendolyn her head. He now called it Diamond Killer.

And Diamond Killer was attached to his waist, hidden by his royal garb.

He took a deep breath, knowing she would have some protection, since he planned to give it to her when they arrived. He had no idea what to expect there, and he had expressed this to her, practically groveling at her bedside for her to stay with him.

With a sigh next to her, he accepted that she was to be his undoing. She was the one person who kept his true power at bay. Cyril had rather confirmed as such, even campaigning for Dalton to ask her to come with them.

Cyril probably knew that it would take the edge off of him too.

Without warning, the carriage came to a stop, and without his eyes leaving Charmaine, he noticed she had paled a bit.

"It's okay," he mouthed.

She nodded in reply.

As they stepped down out of the carriages, Dalton was shocked at the decimation of the village. Yes, it was tiny. But nothing remained. He reached for her hand, but she was already mounting her horse. Pride swelled within him at her resilience. He did not know if he would ever be able to carry himself the same way. He had survived being locked up for five years, but he had Cyril. He had his books. He even had his home.

Randolph's voice chimed from up ahead, breaking his stream of consciousness. "We start here and we ride to the next town of Valhiem, so we can demonstrate peace and strength for those who lost their homes here."

Randolph's eyes went to James, who had taken his spot next to the King at the front of the line. Lawton stood by him too, not missing a beat of the action.

Randolph circled back to ride with Dalton, fidgeting

with his reins uncomfortably next to Charmaine. It was clear to Dalton that Randolph was there for his own protection, and Elena's. Dalton laughed that his father put Randolph in charge of knightly duties so freely, given his raw reality. Dalton would never admit that Randolph was good at being a knight, but a part of him would always resent Randolph from shirking his duty designated at birth. Dalton had known for three years who Randolph really was, and it was hardly a secret among the royals. But somehow, without a formal rule, all those who wore the crown were keen to keep his truth hidden.

Elena gasped and covered her face as they moved throughout the burnt and collapsed rubble. The remains of Brinn's citizens and homes were infiltrated with buzzards and sadness alike. It took a lot for Dalton not to look at Charmaine, but he did not want to draw attention to whatever she was feeling. He had learned there was strength in enduring alone.

As Dalton turned his head to look at Elena and ask her to say a prayer with him, he heard a loud scream. His head whipped to the side as he saw mercenaries explode out of the rubble, running directly toward the procession.

He lifted his sword, as did everyone else in the grouping, but he knew it was too late.

Dalton was in front of Charmaine, reaching for his sword as he moved to dismount. The familiar surge of power awakened beneath Charmaine's skin, gripping her as it had the last time she was in Brinn.

Her breath ragged, she dismounted, and tried to join the chaos ahead.

"Where is she?! I need the girl with the raven hair," a

mercenary screamed among the explosion of the battle.

This was an ambush. They came for me.

"DALTON!" she screamed as the man bolted toward them.

Without another thought, she gave into her power. Completely. Running toward Dalton, she grabbed his arm. Shock registered through him as her power flowed through her hands into his, and Charmaine took Dalton with her.

Charmaine grabbed his arm and Dalton felt it.

He felt *her*.

The reason for this draw. The reason he felt so connected to her. The reason he could not stay away from her still unknown, other than some sick of fate where the only person to make him feel normal and alive had secrets like his own.

She had power too, but she was *using it*.

"Charmaine."

Suddenly, there was an explosion. The mercenary ran straight for the first group and smoke was rising fast from the blast. Swords clanged in front of them as their sight became blocked by the blast's remains. Dalton could barely hear screams and cries over the deafening of whatever Charmaine had dragged him into with her power. He could hear wailing. Pain.

He went to move, but he could not move his legs.

He was frozen now.

And he was entirely at her mercy.

"Charmaine!" he yelped, trying to tug away. He twisted his head from side to side, clearly having use of his neck, but not his legs. He swore, looking at the terrified girl who clutched his hands for dear life.

And then he heard it and saw him. Lawton was covered in blood, standing mere inches from them. Dalton gasped at the sight. Lawton's skin was bleeding and part of his knight's garb had been shredded from the blast.

Lawton ran toward Randolph, yelling, "Where in the Ten Kingdoms is the Prince?"

Randolph spun around wildly, running a hand through his hair as he roared, "CHARMAINE?"

He could not see us.

Where was James?

Charmaine could not breathe. She could not see anything up ahead, except for knights running toward the smoke, toward the pile of bodies that tried to escape the clutches of the dark cloud. She needed James, her *anchor*.

He could bring her out of this.

But she could not move.

She saw Randolph look around wildly, his eyes ablaze.

You have to breathe, Char. Breathe.

"Charmaine, can they not see us?" Dalton asked loudly, his voice rising in alarm.

But he knew. I could see the recognition in his eyes. Why he felt this draw too, why he felt like he could trust me... Our powers. Destiny had brought us together, invisibility and snow.

Her gaze flickered around her, looking for anyone she loved. Randolph had rushed into the cloud with Lawton, trailing him in a roar of hatred.

"Charmaine, come back to me," Dalton said, seeing her so far away. "Charmaine, I see you."

Dalton did what Charmaine had done for him in the

throne room when he had been at the mercy of his power. He kissed her.

He smashed his lips against her mouth, willing her to feel him, to hear him, to pull them back into the light. He wanted to show her that he was there for her, always and forever. If anything happened to Elena, or even Gods-damned Randolph, or her brother while her power froze them both... He did not know if they would forgive themselves. If anyone could forgive themselves.

Her power thundered against his own. Where he was all ice, she cracked it open with invisibility, a secret weapon against his own. They were in unison, their gifts pushing and pulling as they peeled back one another's layers, only to expose themselves to one another in the rawest of truth.

She gasped against him, desperate as tears fell from her eyes in fear.

She was scared of what? Of me?

His heart cracked at the realization. All the nervous moments. All the gazes from James. The constant twiddling of her thumbs as if she was consistently on the verge of taking a deep breath.

How in the Ten Kingdoms could I not see it before?

Cyril taught him all the signs, things that he was able to do to quell his own gifts. She had been breathing, keeping her power at bay with all that she knew.

She could turn invisible.

Did Randolph know?

If he did, Dalton swore he would kill him for keeping this shit from him. From keeping the real Charmaine from him, when Dalton knew damn well *who* he was.

She was magnificent. And she had nothing to fear. Never again.

"I will never hurt you," he mumbled against her as he felt her power undo itself.

Her arms interlaced behind his neck as she pulled from him slowly, tears streaming down her flushed cheeks.

"Dalton, I need you to be safe," she said quietly against the roar of battle that took place around them.

The smoke began to disappear, but he still could not see through it.

"Charmaine, I am. You saved me. I am hidden. But we must go back now."

She nodded, tears running down her face in recognition.

We must go back.

Lawton ran out of a heaping pile of bodies as fast as he could. He thought about jumping, but he did not want to draw attention to himself. Using his power was not always safe in battle. He could accidentally jump into someone's weapon. And he was pretty sure Randolph would kill him if he tried anything stupid.

He knew the brute loved him like a brother, but he accepted he was never going to get an admittance.

The brutality of these mercenaries was an absurdity even Lawton could not comprehend. Ten Kingdoms, Randolph himself could not even comprehend it. And Randolph was his best friend. He had killed more people than he was even aware of.

Lawton pushed all of that away now, the daze of the end of the battle taking control of his limbs.

A mass murder was a low blow, even for the mercenaries.

He ran straight for Randolph when he spotted him, his eyes wild and jaw set. He did not need to say much, but he needed to tell him before the other knights knew. Before the Prince had to become who he was born to be.

"Where in the name of Ciara is the Prince?"

Randolph surveyed him. He was too damn smart, too damn familiar with the role of power to understand what he was saying without saying it. His eyes said it all.

The King and Queen were dead.

"No time to mourn your King, Rand. We have to find him."

Randolph read Lawton like a book. He was a rat bastard sometimes, but he was an intuitive leader. Despite being so destroyed by things he had no part in caring to remember anymore, he cared about people. Because he was a King in his own right.

"No mourning those who deserved to meet their end," he spat, violence blazing through every word. Lawton flinched at his insolence, but figured he would find out the reason behind such venom later. He always did.

Randolph touched Lawton's shoulder as he said, "Now, let us look for our sovereign."

Randolph dragged his sword against the rubble of the battle and Brinn. His eyes were so heavy with the stain of battle, his brain full, his heart tainted by more kills at his sinful hands. At least, if it was a mercenary, he did not need a reminder.

He walked slowly as he and Lawton came out of the battle. They scanned for Charmaine and the Prince. Randolph knew they were together. They were the only two people missing during the battle, but not in vain. He was glad, if anything, that they had one another.

It was good they did not see what he had.

Elena was a mess, and it killed Randolph that he could not protect anyone from this. In part, that was why he became a knight. He wanted to have the opportunity to make a difference, to save people. And he had failed today, miserably. The horrors of war touched everyone, and it was a matter of time before their decent luck ran out. Yes, they had been attacked numerous times at the castle, but loss had not hit Randolph deeply. And Randolph knew that losing people one loves was a battle wound which could not be healed by magic.

Elena's wails sounded in the distance. Lawton had dragged her elsewhere and put her in a carriage with that serving boy, Athelred. Randolph wandered a little further, blinking once and seeing nothing in front of them. He cursed and took another two steps, to which they unveiled before him, wrapped in one another's arms.

Dalton was crouched in front of Charmaine, holding her hands as they sat wrapped on the ground together. A sigh of relief rushed through Randolph, for neither of them looked to be harmed. Neither of them even looked to be touched by the devastation of battle. On another day, Dalton's precarious obsession with Charmaine would have irritated him, especially since now his wife sat in a carriage losing her mind to grief. Today, it did nothing. Everyone would be touched by what happened in Brinn. Sadness flooded through him as he took more steps toward them, cautiously thinking of what he was about to do. He was about to be thrust into a role that would change everything.

But he claimed his destiny. He was done hiding from who he was. This was what he did. He took people's lives from them. He had sworn to Lawton that he had to be the one to do this. He had to be the one to tell her.

Randolph had wreaked devastation before, torn

Kingdoms down with his bare hands. Yet, this was the hardest moment of his life. He approached them slowly. Blood crusted all inches of his body. This was harder than telling anyone the truth about his identity. This was cruel, but it was his news to give because he wanted to bear the burden.

He already had so many. What was the weight of one more?

Charmaine lifted her head, noticing his slowed approach. Her violet eyes were red as if she had been crying. She smiled slightly and Randolph wished she had not.

"Charmaine," he said softly, trying to put on his bravest of faces.

Dalton stood up to leave and Randolph beckoned him to stay seated, his hands wrapped in hers.

Randolph bowed his head before his King, silently conveying to him all that Dalton needed to know. He did not need to use his lips to converse with Dalton. Despite their differences, they were more similar than not. The silence was deafening, but it rung with truth and understanding. Dalton bowed his head in response, accepting what Randolph was silently saying.

The King and Queen did not survive the blast. Dalton did not look shocked.

"What else is it?" Dalton asked, his voice wavering.

Charmaine sat clueless below, her eyes filled to the brim with worry as Randolph took a rattled breath.

"It is James, Char. He is dead."

THE DEATH OF THE
SEVENTH KINGDOM

ark power cracked against the cold air that whipped through the Seventh Kingdom. It was merciless, tired, and vengeful.

The man whose hands the power erupted from were slightly shaken by the display of the Old powers, for he had not inherited them. He had stolen them many years before.

He hissed as he let his daughter's darkness wander forward. The effort strained him. He was expanding his domain with the castle he had overtaken; therefore, he could not stop.

Not now.

Maybe not ever.

It had been a brutal fight to the death with the Seventh Kingdom. The man had almost taken the First Kingdom in its stead. But there was something beautiful about stealing the light from a kingdom which he never had much of a taste for. As much as he did not want to admit it, the First Kingdom would always be his home. And he would save it for last.

He laughed, a cruel and wicked cackle against the whispering winds. He relished the remembrance of brutality he had demonstrated against the fortress of the Seventh and the home of their last remaining monarch, Princess Reine. Her sun-kissed skin and brown eyes had flashed in horror as the man's forces stormed the castle. Nobody had believed the man, even in his own ranks, even when he was *alive*, that the Seventh Kingdom could be besieged. The people with their tattoos of sorrow and devotion to their monarchs honestly disgusted him. They had an unwavering loyalty to their customs, and he looked forward to shattering their ways. Castle Dead was a beacon for all that they were and all that they held true.

He had taken Princess Reine into his custody. His dark power shackled her majesty and the other members of her court to his confines. They would remain there until he noted otherwise. He only wished he could have found the lost King, for that would have been a prize to bestow indeed.

Princess Reine had given him no further information on what he wanted to know. She had only confirmed his suspicions that the Gods had allowed monarchs to have powers again, for what reasoning he was unsure. She had lashed out at him without hesitation. Fire spewed from her fingers and mouth in a rage so passionate that the man almost applauded.

His original intention had been to murder the young princess and take the throne for himself. If the lost King was truly what the stories had said, *lost*, then he would be able to reclaim one of the ten crowns before he even got to the First Kingdom.

And he wanted to rejoice in the First Kingdom's demise, comeuppance for all the pain his daughter had caused during their too-short lifetimes.

He smiled to himself, cold. His jaw was set. There was a beauty that he could not deny in his own arc of Kingly redemption, saving the First Kingdom for last. The man wished his daughter had been there to see all *this,* without her petty husband to bring her toward the light. He wanted her to see the world fall and be restored to the glory he had always envisioned for it.

He had died in his first lifetime, for this world to be reborn in his innovation.

He breathed in the fire and smoke around him, which had begun to rise to meet him. He savored the death and destruction that his darkness brought him. He had missed it like a dear friend. This new lease on life, and the promise of his restoration coming to fruition, left a devilish smile on his face.

"Sarridolon," he whispered the name of the realm he wished to reforge. He ran a hand through his long red hair, overwhelmed by his desires for control.

"What did you just say?" a voice said below him.

It was *the girl.* The girl who he had forgotten lying at his feet. He had been so obsessed with admiring the ruin of this Kingdom that he nearly stepped on her.

He leaned down. His old mind willed him to stay away from the things he wished he saw when he looked at the girl. His curse reminded him that he did not care how old she was, only that she was his prized possession.

As he crouched down to look into her eyes, he reveled in her expression. She was terrified and fearful of him. It had not been that way when he had met her all those years ago. She had been open then. She had desired freedom from the blubbering idiots of her father's court.

But over time, he had broken her, like he had broken

everyone else he had ever touched.

Her black hair was sticky with blood, and her dark blue eyes were alight with fire, despite the tears that drenched her cheeks. Her pain and fury were like starlight to him—beautiful as it was devastatingly unknown.

"Come, Carinthya," King Finn said, beckoning his darkness to lift her to her knees. "Now, we move to the Sixth."

ACKNOWLEDGEMENTS

Writing a book is the hardest thing I have ever done. It most definitely takes a village. I am grateful to the following people for holding me accountable and making this dream of mine come true. Thank you for being a part of the TPOS village.

To my family, thank you for being so supportive of my desire to do this.

To Will, thanks for reading this in pieces when I felt like sharing.

To Nicole Platania, thank you for believing in TPOS as much as you believed in me.

To Chey Parkerson, thanks for reading random snippets.

To Michaela Bethard, thanks for reading this... multiple times. I owe you.

To Isabel Strychacz, for being an everlasting inspiration.

To Carly, thanks for proofreading and fueling my ego.

To all of bookstagram, thank you for cheering me on.

And to Dalton, Charmaine, Randolph, and Elena... Thank you for all you have done for me. I am sorry for what I have planned for book two.

ABOUT THE AUTHOR

L.B. Divine is a fantasy lover, cat mom, Outlander enthusiast, and has always dreamed about writing stories of the fantastical. The Prince of Snow is her first novel. L.B. Divine can be found on Instagram, Twitter, and TikTok at @lbdivineauthor.

Printed in Great Britain
by Amazon

21287007R00231